Quinn had her at his mercy...

The night Quinn had first met Dulcy, all he'd wanted was a quick roll in the hay. Then he'd discovered she was his best friend's fiancée. Now...well, now he wanted to show her all the things Brad never could. Make her beg for him in a way that made her question her choice in men.

"I've always admired women who are comfortable in their own skin," he murmured, stirring her hair with his breath. "Who feel as comfortable out of their clothes as in them."

Her shudder seemed to ripple straight to the core of him.

"Tell me, Dulcy," he whispered in her ear. "Would you like to be naked with me right now?"

She blinked at him, her eyes swimming with desire and confusion. Her lips parted, as if awaiting his kiss.

Quinn gave ⬚⬚⬚⬚⬚⬚⬚⬚⬚⬚ ⬚⬚⬚⬚. She hadn't put her panties b⬚⬚⬚⬚⬚⬚⬚⬚⬚⬚⬚⬚⬚⬚⬚⬚⬚⬚ ⬚ter in the ladies' r⬚⬚⬚⬚⬚⬚⬚⬚⬚⬚⬚⬚⬚⬚⬚⬚around in public fo⬚⬚⬚⬚⬚⬚⬚⬚⬚⬚⬚⬚⬚⬚⬚er her skirt, air car⬚⬚⬚⬚⬚⬚⬚⬚⬚⬚⬚⬚⬚ck hard.

He didn't know how he was going to pull it off, but he had to convince her that he really *was* the best man....

Dear Reader,

A few years ago, we had the opportunity to drive to California on the infamous Route 66. Haven't you done it? You have to! And along the way, put aside some special time to explore New Mexico. By far, the state was the most magically romantic place we encountered along the way. Once you're there, gaze out at the infinite rolling desert, broken only by breathtaking mesas at sunset, and tell us if you don't see our characters, Dulcy Ferris and Quinn Landis embracing in the distance. (And be thankful you can't see what *else* they're doing....)

In *A Stranger's Touch*, sexy litigation attorney Dulcy Ferris is one week away from entering a passionless marriage...until gorgeous Quinn Landis tempts her with everything she told herself she didn't need but now urgently wants. One blazing night of passion leaves her questioning everything—including the mysterious disappearance of her fiancé, and the realization that her new lover is also the best man!

We hope you enjoy Quinn and Dulcy's sizzling adventure. Let us know what you think. You can write to us at P.O. Box 12271, Toledo, OH 43612, or visit us on the Web at www.toricarrington.com.

Happy (and hot) reading!

Lori & Tony Karayianni
aka Tori Carrington

A STRANGER'S TOUCH

Tori Carrington

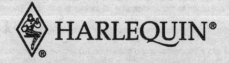

TORONTO • NEW YORK • LONDON
AMSTERDAM • PARIS • SYDNEY • HAMBURG
STOCKHOLM • ATHENS • TOKYO • MILAN • MADRID
PRAGUE • WARSAW • BUDAPEST • AUCKLAND

This one's for the foreign publishers who make our books
available to readers around the world, including, but not
limited to, the warm and wonderful people at Mills & Boon
and Harlequin Hellas. And for those same readers, who
are more similar to us than different. You prove that
romance knows no boundaries....

ISBN 0-373-79041-4

A STRANGER'S TOUCH

Copyright © 2002 by Lori and Tony Karayianni.

Printed in U.S.A.

1

MAYBE THERE WAS SOMETHING to the saying that women reached their sexual peak in their thirties. Dulcy Ferris shakily tried to light a forbidden cigarette as she sat in the bathroom stall of Rage—the nightclub that was all the rage in Albuquerque, New Mexico, that her two best friends had brought her to. The lighter she'd had forever didn't seem to want to produce a spark. Not that it mattered. Lately her body seemed to be sparking enough for a thousand lighters.

Finally a tiny flame. Dulcy pulled deeply on the cigarette, then sat back on the closed commode seat, resting her head against the cool ceramic tiles behind her. She'd be the first to admit that she didn't buy into the whole biological clock scenario. That's not why she was marrying Brad Wheeler in a week. It wasn't the reason why at thirty she was marrying for the first time. But it did strike her as strange that lately her hormones seemed to be running on overdrive, filling her with all sorts of decadent urges she'd never even thought about before, much less entertained. Then there were all the...*weird* physical side effects. Her skin seemed to tingle constantly. Her nipples were eternally taut. Her inner thighs seemed to generate a heat all on their own. And the mere act of taking a shower made her eye the soap in a naughty way, igniting in her a desire to do all sorts of wicked things to her own body.

She glanced at the glowing end of the cigarette, her gaze languidly sliding over her fingers and arm. Even now a light sheen of sweat coated her skin, though the central air system of the hotel that housed the club was likely adjusted to handle the dance-generated heat. If she didn't know better, she would think she was suffering from an early stage of menopause. But she remembered when her mother had gone through her hot flashes. No, she definitely was not experiencing that. Catherine Ferris had been a murder away from becoming a homicidal maniac during that rough two-year period and her activity level had seemed notched up to warp speed. Dulcy, on the other hand, couldn't seem to drum up enough energy to open the jar of dill pickles that had sat unopened in her refrigerator for the past month, despite countless half-hearted attempts that left her staring at the contents as if they were some unattainable dream.

Okay, she absently admitted, so maybe her sexual relationship with Brad, or lack thereof, was partially to blame for her current condition. If only she knew what it was like—

The outer door swung inward, letting in a blast of music. Dulcy stood up and tossed the cigarette into the bowl, then waved the smoke away, hoping she didn't set off an alarm somewhere. A quick rap vibrated the pink metal stall door. Normally she would have jumped out of her skin at such an intrusion, despite her suspicion of who it was. But now she could only sigh and open the door to stare at her friend Jena McCade.

"Can't a girl go to the bathroom?" Dulcy asked.

"Are you smoking? You *were* smoking, weren't you? My God, when did you pick up that nasty habit? People are quitting smoking now, not taking it up." Jena wrinkled her nose, then reached into her purse.

Dulcy tried to avoid the spray of her perfume.

"Only you would steal into the john for a smoke when the place is crawling with grade A men," Jena added.

Dulcy snapped straighter and tugged at the hem of her short black leather skirt, an impulse buy she hadn't had the guts to wear until tonight. The fact that the place *was* crawling with grade A men was all the more reason for her to be in the john. The cigarette she'd bummed off the barmaid was just an excuse, the lighter in her purse an old one she'd picked up eons ago when she'd briefly dated a smoker.

The truth was that all the men in the other room only served to heighten her awareness of her heated condition. She stepped to the sink and splashed cold water over her face. Jena grimaced at her in the mirror.

"What?" Dulcy asked.

"You do know you just messed up your makeup."

Dulcy scanned her features. So she had. So what? She couldn't bring herself to care. She wasn't here to entice any of the guys out there to go out with her. In one week she was officially off the market, married and settled. And it couldn't come soon enough for her. Maybe it was the thought of her honeymoon that was getting her all hot and bothered.

"Here—" Jena rifled through her purse and came up with a compact. Her perfectly made-up face was puckered in disapproval as she dabbed at Dulcy's cheeks and nose.

Dulcy batted her away. "I don't want to look like I'm on the make."

Jena's devious violet eyes twinkled. "This is your bachelorette party, babe. That's exactly how you want to look."

Dulcy wiped off some of the rouge her friend had applied. No, she didn't want to look like she was on the make. Simply because she was afraid that if a particularly good-looking guy did approach her, she'd be hard-pressed not to wrestle him to the ground and have at him. And then where would she be? Or, more accurately, who would she be?

Certainly not the woman she'd spent the past thirty years looking at in the mirror.

Then again, she was already having trouble with *her.*

She slowly touched up her lipstick, finding the silky way it glided on almost unbearably sensual. She squeezed her eyes shut. Now this was going too far. When she started thinking of her own lipstick as sensual, she was in big trouble.

God, Brad would think she was the biggest hussy alive. Brad…

"Are you ready?" Jena asked, crossing her arms under her breasts and tapping her foot.

Dulcy recapped her lipstick then tucked it into her purse. She supposed she'd stalled as long as she could. She had agreed to this night out with Jena and Marie. She'd just have to see it through. She glanced at her watch. She only wished it were later than nine o'clock.

"HERE'S TO HOCKEY PLAYERS!" Jena toasted an hour later, then lowered her voice to a bawdy whisper. "And their big…sticks."

Dulcy blinked and tucked her shoulder-length blond hair behind her ear. Her head felt as if it were stuffed with wool, her limbs felt peculiarly languid, and if she wasn't imagining things, her friend had just made a brazen reference to hockey players'…private equipment. Not that she was surprised. Jena somehow managed to squeeze the topic of sex into any conversation.

Dulcy mentally repeated the word. *Sex. Sex, sex, sex.* She grinned. The magic of the liquor seemed to have squelched her hormone-ridden body. Or, if she was lucky, the unfamiliar feelings had bit the dust altogether.

"Dulcy, you dropped the ball," Jena accused.

Balls and hockey sticks? She scrunched up her face,

opening her mouth to correct the mixed metaphor, but somehow the words never made it out. Instead, she shifted in the corner booth of the nightclub and raised her shot glass, the tequila inside splashing out and coating her fingers, as she waited for Jena and Marie to pick up their shots. "To hockey… Hey, wait a minute. Haven't we toasted hockey players already?"

Jena nearly gave herself whiplash watching three hot guys walk by the table. Well, at least they were what Jena considered hot. Which sometimes seemed to include any male under the age of forty who could financially support himself. These three guys weren't Dulcy's type at all. They were too…muscular, too…alpha, too…smug. She preferred a bit more of a challenge—a man whose own personal criteria in the women he dated extended beyond "breathing."

Jena rolled her eyes heavenward, then groaned in lust. "Yes, we have toasted hockey players already. Three times. First, for their smooth moves. Second, for their large sports cups. Third…for their big sticks. Living in New Mexico, where hockey players are a rarity, you can't possibly be complaining, can you?"

Dulcy glanced around the club, which was conveniently located just off the lobby of one of Albuquerque's better hotels. From the real leather, deep-burgundy colored booths and stools, to the brass fixtures and mid-level rock band playing in the far corner, the place was teeming with NHL pro hockey players from a visiting L.A. team, a result of a season kickoff exhibition game against New Mexico's WPHL division team. The instant Jena had gotten wind of their whereabouts, the location of Dulcy's bachelorette party was a done deal. There was nothing she or Marie could do to change Jena's mind. So all of them had checked into three connecting rooms on the seventh floor of the hotel, and headed straight down to the club to "get their party on," as Jena had put it.

"To hockey players, then." Dulcy clinked her shot glass against her two friends'. Licking the salt off the back of her hand and downing the fiery amber liquid, she grabbed for one of the dwindling lemon wedges on a plate in the middle of the table.

Dulcy shuddered. She'd never been much of a drinker. A beer here, a glass of wine there. And her lips had certainly never before touched a shot glass, much less tequila. Well, unless the glass was wide-rimmed and the contents were called a margarita. But this was her last real night out with the girls as a single, professional female, and she had agreed to give in to Jena and Marie's hearty demands that she do it right.

She only wished they had chosen a better-tasting liquor. "Who said this was supposed to get easier after the second shot?"

"I said it gets easier. I don't know. Maybe it's after the third shot. How many have we had? Has to be more than three… But it will get easier." As the youngest and the third member of the circle, Marie Bertelli had a smile, they all agreed, that could stop Tom Cruise dead in his tracks. Well, all except for Marie, anyway, who thought her looks rated as paper-sack material.

Dulcy leaned against the younger woman's arm, Marie's red hair nearly putting out an eye. She batted the curly strands away. "And you're a terrible liar. Maybe that's the reason why you're *not* married yet."

Marie made a face that only made her look cuter, if that was possible. "Yes, well, you probably wouldn't be getting married either if you were still living under your parents' roof. How's a girl to get any man to stick around in that environment?"

Dulcy conceded the point. Marie's parents, along with her three impossible older brothers, were convinced that sex was strictly reserved for the married—at least, when it came to women. All three Bertelli brothers had always had *very* active sex lives, from what Dulcy could remember. As for Marie, she couldn't even kiss a guy at the end of a date without the entire Bertelli family swooping down and grilling him about his income and investments and religious affiliation. In that order.

"Arranged marriage," Jena said.

Dulcy and Marie stared at her.

"Oh. Sorry. Guess they already tried that route, didn't they."

Not only had Marie's family tried that route, but they had failed, virtually chasing her from town, until Dulcy and Jena had tempted her back.

Marie grimaced. "Anyway, in reference to my inability to lie, I'll have you know that I talked my way out of a traffic ticket this morning, thank you very much. I told the nice police officer that I was late for a court date, batted my eyes and, presto—" she snapped her fingers "—he tore up the ticket."

Jena waved her away. "That's because you're so damn cute, especially when you lie."

Marie looked for support from Dulcy. "Sorry. She's right, kid. You couldn't lie to save your life."

Finally, Marie smiled. "I resemble that remark." She fingered nearly every one of the corn chips in the bowl she'd dragged closer, then picked the smallest one, always counting calories. "When are you two going to stop calling me 'kid,' anyway?"

Dulcy grabbed the largest chip. "I don't know. When you move out of your parents' house, maybe?"

Jena lined up the three empty shot glasses in front of her

and began filling them. "You'll also have to make up for the four years you're younger than us. Don't forget that."

"So, in a word, the answer is never."

Her martyr's sigh never failed to amuse Dulcy.

"Yes, well, I wouldn't be under my parents' roof if not for you two. If you hadn't called me six months ago with that proposal to move back and go into practice with you two and the infamous Bartholomew Lomax, I'd still be in L.A. in my comfortable little apartment in Redondo Beach." She wiped the salt from her hands. "Not everyone has the money you were born with, Dulcy. Or makes a killing setting serial killers free like you do, Jena. I've spent two years keeping L.A. streets safe for John Q. Public by working in the DA's office."

"And making nothing in the process," Jena added, sliding one overflowing shot glass in front of Dulcy, another in front of Marie.

"Yeah. Which is precisely why I have to live with my parents until we start turning a good profit." Marie lifted her glass. "To success."

Jena lifted hers. "To hockey players…and their tight buns."

Dulcy laughed and hoisted her glass. "To love."

She and Marie went through the salt-licking, fire-downing, lemon-grabbing process, then stared at Jena where she sat with her glass in the air.

"What is it?" Dulcy asked.

Jena shook her head so that her sleek raven hair swayed, then fell disgustingly back into place. "You had to go and do it, didn't you. Say the *L* word." She sighed.

"What's wrong with the *L* word?" Marie asked.

"Nothing," Dulcy said.

Jena twisted her lips. "Well, seeing as this is your night,

I'm going to refrain from arguing that point with you.'' She raised her glass again. ''To hockey players.''

''And their tight buns,'' Marie finished.

Marie started giggling, then slapped her hand over her mouth, appalled, which sent Dulcy over the edge. Dropping her head into her hands, she laughed until the bar was blurry. But that could also be a result of the cigarette smoke in the air, and the liquor, too, so she didn't pay much attention.

''God, you two are pathetic.'' Jena's smile softened her exotic features as she pushed her glass away. ''Anyway, Dulc, you haven't told us yet how it feels to be eight days away from becoming a married woman.''

''Probably great.'' Marie turned toward her. ''Brad's an absolute top-of-the-line hottie.''

Dulcy and Jena stared at her.

''What? He is.'' Conviction vanished from her face. ''Isn't he?''

''Yes, he is,'' Dulcy agreed, dragging the back of her hand across her mouth. She stared at it in horror. Had she actually just done that? God, her mother would die if she knew. She picked up a napkin, hoping she wouldn't next be running the heel of her hand against her nose.

Then it dawned on her what Jena might be after. ''Oh, no. You can just forget about it. I am not sharing any…intimate details about any part of Brad's anatomy.''

Not that she could share details. At least, not specifically.

She bit the inside of her cheek to keep from blurting out what she had essentially kept from her friends for the past few months. Namely, that straight off the bat, at the end of their first date five months ago, Brad had suggested they not have sex. First he'd told her he didn't want to move too fast, then after they became engaged two months ago, he'd said they might as well wait until their wedding night.

She'd thought it quaint—for a whole two minutes. Then her overactive imagination began wondering what he was hiding. Could the breathtakingly handsome playboy be a minute man? Done the instant he began? She shifted awkwardly. Then there was the size issue. Something she'd immediately set out to disprove by launching a surprise attack on him after dinner at his mother's house one night. She smiled to herself. Oh, no. Size was definitely not a problem. But at the time, Brad's scandalized reaction was.

So the guy was traditional when it came to the woman he wanted to marry. She told herself she should be flattered. Still, a little part of her thought the whole thing was a bit...*weird.* Not to mention immensely frustrating.

There. That was it. The reason why her hormones were running amok. It was only natural that she'd want to make love with her fiancé, the man she planned to spend the rest of her life with, right?

She swallowed. The only problem was that lately everything but Brad seemed to set her off. Her recent highly charged state had even made her consider acquainting herself with the gag gift Jena had given her for her last birthday. She probably would have if the damn vibrator wasn't so large it took enough batteries to run a small car.

Jena rolled her eyes. "Good, because I, for one, am not interested in hearing about them...it." She snickered. "Whatever. No, I want to know how it feels, generally speaking. You know, your being on the verge of becoming Mrs. Bradley Wheeler III."

Dulcy straightened. "As a bride, in general, I feel pretty good." Damn good, actually. At some point over the past year she'd stopped ignoring her mother's incessant speeches about her needing to find a prosperous prospect before there were none left, and started listening to them. And rather than tossing the bridal magazines Catherine Ferris had subscribed to and had delivered to her condo, Dulcy had started absently leafing through them. Then she'd met Brad at a cocktail party and everything had fallen neatly into place. Too neatly, she sometimes found herself thinking.

She smiled at Jena's frown and waved her finger. "But I know that's not what you're asking. As for that, all I have to say is that his being Bradley Wheeler III has absolutely nothing to do with my feeling good. I'd be just as happy if he were a...bartender."

"That's sweet," Marie said.

"That's dumb," Jena disagreed. "Honey, bartenders don't make Bachelor of the Year three years running."

"Neither do hockey players," she pointed out.

"Depends on which publications you're reading."

Dulcy laughed. "Sorry. My subscription to *Jocks-R-Us* must have run out."

Jena playfully slapped her palm against the table. "Then, you must renew, pronto. These guys take home some whopping salaries."

Dulcy tugged the bowl of chips closer to her. "I've already got a groom. Remember? And money has nothing to do with it. I'm marrying for love."

She caught Jena's cringe and silently chalked up another one.

"That's nice," Marie said, sighing.

Dulcy and Jena stared at her again.

Okay, so Marie got romantic when she drank. Jena grew even bawdier. And Dulcy was a sloppy drunk. Dulcy didn't know how they'd gone so long without discovering this before, but she tucked the information into the back of her mind for future reference. Some night when they were vegging in front of the television with a stack of old videos, frapuccino and popcorn, she'd pull it out and they'd have a good laugh.

She propped her chin on her hand and gazed at her two friends. "Thanks, guys—you know, for doing this for me. I'm...I'm having a great time."

"You're drunk," Jena said.

"That, too. But I meant what I said just the same."

"But we're just getting started, Dulcy Ferris." Then Jena fixed the kind of determined gaze on her that made Dulcy and Marie say "uh, oh" whenever they saw it. That gaze was what made her such a great criminal defense attorney. It's also what made her a downright nosey friend. "So tell me, Dulc. Since in eight days, when you go in front of that altar and profess your undying commitment for Brad Wheeler in front of God and everyone, you'll forfeit all possibility of seeing it come true...tell us, what's the sexual fantasy you'll miss most?"

"Yes," Marie chimed in, the dreamy expression vanishing and an almost voyeuristic interest taking its place.

"And if Brad satisfies all my sexual fantasies?" Dulcy asked. Oh, please let that be the case. Let them get married, hit the honeymoon suite and have Brad shed his conservative behavior and turn into a virtual Tarzan in bed. Images of hard abs, ropes and a leather loincloth leapt to mind, and she sighed.

"Ha ha," Jena said. "I'm serious."

Dulcy dropped her gaze and cleared her throat, then told a bald-faced lie. "What if I told you I don't have one?"

Jena scoffed. "Everyone has a sexual fantasy, even Marie here. Don't you, Marie?"

"Oh, yes. But we're not talking about me. I still have plenty of time to fulfill mine. Dulcy's the one getting married."

Dulcy stared at them pointedly. She'd never been very comfortable discussing items of a personal nature. Being amused and sometimes appalled by Jena's behavior was one thing. Telling her friends when she had her period or how frustrated she was that she and Brad hadn't slept together yet…well, that was quite another. She knew her discomfort was due in large part to her upbringing. You could live in a conservative, emotionally repressed household for only so long before some of it rubbed off on you. In her case, it was talking about intimate matters.

She slumped back against the booth. "God. You're not going to let me off the hook on this one, are you."

"Uh-uh."

"No."

"Okay, then…" Resigning herself to the fact that putting them off would only make things worse, Dulcy searched her mind, trying to come up with something that would please them. "Okay. My secret sexual fantasy is a night of white-hot passion with an anonymous bad-boy."

Jena grimaced. "Been there."

"Done that," Marie agreed.

Dulcy lifted her brows. "You have?"

Jena waved her away. "Never mind us. We're talking about you. And certainly even you can do better than that. Half the female population has that fantasy."

Okay, so she was a cliché. Wouldn't be the first time. She twisted her lips and looked around the hockey-player-choked bar, then through the glass doors to the lobby of the hotel. The silhouette of a man seemed to appear out of nowhere. She swallowed hard. Boy, could her imagination work overtime with a little help from tequila. The silhouette moved closer to the club, then halted in the doorway, his face concealed, his body the stuff of which dreams were made. Tall. Broad shouldered. Long legged. Rock hard.

Every single last urge she had hoped she'd drowned with the liquor came rushing back tenfold. Especially when she realized the guy wasn't an apparition at all, but a flesh-and-blood male who seemed to prowl rather than walk. His dusky skin hinted at a mixed heritage. The length of his longish black hair teased the back collar of his shirt.

All sorts of naughty thoughts popped to mind, suddenly making her task much easier. "Okay," she said slowly, her throat mysteriously tight as she tugged her gaze away from the real thing and focused instead on imagination. "My secret fantasy is a night of white-hot passionate sex with an anonymous bad-boy...in an elevator."

Jena's gaze narrowed. Marie nodded encouragingly.

Dulcy's pulse seemed to slow to a steady thrum as she worked her way through the vision. "I, um, would have on this short short skirt...and I wouldn't be wearing any underwear. And he'd...um, he'd be wearing leather pants...black..." That was good. The guy who still stood at the door had on jeans. Close-fitting faded denim that hugged his crotch and thighs to perfection. "And he'd have leather straps in his pants pockets. Straps he'd use to tie my hands above my head...."

Dulcy couldn't swallow, with the vivid images in her head of open-mouthed kisses and soft moans; the glistening, silk-covered shaft of an erection pulsing in her hands; the scent of sex thick and musky, tanned skin pressing against her sensitive pale flesh.

Jena shifted, and Dulcy blinked her into view. It was the first time she'd seen her friend speechless. Afraid of how much she'd just revealed about herself, she curled her fingers into her palms and searched for a way out of the corner she'd painted herself into.

"Oh, and...there would be another hot guy standing in the corner of the elevator...watching."

Judging by the way Jena's brows shot up and the way Marie's eyes bulged, she'd succeeded in her endeavor.

"You just made that up," Jena accused.

Dulcy rubbed the side of her neck, glad she'd momentarily sidetracked her friends. The fact that the guy in her fantasies was real wasn't improving her finely tuned condition any. "Okay, you're right," she lied. "But you have to admit, I had you two going."

She'd also made herself more than a little hot and bothered. Not because she got into exhibitionism or S&M by any stretch. But the hot passion and the anonymous stranger part had long been a secret fantasy of hers. Ever since she'd graduated from ogling her high school P.E. teacher and had taken to privately rating men in public places on how she thought they might perform in bed. Like having coffee at the café around the corner from their office and summing up the young, athletic waiter in the tight black pants that left very little to the imagination. Or dining out at her favorite Mexican restaurant and watching the hot Latin dancer teach customers how to tango, making her wonder how he danced in bed. Or during lulls at work, eyeing the building's new maintenance man, whose biceps practically split the seams of his shirt while he fixed the rash of broken light fixtures.

Dulcy twisted her lips. Curiously enough, all three examples were from the past week alone.

Her wedding—and wedding night—couldn't come soon enough for her.

Jena folded her forearms on top of the table. "Okay, since you're not interested in sharing your real fantasy with us…tell me, Dulcy, why did you say earlier that you have to lie to get married?"

Dulcy made a face. "I did not."

"You most certainly did."

Had she? She thought back and realized that, yes, she had, when she'd suggested that maybe Marie wasn't married yet because of her inability to lie. "It was a joke," she said.

"No, it wasn't. You don't make those kinds of jokes. Does it have something to do with Brad?"

"Jeez, Louise—Jena, give a girl a warning before you go back to something we talked about two days ago." Had she really just said 'Jeez, Louise'? Horrified, she realized she had.

"It was five minutes ago, not two days. And are you going to answer my question?"

Dulcy grimaced. "I plead the fifth."

"It's impossible to incriminate yourself with us, Dulc."

When Dulcy merely smiled, Jena sat up. "Would you like me to rephrase the question in a simple yes-or-no format?"

Dulcy pursed her lips, then said, "Yes."

"Okay. Did you lie to your groom, your husband-to-be, one certain Mr. Hottie," she glanced at Marie, having used her name for Brad, "today?"

"Yes."

"Did it have to do with sex?"

"No."

Jena frowned. "Damn. Okay…did it have to do with your friends, one Ms. Jena McCade and Ms. Marie Bertelli?"

Dulcy went completely still, the question hitting a little too close to home. "Well…it's more complicated than that—"

"A simple yes or no will do, Ms. Ferris." Jena looked to Marie. "May I request Your Honor instruct the witness to respond in the manner requested and agreed upon?"

Dulcy looked to Marie, the session's judge, hopefully.

"Answer the question, Ms. Ferris."

Dulcy gaped at her. Marie never sided with Jena. "Okay, then…yes. Yes, the lie I told to Brad had to do with you two."

She didn't realize the weight of the question and corresponding answer until silence settled on the table. She blinked to stare at her empty shot glass, avoiding her friends' curious looks.

Jena had warned her last month during a cocktail party at the Wheeler estate that Brad would try to break up their friendship after he placed the old rock and ring on her finger. Dulcy had laughed at her, thinking the prospect ridiculous...until Brad had asked her earlier today why only Jena and Marie were involved in her bachelorette party. And why his mother Beatrix—who looked remarkably like Betty White on steroids—wasn't included, as she wanted to be. During the drive into town, she, herself, had begun to wonder whether or not Jena's warning held any water. If Brad did disapprove of her friends now, what would happen after they were married? Would he begin by suggesting they leave one or the other of them off the list of dinner invites in deference to one of his friends or family members? Would he suggest they go to his family's for the holidays, essentially banning her from spending time with Jena and Marie?

She'd snapped her mouth open to make it clear to Brad that her friendship with Jena and Marie wasn't up for debate. But there weren't enough words in existence to convey the special bond that had developed among the three of them when they were kids. A tragic incident with Jena's parents had inspired in each of them an interest in law, and that interest had taken them through the bar exam and eventually to their recently formed law practice in partnership with Barry Lomax. Then she'd decided that she wasn't going to be placed in the position of defending her friendship with Jena and Marie. It was a fact he'd just have to accept.

Concerning her mother-in-law to be, she'd told Brad that bachelorette parties were traditionally for the bride's peers. Besides, Beatrix scared the living hell out of her.

As for the lie...she'd told Brad the three of them were

going to dinner and a movie, then staying at Jena's afterward.

"Let's dance."

Startled, Dulcy looked up to find Jena getting up from the booth. "What? Without—"

"Men? Absolutely." Jena tugged on Marie's hand; Marie in turn grabbed Dulcy's.

Giving a protest yip, she found herself stumbling down the aisle toward the dance floor set up in front of the band. They were playing Seger's "Old Time Rock 'n' Roll" and the decibel level was ear splitting up this close.

Jena easily found her groove, shimmying and shaking in that spontaneous way Dulcy had always secretly admired. Marie began clapping her hands, not nearly as graceful and slightly out of step, but having a good time.

Dulcy shrugged. Why not? She could do this. After all, it was her last real night as a single woman. Surely even she deserved to cut loose and have a bit of fun with her best friends.

With that, she threw her hands up in the air and began shaking her hips in a way she hoped wasn't too ludicrous.

GREAT. HIS FIRST NIGHT OUT in three months and he had to pick a gay bar.

Quinn Landis leaned against the highly polished bar and eyed three men standing nearby. They looked like models from a Gap commercial—as did every other male in the place—and they didn't seem to mind that there was nary a female in sight. He frowned, then asked the bartender for a beer. When he was handed an ice-cold bottle, he leaned across the bar. "What's going on tonight?"

"Sir?"

Quinn gestured with the neck of his bottle toward the guys.

The tender grinned. "Hockey team staying in the hotel."

"Oh." He paid the man, including a generous tip. "Thanks."

Gripping his beer, Quinn made his way toward the only empty table in the place, a small one near the dance floor. He hooked his foot around a chair leg, pulled it out and sat. Okay, so the joint wasn't a gay bar. But considering the low percentage of female clientele, he might soon wish he were anywhere but here. His odds of snagging a prime, long-legged woman interested in spending an hour between the sheets with him were looking slim, with all these jocks roaming the place. He glanced to where a waitress was taking a swat to the bottom from the guys at the neighboring table. Her grimace made him grin. Then again, maybe his chances weren't that bad, after all.

Good. After three months on the range, with nothing but fellow weathered ranch hands as company, he needed to get laid. As soon as humanly possible. Tonight. It was the reason he'd stopped at the hotel for the night rather than heading straight for his best friend Brad Wheeler's family estate. He needed the release before he could even think of facing his friend and hearing all the details about his upcoming nuptials. Besides, merely thinking of Brad's mother Beatrix Wheeler made him roll his eyes. Would the self-proclaimed Queen of Albuquerque appreciate his having trimmed his hair for the occasion, rather than relying on a simple leather cord to hold it back? He doubted it. To her, he'd always been that offensive boy Brad had dragged home when they were kids, no matter the style of his hair.

Married.

Quinn settled back more comfortably into the chair. He couldn't believe Brad was getting married. Of the two of them, he'd figured he'd be the one to settle down long before his restless friend. Well, he supposed he had settled before Brad, at least in an important way. Only, his lifestyle didn't include a woman. Not many females were interested in life on an isolated ranch where you had to drive over an hour just to go to the market. He'd thought he'd roped one, once. He wasn't about to make that mistake again. But Brad...

He shook his head and took a hefty swallow of beer. Since he was a kid, Brad's mother had tried to force him into a mold that spoke of wealth, power and kowtowing...mostly to her. But while Brad could wear a tuxedo like he was born in one, he'd also thought nothing of hanging out with wrong-side-of-the-tracks Quinn. And while Brad had the latest model Jaguar, the fifth one he'd gone through since coming of age, Quinn still had the old Chevy in need of some TLC that he'd bought when he was sixteen with money he'd made breaking his back on his uncle's ranch.

And while Brad had embraced the idea of running his family business, Wheeler Industries, Quinn was satisfied with the spread he'd bought from his uncle three years ago. He enjoyed getting his hands dirty—literally—and working a muscle other than his brain.

He peered through the scant couples on the dance floor toward the band. The sax player wasn't bad. Hmm...neither was the female backup singer. He had just shifted to get a better look, when three women passed in front of him, blocking his view—correction—improving the view. Taking a long, slow pull from his beer bottle, Quinn considered the threesome, who were obviously minus three guys.

The black-haired one definitely had possibilities. She moved that slender body of hers in a way that virtually guaranteed she'd be killer in bed. His gaze slid to the redhead. She wasn't bad. Obviously shy but with the pink tinge to her cheeks and a fire in her eyes that revealed she could be coaxed to take risks.

He put his bottle down on the table and sat up, trying to see around to the blonde's face. She put her hands up in the air, attempting to emulate the brunette's steps…then fell smack-dab in the middle of his lap.

He grinned.

Bingo.

2

ONE MINUTE Dulcy was dancing—at least she preferred to call it dancing while Jena called it clucking—and the next minute she was sprawled across the very warm, very hard lap of a guy sitting next to the dance floor.

Okay, no more tequila for her.

She laughed at her silent quip, then tried to gain a foothold. "I'm sorry. I...must have tripped."

She twisted to get up, her bottom rubbing against the man's...strategic area.

His groan caught her off guard and she blinked up into his face. Then blinked again. Not because she was having difficulty seeing. But because if she wasn't mistaken, she had just landed on top of the star of her most recent fantasy—the guy from the door. And, oh boy, he was even better this close up. Not since she was a teen and had plastered pictures of Sting all over her room—posters her mother had immediately taken down—had she reacted so strongly to the mere sight of someone.

Either that, or she was completely smashed.

"No hurry," her fantasy lover said in a deep baritone, drawing the words out, sounding better than even her imagination could have supplied.

A delicious shiver ran the length of Dulcy's spine, then inched back up again, leaving her stomach quivery and her breasts achy. She brazenly allowed her gaze to flick over the guy's features. Over his broad forehead and thick shoulder-length jet-black hair, the type of hair a girl could lose her hands in. She took in his strong, tanned silk-covered jawline and criminally generous mouth, the kind a woman might be tempted to run the tip of her tongue along the rim of. Then she skimmed her gaze up along the length of his nose to lash-rimmed eyes the color of the amber tequila she had just gulped down with her friends, the sort of eyes that should bear a warning Dangerous Waters Ahead.

She blinked, just then realizing he was returning her gaze with equal intensity, his strangely penetrating, preda-tory…hungry.

But it was his grin that made her stomach yo-yo to the floor right next to her high-heeled shoes, then bounce back up again.

He cleared his throat, the bobbing of his Adam's apple mesmerizing. "I was just sitting here, trying to come up with a good come-on line to use on you and, bam, you fall straight into my lap." He straightened her when she would have slid to the floor. "If that isn't a sign, I don't know what is."

Dulcy clutched his shoulder to straighten herself, in-trigued by the rock-hard muscles she felt bunched beneath the soft, beige chambray of his shirt. Brad wasn't exactly soft, but he wasn't this hard, either.

She noticed she had a good portion of the shirt clutched in her fist. She set about smoothing out the wrinkles, her huge diamond engagement ring flashing in the lights from the dance floor.

She snatched her hand back as if scorched. "I'll say it's a sign. It's a sign that me and tequila don't mix."

She finally struggled to a standing position, finding the strange *thunk-thunk* of her heart disconcerting, and the burn-ing in her lower abdomen completely foreign and as intoxicating as the tequila. She felt as if she'd barely escaped being hit by a charging horse.

"You can dress her up..." Jena's voice edged its way through the silken cobweb crowding Dulcy's mind. "Well, since you've already been personal with the man, don't you think you should properly introduce yourself?"

Introduce herself? What was Jena talking about?

The man stood. And it seemed her gaze had to travel up and up, and up again before she could see his grin.

"I'm Quinn."

Dulcy made a face. "Quinn? That's the name of my—" She yelped when Jena elbowed her strongly in the ribs, the words "groom's best friend" effectively lost.

Not that it mattered. Even though she'd yet to meet Brad's mysterious friend, no exclusive, blue-blooded Wheeler associate, much less Brad himself, would ever be caught dead in a meat market like Rage. And the connecting hotel didn't have nearly enough marble to be considered fashionable, which was one of the reasons why Dulcy had given in so easily to Jena's demand that they come here. For one last night, she wanted to be in a place where no one gave a hoot who the Wheelers were. And the man in front of her, with his longish wild hair, his brawny body and decadently suggestive grin, would not only not care who the Wheelers were, but also effortlessly make *her* forget about them.

"I'm Jena," her friend said, shaking the man's very tanned, very large, very fascinating hand, and shaking Dulcy out of her reverie.

"Hi. I'm Marie."

Dulcy watched dumbly as Marie followed suit, then stood back expectantly. Another nudge. She glared at Jena, then smiled at the stranger. What had he said his name was? Oh, yeah. Quinn. "I'm sorry to have—" she looked around, but saw that the other chair at the table was empty "—to have interrupted your evening, Quinn."

"No name?"

"Oh. I'm—"

"Dee," Jena said quickly. "Her name is Dee."

Dulcy made a face at her. Why would Jena give him a name that she and Marie had used when they were kids? God, Dulcy couldn't remember the last time either of them had called her that. Of course, she'd been the one to insist on the nickname when she was a teenager, hating that her given name was so different from everyone else's. Jena was a derivative of Jenny or Jennifer, Marie...well, it went without saying that her name, as well, was common. Only Dulcy had been stuck with a peculiar name solely because it had belonged to some dead ancestor and her mother had liked it.

The man's large, rough-skinned hand completely dwarfed hers as he took it, knocking her train of thought completely off track. Dulcy felt a strange vibration move up through her fingers, swirl around her arm, then travel the entire length of her body. Good God.

"It's nice to meet you, Dee."

"Me, too. I mean, it's nice to meet you, too...Quinn." The song "The Mighty Quinn" popped into her mind. Oh, yeah...the Quinn standing in front of her would, indeed, be mighty in all the ways a woman needed. She started at the thought, then grimaced. "Um, if you'll excuse me...I think I'm going to be sick."

WELL, AS FAR AS COMEBACKS WENT, Quinn had to say that Dee's ranked right up there with some of the most memorable. While he wasn't arrogant enough to think himself capable of charming any woman, he could safely say he'd never made one feel sick before.

Still, he couldn't help grinning, as Dee teetered back on her heels. He hoped she didn't plan to be sick that moment. On him.

Only she didn't look sick to him. She looked…well, damn good. Rather than being bereft of color, her cheeks were flushed, and while her eyes were bright, he suspected it was more a result of their very close encounter just now than from whatever she'd had to drink.

"Okay, I think I'm going to be all right now," she said, obviously relieved as she pushed her blond hair back from her face. "Yes. I'm fine. I just got…a little dizzy, that's all."

Dizzy was good, Quinn thought. Dizzy was real good.

The redhead stepped up and wrapped her fingers around Dee's arms as if to steady her. "Are you sure? Would you like some water? Maybe you should sit down."

Quinn deftly pushed the chair opposite him out. "Be my guest."

The blonde looked from the small table to the empty chair to his face again. "I couldn't," she said, trying to back away.

"You can," Jena said and steered her toward the table.

Quinn noted the interesting behavior. The brunette pushed and the blonde skidded a couple of inches, then stopped again. "I can't," she said, staring at her friend.

The other woman rolled her eyes to stare at the ceiling and sighed gustily. "Talk about wet blankets."

Oh yeah. Sheets…silk ones…black, to contrast with the paleness of the blonde's skin. Quinn waved a hand toward the empty chair. "Please. At least until you get your feet back under you."

The brunette grinned, the blonde grimaced and the other one… Quinn looked to see her pirating a glass of water from a waitress's tray. With a tad too much enthusiasm, she plopped it down on the table next to his beer.

Interesting…the two women appeared to be trying to hook their friend up with him. Which should have pleased him, if solely because it would make his job that much easier. But somehow the obvious attempt left him feeling a little ill at ease. He squinted and looked at them more closely. What were they up to? The one named Jena gave him a catty smile, Marie immediately avoided his gaze and the blonde…

Jena grasped Dee's shoulder and firmly pushed her into the empty chair. Dee appeared as mystified by her friends' behavior as he was. Quinn slowly sat back down in his own chair.

"We'll be right over there," Jena said and smiled. "You two have a good time…getting acquainted."

The blonde made a grab at her friend's arm, but the brunette seemed to anticipate the move and maneuvered around it. The redhead followed quickly behind her.

Quinn shook his head, then glanced at the woman across from him. "I think we've just been hooked up."

She stared at him as if now remembering he was still there. She nearly knocked the chair over in an attempt to get up. Quinn quickly grasped the back of it. "Whoa, there. I don't bite." The soft silk of her blouse was warm to the touch as he steadied her back into the chair. "Although I have been known to nibble a little. Upon a lady's invitation, that is."

Her cheeks burned bright, heightening the hazel of her eyes. She looked caught between wanting to bolt…and longing to stay.

Quinn looked at her more closely. Oh, it had been a long time since he'd been with a bad-girl playing good. And this one was definitely a bad-girl. It was evident in the delicious curve of her neck when she turned her head just so. In the enticing jut of her erect nipples against her blouse. In the way her decadent tongue dipped out to touch the corner of her mouth as if eyeing a treat she really wanted but didn't dare take.

The heat that had accumulated in his groin when she had dropped into his lap ignited into something hotter, and difficult to ignore.

"Oh God," she murmured, trying to get up again and this time succeeding. "Nothing personal, but…this just isn't something I should be doing."

Quinn allowed his gaze to travel over her from forehead to ankle, liking every incredible inch of her but knowing the chances of his getting to sample any of her wares had just dwindled to zero. "Are you sure?" he asked.

She nodded so emphatically she nearly fell back into her chair. "Oh, I'm very sure." She bit her plump bottom lip, then glanced in the direction her friends had gone. "Absolutely…positively…" Her gaze settled on him. "Um, sure."

Quinn grasped his beer bottle, trying to cool himself with the condensation running down the green glass. "Well, it was nice meeting you, then."

She gave him a fleeting smile that made him want to groan, then left him staring after her, even more in need of a woman than he'd been a half hour ago.

"ARE YOU INSANE?" Dulcy repeatedly splashed water over her face and stared in the rest room mirror at Jena, who was skillfully freshening her lipstick. She felt…anxious, shaken, and one-hundred-percent sober.

Jena pursed her lips and tried to hand Dulcy her lipstick. "Actually, I was just asking myself the same question. Of you."

Dulcy violently yanked paper towels from the holder one after another. "For God's sake, Jena, you can't possibly be implying what I think you are." She realized she'd accumulated a small pile and forced herself to stop, blotting her skin with a handful.

"What? That you spend your last night as a single woman in the arms of a complete stranger?" Her smile was decidedly wicked. "Absolutely."

The flushing of a toilet sounded, then one of the stall doors opened and Marie's curly red hair sprung into view. She claimed the sink on the other side of Dulcy. "In retrospect, it probably wasn't a good idea," said Marie.

Dulcy slumped against the sink in relief. "Thank you. At least someone sounds reasonably sane."

Marie smiled at her in the mirror. "But you have to admit, the guy was downright...tempting."

"Native American."

Dulcy stared at Jena.

"What? Didn't he look Native American?"

Marie nodded.

"Not full-blooded, mind you. But he definitely has some of that hot Native American heritage in his background."

Dulcy really didn't want to discuss this. She wadded up the towels and rounded Marie to stuff them into the wastebasket.

"That's exactly what I thought," Marie said, washing her hands and drying them. "All that wonderful brown skin. Those chiseled features. That...that mouth."

"He's not," Dulcy said, closing her eyes against the seductive image that her friend's words conjured. "Just because a guy has long dark hair and a great tan doesn't mean he's Native American."

Jena's gaze homed in on her in the mirror. "So you did notice what a wowie he was."

Dulcy raised her chin. "I'm engaged, not blind, Jena."

"Yes, but you're not married yet."

She rolled her eyes. "I can't believe I'm even discussing this with you." She held up her hand. "No, let me rephrase that. I am through discussing this with you. I am not going to do anything with any strange man just because I'm getting married in a week. Get it?"

"Got it."

"Good."

Marie smiled and linked her arm with hers, then Jena hesitantly did the same on the other side of her. "Now that that's out of the way...let's go have some fun."

FUN. THREE HOURS LATER Dulcy supposed that someone might have found the molten temptation flowing through her veins fun, but she found it downright alarming. A woman in love with the man she was about to marry wouldn't salivate over another man, would she? She'd always thought love made one blind to all others, no matter how tantalizing...or how much one had had to drink.

In hindsight, she should have insisted she, Jena and Marie go up to their rooms and settle in with every last item on the room service menu and a pay-per-view movie immediately after the "anonymous male" incident. But she hadn't. No. Instead, she'd downed more tequila—in moderation— scarfed down more corn chips and a large number of the nachos they'd ordered, and danced until she was sure her feet would fall off.

And during every single move she was heatedly aware of the stranger watching her from across the room. That is, when she didn't catch her own gaze plastered to him and his strikingly manly physique.

Did he have a Native American background? She admitted that with his dark hair and eyes and skin, all made darker still by the intimate lighting in the club, he very well could have. And the contrast between his provocative dark looks and Brad's handsomely waspish features couldn't have been more profound.

Dulcy absently fingered the sexy silk negligée in a box at her elbow, a gift from Marie, and watched a woman approach the man she couldn't seem to tear her eyes away from. He'd talked to no fewer than four other women during the course of the night, and danced with two others, but she couldn't deny her relief when none of them joined him at his table. As if sensing her attention on him, he slid a dark, suggestive glance in her direction, and then led the woman onto the dance floor. She felt as if she were about to swallow her tongue whole when he skimmed his hands down the woman's back as he pulled her close, even as his gaze was fused with Dulcy's. Good God...

"Don't be such a prude, Marie," Jena was saying across the table. "Of course it's all right to bring sex toys into the marriage bed."

Dulcy forced herself to pay more attention to her friends, and less to the man who was touching another woman but seemed to be suggesting he'd rather be touching her.

Marie was twirling a spiked dog collar around her finger. "But there are sex toys...and then there are implements of torture."

Jena smiled. "You mean there's a difference?"

Dulcy caught herself rubbing her index finger and thumb against the decadent material of the nightgown and forced herself to place the lid back on the box. "I hope you got a receipt for this stuff, Jena," she said softly, indicating the array of materials that seemed cruel even for a pet.

"That depends."

"On what?"

"On whether or not you plan on returning the items yourself."

Dulcy made a face and peered into the bag in which she'd instantly stuffed the highly wicked items that served as Jena's gift. "Tell me you got them on the Internet?"

"Nope. There's this great little shop downtown I know you're going to love."

Dulcy groaned and snatched the collar from Marie. "I don't think so."

"What's this one for?" Marie asked, poking at a miniature version of the dog collar about two inches in diameter.

"Never mind." Dulcy took that one, too, then put it in the bag with the other items that gave a whole new meaning to the word *unmentionables*.

She was aware of the slow song ending, which probably meant another fast song would soon start up. And Jena would undoubtedly pull them up for another fifteen-minute set. Dulcy didn't think her feet could stand it. She found herself glancing toward the dance floor, only realizing why she'd done so when she spotted the man named Quinn being led off by the woman he'd just danced with. But rather than heading back toward his table, she was navigating a path toward the door and the lobby beyond. Dulcy quickly averted her gaze. She didn't have to guess where they were heading. She looked down to find her hands clutching the bag, and released her grip. No doubt *that* couple could find something interesting to do with these items.

As expected, the band launched into another dance number and Jena virtually popped up from her seat. "Come on."

Marie groaned but slid from the booth, while Dulcy shook her head. "I'm just going to go run these things up to my room before someone sees them and gets the wrong idea about me."

What she really wanted to do was go strip out of her

clothes and her heels, brush her teeth, pull the sheet up to her chin and veg with a really good movie…and think about what she could have been doing tonight had she had enough guts.

Jena leaned over the table toward her. "You'd better be back in fifteen or else I'm coming up after you."

Dulcy smiled, knowing that despite her friend's threat, she'd be more likely to curl up on the bed with her and steal whatever she was eating, along with the remote. "Deal."

She gathered her gifts together and slid from the opposite side of the booth, giving Marie a sympathetic wave as Jena led her toward the dance floor. Well, she did have to give Jena some credit. The place was teeming with men who were exactly her type, but she hadn't once wavered in her promise to make this Dulcy's night. There had been one moment when Dulcy was afraid they were about to lose her—when a fresh-faced hockey player with a lopsided grin, a chin dimple and devilish eyes had stolen her for two whole dances—but Jena had finally peeled herself away from him and rejoined the party. Dulcy had decided to let slide the bit of paper, no doubt holding the player's phone number, that Jena had slipped into her pocket.

The difference between the smoke-choked atmosphere of the club and the brightly lit, sparsely populated lobby was like night and day. And Dulcy felt immediately better. More like herself, more in control. She took a deep breath of the hotel air and blinked, slowing her step as the pulse of the music drifted farther and farther away. It had been so long since she'd actually been to a club, she had forgotten what it was like. The intimate lighting. The heat of too many young, single, needy bodies filling the room. The rhythm of the drum that seemed to vibrate across the floor and grip her heart. She and Jena had gone a few times when they were in undergrad school together. And again when Marie had come of age. But it had never really been her thing. Going to the theatre or out to a nice dinner, visiting with her friends—those had always been her preferred styles of entertainment.

And now she knew why. There was something about the wild environment…about merely being in a club that seemed to emphasize wantonness and willingness for experiences she only allowed herself to fantasize about, and never indulged in. What others, like Jena, saw as challenges, she saw as strictly dangerous.

She started to walk by the concierge's desk, then backtracked, clutching her packages tightly to her side. "Excuse me, when does room service close for the night?"

The young, attractive man behind the desk openly eyed her and grinned. "Never, miss. They're open twenty-four hours. With a limited menu after midnight."

She found herself smiling back at him. "Good. Thanks."

"Don't mention it."

She turned back toward the far hall and the elevators there, her heels clicking against the marble tiled floor. See, the concierge's overt reaction to her, probably after having seen her come from the club, was proof positive of her verdict on clubs and clubbing. She thought the appropriate word nowadays was *player* but she couldn't be sure. Whatever it was, she certainly wasn't one, and never would be.

She punched the elevator button, then stood back to wait. No. In eight days she was going to be Mrs. Brad Wheeler III. She grimaced. Why had she thought of it that way? She shook her head and dug through her purse for her room card key. But even she had to admit that while Brad's financial status hadn't influenced her decision to marry him one iota, it would certainly impact her life from here on out. She'd just gotten used to balancing her own checkbook, yet now she'd have an accountant and house manager to look after all that for her. It had been a challenge to remember when she'd last had the oil checked in her car, yet now she would have use of Brad's in-house mechanic, who looked after his half dozen or so cars on a daily basis.

She pulled out her card key. Oh, yeah. Her life from here on out was definitely going to change. For the better, she firmly told herself. Who cared if personal privacy would be virtually nil? Her mother would have the money she'd had to do without for too long. And Dulcy would have Brad. That's all she needed.

The elevator dinged open, and she stepped inside and pressed the button for the seventh floor. The mirrored doors began sliding closed and she leaned against the back of the elevator and sighed. An inch before the doors would have closed altogether, a hand snaked through the opening. The doors bounced, then jerked back open.

Dulcy stared, suddenly dry mouthed, at the new arrival— all dark skinned, big grinned and looking so good she could eat him with a spoon.

Oh, yeah? If Brad was all she needed, why was she looking at the guy from the bar as if she wanted to order him up from room service?

3

TWO TIMES LUCKY, Quinn made a mental note to himself, because something like this didn't happen to him every day. First this girl who could have come from one of those 1-900-babe hotline commercials literally drops into his lap…now he runs into her, alone, in the elevator.

He held the doors open with one hand and watched Dee scramble from where she was leaning against the wall. Her relaxed position had caused her skirt to inch farther up her long, long legs. The design of her white blouse was far too conservative to be called sexy, but the leather skirt hugged the body it was wrapped around to delectable perfection. No matter how hard she tried, he'd bet, she was never quite successful in covering up the sensuality that emanated from her like a seductive scent. A mystifying, evocative sexuality had ensnared him so completely in the scant few minutes they had spoken that he hadn't been able to drum up enthusiasm for anyone else. He'd thought he might have something with the last girl he danced with. But when she propositioned him, he turned her down. So then she'd asked him to do her the favor of walking out of the bar with her because one of the hockey players was coming on a little too strong for her liking. He had, and after stopping off at the hotel gift shop to pick up a fresh razor, he'd decided to go upstairs…alone.

At least, that had been his intention. But now that he stood staring at the fantasy-in-heels staring back at him like she wanted to eat him whole…well, maybe the night wasn't yet over.

"Hi, again," she said, her voice soft and hesitant.

He noticed she was nearly bending in half the box she held, and his grin widened.

"Where's…um, your friend?" she asked.

He cocked a brow and stepped into the elevator, allowing the doors to close behind him. The simple move caused her to step back farther.

"Friend?"

She nodded and tucked her hair behind her ear, looking everywhere but at him. Correction. Looking everywhere on his body except his face.

"Oh. You're talking about the girl I left the bar with." He shrugged. "I don't know where she is. I guess she went to her room. Alone."

Something he'd been facing himself until ten seconds ago.

He glanced at the control panel, then pressed the button for the sixth floor. "Your birthday?" he asked.

"Huh?"

He pointed to the boxes she held.

"Um, no, but…something similar."

He turned so that he was facing the doors alongside her. The scent of something fruity, something fresh, reached his nose and he breathed it in. While city girl was stamped all over her, she smelled amazingly like the outdoors. And infinitely edible.

Quinn had never noticed how quiet elevators were before. Or how small. He swore he could hear the sound of his blood rushing full speed to his groin. Feel the heat of his body increase the temperature of the enclosure. Sense Dee's growing tension as she swallowed.

How did one close a deal of this nature in the negligible

amount of time it took for the elevator to climb to the sixth floor? He'd already guessed that one-night stands and becoming intimate with strangers went against Dee's principles, although he suspected that if she listened to her heart, she'd probably follow it. But her running away from him in the bar proved she wasn't anywhere near ready to do that.

But he also knew that she was as attracted to him as he was to her. Had watched her watching him all night. Had stared at her as she licked salt from her hand with that naughty pink tongue of hers, her gaze steadfastly on him, then downed tequila along with her friends.

The elevator bell dinged. The doors slid open.

Damn.

The way he saw it, he had two options. Push the emergency button and thrust her against the wall and have his way with her. Or leave.

He began to exit. He heard her intake of breath, as if she was about to say something, and hesitated on the threshold, another option emerging.

He turned, butting his shoulder against the open door. He gazed at where she still stood rigidly straight, clutching her packages as if they'd somehow protect her against him. Protect her against her attraction for him. An attraction that widened her pupils until her hazel eyes nearly shone black, and left her moistened lips parted.

Quinn cleared his throat, then smiled. "You, um, wouldn't happen to want…"

He purposely let his words trail off, allowing her to define the parameters, if she chose any.

She quickly shook her head. "No. Sorry. I can't."

He glanced at his boots. "My loss, then, huh?"

The elevator door bounced against his shoulder. He started to straighten. Then out of the corner of his eye he saw the woman throw the packages she held to the floor. And suddenly she was up close and real personal.

Quinn wasn't all that clear on the details of what brought her from the far end of the elevator to flush up against him, but he wasn't going to look a gift horse in the mouth. Almost instantaneously, her fingers were in his hair, tugging the strands from the leather strap. Her mouth rested awkwardly against his, the stiff peaks of her breasts jutting through the chambray of his shirt. Acting on pure instinct, he groaned and pulled her closer, slanting his mouth more comfortably against hers. With the tip of his tongue, he traced the seam of her lips, coaxing them open. And just like that, they were.

God, she tasted like pure temptation, just the way he knew she would. Mischievous, sweet, and hot as hell. He slid his tongue along the length of hers, reveling in the texture of it, the taste. He'd all but given up hope of kissing her like this. Now that he was…well, it was even better than he had imagined. In an instant he was rock hard and wanted her in a way that made him forget where they were—a condition that intensified when she wriggled and shimmied hungrily against him.

Quinn slowly slid his hands to her hips, holding her still as he pressed his erection into her soft flesh, leaving little doubt about how he was feeling and what he had in mind. When she not only didn't object but shivered in response, his body temperature leapt another few degrees. He skimmed his hands from her hips, up along her slender midriff, then created a wall on either side of her full breasts with his palms. At her gasp, he stepped up the force of his kiss, then drew his hands all the way over her breasts, squeezing the straining tips between his thumbs and palms.

Take it easy, buddy. You don't want to scare her off.

And he was all too aware of the risk of scaring her off.

Of moving too quickly and having her balk. She had run from simple conversation in the bar. Pushing her too far too fast here, alone in the elevator, might ruin his chances altogether. But he simply couldn't help himself. The instant he'd been given a taste of what he'd been longing for all night, he was filled with the need to take it all the way. For the past two hours he'd mentally envisioned every last thing he'd like to do to the woman now in his arms. And, by God, he couldn't stop himself from making those plans a reality.

A slight pulling of fabric and her blouse opened. A dip of his hand and the material bowed, revealing a snow-white lace bra. He briefly broke off the kiss to gaze at the small mounds of flesh accented to perfection by the half-cups of fabric. Her nipples poked against the material, begging to be set free. And he found more than anything that he wanted to grant them that freedom. Dipping his index finger inside the cup and under the stiff peak, he lifted. The rosy tip popped up. He wasted no time fastening his mouth around it, licking and tugging and pulling until Dee's breathing was so erratic that it nearly tore the succulent bit of flesh from his mouth. He blindly found and liberated her other nipple, groaning at the decadent way she held her shoulders back, straining for his attention. He caught the stiff peak between his thumb and forefinger and pinched, reveling in her sharp intake of breath.

Quinn closed his eyes. God, but her responsiveness was killing him.

Stroking her right breast, he dropped his other hand lower, skimming the backs of his fingers down her hip, then lower still, until they rested against the skin of her leg. The bare skin of her leg. The fact that she wore no nylons surprised and excited him. Maybe this bad-girl in good-girl clothing had a naughty streak she didn't even know the breadth of. He drank in her moan. Oh, he was going to enjoy not only introducing her to that naughty side, but making her love it. He edged his fingers upward, slowly lifting her skirt until he was mere millimeters away from her sex. He paused, measuring the hunger in her kiss, the rapidness of her breathing, then he brushed the backs of his fingers against the crotch of her panties, finding her hot and wet and ready.

She shuddered so violently that for a moment Quinn thought she might have climaxed. But rather than collapse against him for support, she grasped his shoulders and pressed her hips more solidly against his, cradling his pulsing erection between her thighs. Quinn stretched his neck and groaned. Sweet Jesus, but she was going to end him right here and now.

WILD…hard…wet. Dulcy had never felt so out of control in her life. Yet so completely in control. Of herself. Of Quinn. Of the powerful emotions surging through her body, bringing to life a hunger, a need, she hadn't known existed. The instant her sex made contact with his through their clothes, she knew she had to have him. Gone was any rational thought. Vanished was every last shred of self-doubt or concern about tomorrow. She completely gave herself over to the power of feeling. Nothing more. Nothing less. Of listening to her body and following its lead, trusting it not to lead her in the wrong direction.

She began fumbling with the buttons of his shirt, then gave up and tore at the material, sending buttons ricocheting through the elevator. Finally, the smooth, hair-peppered chest was bared to her gaze. She tugged the soft material down over his shoulders, marveling at the toned, sculpted quality of his pecs. She'd sensed his hardness when she'd fallen into his lap, but somehow not even that brief contact had prepared her for this. She placed a hesitant kiss against the heated flesh, then opened her mouth for a more thorough taste, thinking that if, instead of air, she could breathe *him* right that moment, she would.

She shamelessly jutted her hips against his, absently wondering what felt better—the fire licking through her veins, making her aware of every pulse of her heartbeat, or him. The long, thick ridge of his erection pressed against her swollen flesh, and she shivered, deciding that there was no longer any differentiating between the two. His actions fanned the flames, provoking even bolder reactions from her.

His fingers seared her bottom, tunneling under the edge of her panties and cupping her. Dulcy reached for the front of his jeans and the button there. Her fingers brushed something, and she swallowed hard, realizing that the tip of his arousal was right there, peeking from the waist of his jeans.

Dear Lord...

She skimmed her thumb over the velvet tip, rubbing the bead of moisture over him, then shamelessly lifted her thumb to her mouth, tasting him. She blinked to look into his eyes. The sight of his enlarged pupils, the sheer desire on his face, enhanced her own skyrocketing feelings.

The elevator door bumped against her arm. Dulcy grasped the gaping edges of his shirt and pulled him inside the mirrored enclosure. The doors immediately slid closed, but when the elevator started to drop, Quinn reached behind him and pulled the emergency button, stopping it from going anywhere.

One of his fingers traced the length of her fissure from behind, coaxing her right leg up in order to allow him freer access. Dulcy hooked her foot around his calf. She nearly collapsed as the same finger found the pulsing bit of flesh at the apex of her thighs. She gasped as the finger dove into her dripping recesses.

Forgotten was her own quest as she grasped his shoulders, afraid she might faint from the headiness of it all. She broke contact with his mouth and rested her cheek against his bare shoulder. Through heavy-lidded eyes she watched their reflection in the smoky wall mirror. Somewhere in the depths of her mind, she thought she should be shocked to find herself standing there, her blouse open, her engorged nipples peeking out from the top of her bra, her leg hiked up revealing more than was decent and Quinn's dark-skinned hands branding her pale flesh. But the image only served to turn her on more.

"Reach into my back pocket," he said savagely into her ear. "Now."

Dulcy slid her hands down his back and into both pockets, moments later tugging out a foil packet. In one swift movement, he freed her of her panties and undid the front of his jeans. Not wanting to let go of him, Dulcy put the corner of the packet between her teeth and ripped, praying she hadn't damaged the latex. She moved to sheath him, but he took it from her fingers.

"Oh, no, darlin'. If you do that, we'll never get a chance to use it."

He covered himself with the latex condom, then thrust her against the back mirror of the elevator. Dulcy braced herself against the cool surface even as he circled his hands to her bottom and pulled her legs up to rest on either side of his hips. She crossed her ankles behind him, then sighed as he entered her in one, long, thrust.

The flames that licked through her veins exploded to engulf her entire body. Her breasts throbbed. Her stomach tightened. And the sensation of his erection filling her seemed, oh, so right and made her hungrier for more.

She tilted her hips, taking him in even deeper. He groaned and thrust again, moving her back up the smooth mirror even as she steadied herself with her hands. He thrust again, each stroke edging up the chaos swirling inside her stomach, further tightening her nipples. She moved her head restlessly from side to side, able to do little more than anchor herself to accept his long, deep thrusts. She caught their reflection in the glass again, the vision chasing the air from her lungs. His legs were slightly bent to balance their weight, his dark shoulders glistened with sweat, her breasts swayed with each long stroke.

She swallowed hard, thinking that *long* was the key word. Long…and hard…and thick. His dark hair fell over his brow, half concealing the fierce expression on his face as he plunged again and again into her swollen, welcoming flesh. She'd never felt so naughty, so elemental…so mind-blowingly sexy as she did when he grasped her hips tighter, grinding against her, and forcing her right over the edge into oblivion.

A HALF HOUR LATER, Dulcy paced the length of her hotel room, then back again, barely seeing the patterned bed-spread that matched the draperies that matched the wall hanging that went with the lamp. Her breath came in irregular gasps, her muscles felt oddly electrified, and despite the thirty minutes that separated *now* from the erotic moment in the elevator, she was still on fire, her body hungry for a nameless something that only the stranger who had awakened the hunger could give her.

What had she done?

She glanced at the packages she'd tossed onto the bed, then at the clock, then at the telephone. She was distantly surprised neither Jena nor Marie had come after her yet. Then again, for all she knew they'd caught one of the elevators while she and Quinn had been stopped in theirs on the sixth floor, and were already in their rooms. She stalked to the connecting door and listened but couldn't hear anything. Not prepared to face either of her friends if they were there, she opted against opening the barrier.

She moved to the other side of the bed and the phone there. The red light was ominously dark. But just to be on the safe side, she punched the button to retrieve her messages, only to be told by a cold, automated voice that her voice-mail box was empty.

She hung up the receiver again and stared at the clock. It was after one o'clock. She didn't care. She needed to talk to someone. And the perfect someone for her to be talking to right now was Brad.

She picked up the telephone receiver again, punched the button for an outside line, then followed with his number. Ten rings later, she hung up the receiver again, then sank down onto the bed, rubbing the heels of her hands against her eyes.

What had she done? She groaned. Oh, she knew what she had done, all right. She had effectively mauled the most dangerously enticing man she'd ever seen in her life, in a hotel elevator. Tempted the man of her fantasies. Welcomed him into her flesh. She clamped her eyes shut even farther, until she saw stars. One minute she'd been congratulating herself on making it through her bachelorette party intact. The next she'd been living the made-up fantasy she'd shared with Jena and Marie earlier in the night.

Well, it hadn't been completely made up, but the elevator part of it had been. But, oh boy, what she had been missing out on with that little addition.

"This is crazy. Absolutely, stark raving, lunatic mad."

She could still see Quinn's sexy grin as he emerged from the bright blinding light of orgasm to stare down at her. Then reality had dawned and her eyes had widened—and his sexy grin had turned into a distinct expression of disappointment. Dulcy couldn't have moved fast enough, far enough as she shakily tried to put herself in order while she released the emergency button.

They'd reached his floor first. "I'm in room 613 if you change your mind," he'd said, just before the doors closed.

Was it possible to love one man and want to marry him, but want a completely different man only eight days before her wedding?

Well, that was certainly a stupid question, wasn't it. For if there was one thing she had just proven, it was that.

Pushing from the bed, she stormed into the bathroom and turned on the shower full blast. Refusing to look at herself in the mirror, she stepped back into the other room to where her overnight bag rested on the table, and had to take out nearly everything else before she found her nightgown. For several moments she stood there, staring down at the familiar material—the familiar, boring material. The expensive, light blue cotton nightgown with the little satin ties at the throat. The sound of the shower echoed in the bathroom. But she could concentrate on nothing but the steady pulse of her heartbeat. The smell of her sex, their sex, filling her nose. The throbbing of her womanhood and the hunger that remained. She knew she should undress and head for the shower.

Instead she moved toward the door. Whatever happened, she knew she had to see this thing through to its natural conclusion. And that meant having sex with Quinn until the hunger that raged inside her was satisfied. Or until something other than her own needs clamored for attention. The rest of it…well, the rest she'd figure out later. All she could think about was having Quinn's tongue in her mouth. His hot hands grasping her breasts to the point of pain, his fingers rubbing her nipples. His long erection stroking her inside and out, edging her to a place she had never visited before but curiously wanted to stake a claim on. Now. For as long as he could physically manage it. Until she couldn't walk. Until neither of them could stand the sight of the other. Until she'd cried out in orgasm again…and again… and again.

Or until one her friends hunted her down and tore her away from him.

INCREDIBLE…

Quinn slowly drew the very tip of his finger along the sweat-dampened valley of Dee's back, then down farther until he rested between the sweetly shaped cheeks of her bottom. She moaned in her sleep, instinctively rocking against his touch. He curved his fingers around her swollen sex and squeezed. Even in sleep she responded to him in a way that touched the most fundamental part of him.

He lay back beside her, thinking over the past four hours and wondering if he'd ever view the world the same way again. He didn't even have to close his eyes to see her straddled across him, her face full of decadent wonder as she watched his flesh disappear into hers; or under him, her arms stretched up above her head, allowing him to take control; or with her tush grinding back against him, the mingling of her pale pubic hair with his dark, sheer ecstasy on her face when she reached climax again…and again…and again.

He glanced down to find his member pulsing back to life against his bare stomach. Of course, he'd essentially had an erection ever since she'd landed in his lap earlier. He had the feeling that if they continued for the next two days, he wouldn't go limp. And he didn't think his reaction had anything to do with his teenage tutelage in the hands of his older next-door neighbor, who had taught him the finer points of tantric sex. He'd simply never wanted someone as much as he wanted Dee. Which should have puzzled the hell out of him considering that normally he would be lying next to his latest conquest planning his escape route. Then again, he didn't think he'd ever had sex with a woman who dropped off to sleep as quickly as Dee had. The action implied trust. And he found himself extending it to her, as well. He hadn't encountered much of that in his thirty-four years. If the women he usually bedded weren't making sure he didn't sneak out, they were trying to come up with inventive ways to get him to stay.

Not that Quinn thought he was such a great catch. No. As he'd gotten older, so had his bedmates. And he was coming to notice a certain desperation in his partners where there had once been only a warm afterglow. He gazed at Dee leisurely, thinking he'd love to see all that pale hair and skin of hers resting against his black satin sheets. See her toned, turned-on body against the backdrop of his bedroom instead of a cold hotel room. He lazily drew his finger up along Dee's side, over her breast, then her left arm. She shivered in her sleep, then shifted, bringing her side against his and draping her arm across his chest. He watched as her slender fingers tunneled through the hair there, then stilled. The rock on her ring finger seemed to flash at him in the dim light from the balcony door. He'd noticed it earlier in the bar. Engaged? He suspected so. He also suspected that the gathering with her friends wasn't a birthday party, but was instead a bachelorette party. Which meant that the wedding wasn't that far off. Might even be this weekend.

A pang of something he couldn't immediately identify skated through his stomach. He couldn't identify it simply because he'd never encountered it before. Jealousy. Pure and biting. The thought that the incredibly sexy woman lying next to him was about to marry another man filled him with a heat that had nothing to do with sex and everything to do with possessiveness. Which confounded him even more.

He'd bedded a couple of married women. Even an engaged one. On the day of her wedding. Was he proud of it? No. But, hey, sex was sex. And women committed to other men understood that more than single women. When he spotted the ring, he knew from the get-go that his time with the woman would be a one-shot deal. Which was all he was in the market for. The women from whom he'd wanted more had been few and far between. And they had always been single. New to him, however, was the desire to have a woman who already belonged to another man.

Dee murmured something. He shifted his head to watch her sleeping features. Her damp blond hair curled wildly around her heart-shaped face, her full, pink lips were swollen from his kisses, and when the tip of her tongue dipped out to lick the corner of her mouth, he nearly groaned. Oh, the incredible things she could do with that mouth. Just remembering made his blood surge through his veins triple time and his erection grow to painful proportions. He put her hand to rest on the bed and turned onto his side. If this was all they were to have, this one night, he was going to take his fill of her. And, he hoped, give her a memory she wouldn't soon forget.

With a languid hand, he trailed a path down over one curved cheek, then slid it into the crevice beyond. She made a soft whimper as he flicked his thumb over her swollen bud. He reached down and nudged her thighs open, baring her sex to his gaze for only a moment before he positioned himself there, between her legs. Within moments he was sheathed with a condom and he rested the tip of his erection against her engorged portal. He grit his teeth against the desire to thrust into her to the hilt. Slow. Nice…and…slow.

He fit the tip inside her slick flesh, then withdrew. She

murmured again and turned her head, but still didn't awaken. Gently grasping her hips, he slid his hands under her and slowly began to stroke her from the other side. He entered her again, this time a few millimeters deeper.

He knew the instant she awakened from her low, blood-stirring moan. She looked over her bare shoulder, her eyes sleepy and full of desire. He thrust again, this time even deeper. Her back arched, bringing her sex directly against his. Quinn stretched his neck and groaned as she began straining against him, seeking a deeper, more meaningful meeting. He was only too glad to oblige. Grasping her hips, he plunged in all the way, the explosion of light behind his eyes astounding him as he reached the edge of orgasm faster than he ever imagined possible.

4

DULCY JUGGLED HER BRIEFCASE along with her "grande" cup of Starbucks coffee and a small pot of African violets she'd picked up on Saturday—the day she was supposed to pick out china patterns. Instead, she'd lingered in the open-air market, choosing fruit she usually didn't keep around the house and buying violets. There was something about the flowers' raw beauty, their vivid colors, that drew her to them, although she told herself she simply thought they would look good on her desk. She turned the lock and shouldered open the glass-and-chrome door to Lomax, Ferris, McCade and Bertelli, Attorneys-at-Law. Monday morning. Two whole days since she'd kissed Quinn goodbye at the door to his hotel room...twice. The first time, she'd never made it into the hall. No promises. No regrets. No lingering what-ifs. She mentally braced herself, waiting as she'd been waiting all weekend, for one of the three to hit her. They didn't. She sighed, wondering what, if anything, that said about her.

The door whooshed shut behind her and she took in the neat, rustic waiting area of the law offices. A colorful south-western area rug covered the pine floor while rough-hewn furniture sat off to the right, including a coffee table that had legs as thick as tree trunks. In fact, they *were* tree trunks.

A glance at the empty secretary's desk told her that Mona wasn't in yet. Instantly, Dulcy relaxed her shoulders. Good.

She'd been dreading coming to the office for fear that there was something…different about her. Something the no-nonsense fiftyish secretary would immediately home in on and identify. And the last thing she wanted right now was anyone scrutinizing her. Not when she was having a hard time figuring herself out.

She stepped toward the first office to the right that bore her name on a brass plate.

"Happy Monday, Miss Ferris."

Dulcy gave a little squeak and nearly dropped the violets as she swiveled around to face Mona, who'd stepped out of Jena's office. The older woman immediately narrowed her gaze. Dulcy bit the inside of her cheek. Well, how did you like that for keeping things normal? The first voice she hears and she nearly jumps out of her skin.

"'Morning, Mona." She swung her door inward and laid her briefcase along with her coffee on the filing cabinet just inside. No matter how many times she'd asked, the older woman refused to call her by her first name. "Early this morning, aren't you?"

Mona fingered through the folders in her arms. Jena had once asked the ageless secretary if she had an entire closet full of navy skirts and plain white blouses. Dulcy had balked at the personal attack. But since then Mona had begun varying the color of her skirts, though they were all cut the same. Straight. Long. Basic. Much like the woman herself.

"I was just going to make the same comment about you," said Mona.

Dulcy waved her free hand, trying to come up with something witty to say, anything to divert the woman's attention, but failing miserably. Instead, her gaze focused on the violets in her hand. She glanced back at the secretary. "Here—I brought these for you."

Mona's face immediately brightened, making the fact that

she wore no makeup almost a nonissue. She put down the files and accepted the small pot. "For me?"

Dulcy smoothed her hair and checked the simple twist at the nape of her neck—a nervous gesture she hadn't used for at least five years. She frowned and forced her hand back to her side, fisting it to make sure it stayed put. "Yes. I was, um, at the market the day before yesterday and thought they'd look nice. You know, on your desk."

There it was again. The gaze.

Dulcy wasn't sure if it was the severe way Mona pulled her salt-and-pepper hair back into a bun, or the fact that she'd worked in a law office for so long, but Mona Lyndell had a stare that any prosecuting attorney would envy. And under which any witness would cave.

And Dulcy would do well to remember her own advice to clients. Less was more when it came to answering questions.

A door from the opposite side of the offices opened and Barry Lomax's substantial frame filled the empty space. "I thought I heard your voice. How's my girl doing this morning?"

Dulcy's tense smile relaxed into a genuine one. She crossed the area rug and fondly kissed Barry's cheek. He'd always reminded her of a cross between Kirk Douglas and Sean Connery in his bearded days. And he always made her feel good about the choices she'd made in her life.

Barry had a large hand in her ever making it as a practicing attorney, and was the sole reason she, Jena and Marie had been able to form their own partnership. At sixty-seven, the renowned trial attorney was long overdue for retirement. But with no children of his own and his original partners having retired long ago, he wanted to guarantee that everything he'd built up wouldn't disappear along with him. When Dulcy, Jena and Marie signed on as partners six months ago, they'd done so with the express stipulation that the firm would always hold Barry's name. In return, they received a boatload of wealthy, established clients, a swanky downtown address and the best working environment they could have hoped for.

Her smile widened. "You know, you're going to have to watch that 'girl' and 'honey' stuff from here on out. We wouldn't want anyone getting the wrong idea," she admonished.

Thrice divorced—twice to women who had started as paralegals at the firm—Barry wasn't a newcomer to the gossip mill. He pulled at the waist of his slacks, a habit he'd picked up a while ago after dropping twenty pounds. "Actually, I think that's more incentive to keep calling you 'girl.' There are worse things I can think of than having everyone believe there's a little hanky-panky going on behind the scenes here."

Dulcy crossed her arms. "Oh, that's just what I've always aspired to. To have everyone think I slept my way to the top." She laughed. "Anyway, that's not what I'm talking about. If you call me those cute little endearments in public, the entire legal establishment will be calling me 'girl' in no time flat. I can hear it already. I'm arbitrating an important case and the opposing attorney asks, 'Is that all, honey?'" She shuddered. "No, thank you."

"Oh, I don't know. You could try what you did with me the first time I slipped and called you 'honey' in public."

Dulcy's face went hot as she recalled the incident. She'd been all of twenty-one, participating in a mock trial. With solid ties to University of New Mexico School of Law, Barry had been visiting counsel and had agreed to sit in as the judge. "Any more questions, honey?" he'd asked. She'd bristled, then shot back, "No, I think that about covers it, pookems," and the entire room had erupted in laughter. Including Barry.

It was the beginning of a mentor-student relationship and, even more important, a friendship that Dulcy cherished.

"Can I get you two some coffee?" Mona asked.

Dulcy uncrossed her arms. "Thanks, but I can get it myself," she said as she had nearly every morning for the past six months.

Barry held out his white handmade ceramic cup with a real antler as the handle. "Mighty fine of you to offer, Miss Lyndell."

The instant Mona had taken the cup and disappeared down the hall, Dulcy lowered her voice. "I still think she has the hots for you."

Barry's deep laugh boomed through the room. "And I still think you're off your rocker, Dulc. Mona's been my secretary for thirty years. Don't you think I'd know if she had the slightest bit of interest in me?"

Dulcy patted the front of his starched shirt. "I don't think you'd notice if the woman stripped down naked right in front of you."

"Which would never happen."

She started to walk toward her office. "How would you know? You never look up from your latest case file long enough to see if it already has."

Another chuckle. "Did I know what I was letting myself in for when I signed you gals on as partners?"

Dulcy winked. "Actually, I still suspect you did it just to give half your clients a heart attack."

"Speaking of partners in crime, where are yours this morning, anyway?"

Dulcy glanced at her watch. "I'd say Marie's doing the parking spot hunt outside the county courthouse right about

now. And Jena…'' She smiled. ''Well, Jena's probably running late, as usual for a Monday morning.''

Which was exactly what Dulcy had been counting on.
She hadn't dared breathe a word to either of her friends
about what had happened two nights ago. And, thank God,
neither of them had pursued the matter. From what she understood, Jena and Marie had closed the club down. By the
time they'd made their way upstairs and knocked on her
door, they'd figured she was dead to the world and had let
her be. After all, everyone knew Dulcy was as boring as
they came.

If they only knew… She tightened her hand on the door
frame. Yes, well, if she had a say in the matter, they would
never find out.

The recollection of her reckless behavior sent a shiver
shimmying down her spine. She didn't even know Quinn's
last name. And he didn't know hers. Which was the way
she'd wanted it, wasn't it? She worried the back of her engagement ring with her thumb. After all, she was a scant
five days away from marrying someone else.

Barry stepped closer to her, a curious expression on his
face. Dulcy focused her errant gaze on him, wondering how
much she'd revealed by standing there reliving the past
weekend.

He lowered his voice. ''You know, as long as I have you
alone, there's something I want to talk to you about,
Dulcy.''

Oh God. Here it was. Everyone knew about what had
happened and she was going to hear about it.

''What—'' She cleared the frog from her throat, ''what
is it?''

He stared at her for a moment, then nodded in the direction Mona had gone. ''It's just that…I was wonder-

ing…have you noticed anything odd about Miss Lyndell lately?''

Odd? "No," she said, drawing out the word. "I can't say that I have. Then again, I really don't know Mona that well. You'd probably be the better judge of that."

He repeatedly smoothed down his tie. "I don't know. Maybe I'm overreacting but I think something's bothering her."

"Oh, maybe the world at large?"

He frowned.

"Sorry. Tell me, what makes you think that?"

He shrugged. "She seems to be forgetful lately. Failing to remember to call and cancel appointments. Ordering up the wrong thing for lunch."

Dulcy clucked. "Poor baby."

He had the good grace to redden slightly. But Dulcy also noticed that he was genuinely worried. She tilted her head to the side and considered him.

"And you know how she is. She'd never share anything of a personal nature with us. Do you suppose she's having problems at home?"

"Honestly, I couldn't tell you, Barry. You're right, she doesn't share anything personal. Would you like me to talk to her?"

Footsteps sounded on the floor between area rugs. Barry snapped upright, gave Dulcy a steady gaze, then stepped back to his office door and turned to his secretary.

"Ah, there she is," he said. Dulcy watched him accept his coffee cup, the way Mona waited to see if it was all right, then turned and walked into her office. Was there something bothering Mona? If so, Dulcy didn't know if she was the one to find out. Right now, her own plate was overflowing with items requiring her attention, not the least of which was her upcoming nuptials.

She debated closing her office door, then opted against it since she never closed it and the mere action itself might raise Mona's brows and start her to snooping. The last thing she needed was Mona on the prowl. She reached out and opened the door farther, just to be on the safe side, then rounded her desk and sat down. There was the Travers case to work on, a legal brief to proof and tweak and approve, and a court appearance to prepare for later in the week.

Still, all she could seem to do was drum her fingers against the empty desktop.

"Oh, for God's sake, just call him," she ordered under her breath. "He's your fiancé."

She glanced at her watch, though she was very aware of what time it was. A few minutes after eight. That meant Brad should be just getting into his office. She plucked up the phone, put it back down, then picked it up again. She'd left two messages on his home answering machine over the weekend, asking him to give her a call if he had the chance. He must not have had a chance. She put down the receiver and scratched her arm through her suit jacket.

"Miss Ferris?"

Dulcy nearly catapulted straight from her chair. Which didn't improve the secretary's dour expression as she stood watching curiously from the open doorway.

"What is it, Mona?"

"Miss McCade just called. Said she was running late and asked if you could sit in on an eight-thirty conference to finalize the details of a prenuptial agreement. She said that everything's already ironed out, and it will only be a matter of crossing the t's and dotting the i's."

Dulcy grimaced. Sure, Jena routinely ran late on Monday mornings, and while she'd been known to reschedule an occasional appointment or two, she'd never asked Dulcy or Marie to sit in for her.

She absently rubbed her temple. The fact that this particular case involved a prenuptial agreement so close to the exchange of her own nuptials didn't escape her notice, either.

What was Jena up to now?

"I can put the conference off until she arrives," Mona offered. "But it's too late to call and reschedule."

Dulcy considered her options, trying not to be too skeptical of her friend's motives. Finally, she shook her head. "No, that's okay. I think I can handle it. Thanks."

"Certainly."

Dulcy pulled the Travers case file in front of her and flipped it open. Moments later, she realized Mona still stood in the doorway. She looked up. "Is there something else?"

The older woman appeared ready to say something, then sighed. "No. No, there isn't."

Remembering her conversation with Barry, Dulcy was raising a hand to stop Mona from leaving, when the phone chirped. For the second time in as many minutes, she nearly leapt from her chair.

Of course, Mona didn't miss the reaction, and her eyes narrowed. "I'll get it for you."

"I've got it. Thanks again."

The secretary nodded and left the room.

Dulcy wiped her damp palms against her skirt and reached for the receiver. "Dulcy Ferris."

The caller identified herself as having been referred by a fellow attorney. Dulcy swallowed hard. Not Brad.

For the next five minutes she spoke to the potential client and somewhere over the course of the conversation she actually forgot about the past weekend. Put out of her mind the murkiness of the future. Managed to concentrate on nothing but the here and now. Devote herself completely to her career. Which was exactly what she had hoped would happen.

A half hour later she no longer recognized the woman who had been so impulsively wild the other night. She collected the file on Jena's prenup case from Mona, then joined the bride and groom and the groom's attorney in the smaller of the two conference rooms.

She explained Jena's…detainment and then introduced herself. It appeared the bride, one very blond, very busty Mandy Mallone, was to be her client, however temporary.

"So," she said, taking the seat next to Mandy and trying not to wrinkle her nose at the overpowering smell of perfume. "Jena told me that all the hard work's done." She flipped open the file and extracted the prepared contracts. A set of originals and another file copy with red arrow stickers indicating where signatures were required. "We're just here to sign, is that right?"

"Right," said the groom, a twenty-something, handsome, stuffy-looking Jason Polansky.

The bride crossed her arms, pushing up her already pushed-up breasts in her tight white suit. "Wrong."

Dulcy blinked, once, twice, and hoped like hell she was hearing things. She silently cursed Jena, who was probably even now laughing at her expense in a coffee shop somewhere.

The other two in the room instantly spoke up. Dulcy was somewhat familiar with the middle-aged lawyer sitting next to Polansky, simply because the services of Steve Saragin and Associates didn't come cheap. And because he starred in his own cheesy commercials advertising his services on TV. He was the legal equivalent of a used car salesman. An attractive equivalent—but why was it men were never as handsome when they did something sleazy like that?

"Oh, come on, Mandy. This is the fifth time we've been through this," the groom objected.

Saragin added, "Miss Mallone, I have to remind you that a verbal agreement is just as binding as a written contract."

Dulcy bit her lip to keep from responding. She slanted a hopeful glance at the brassy bride next to her. Neither comment seemed to move her from her position. If anything, they seemed to make her attractive chin snap up higher, and the scarlet-painted nails dig deeper into her arms.

"I've changed my mind. So shoot me."

"Don't tempt me," Polansky said under his breath, obviously exasperated. He turned on an impressive grin that Dulcy suspected had attracted his bride to begin with. "Mandy, honey, we're getting married in five short days. Don't you think we'd both breathe much easier if we got this out of the way?"

Dulcy stared at him, trying not to think about the fact that it was the same day she was to marry Brad.

"We don't have time for this. Really, we don't."

Saragin slid the contracts out from in front of Dulcy and tried to hand them to Mandy. "Mr. Polansky is being very generous, Miss Mallone. Exceptionally generous. My advice is that you should sign."

Mandy appeared to waver. She slowly released her grip on her arms. The groom smiled at her encouragingly, Saragin cleared his throat, and she hesitantly moved to take the contracts.

Dulcy was unable to sit on the sidelines any longer. Call her a masochist, or just plain aggravated by the groom and his attorney's behavior, but if the firm's client was hesitant, she should find out why. She took the contracts from Saragin and gave Mandy a sympathetic smile. "Good thing you're not serving on behalf of her attorney then, isn't it, Steve." She gave the two men a pointed glance. "You don't mind if I take a minute, do you? Since this isn't the brief meeting we all expected.''

The opposing attorney moved to object, then snapped his mouth shut when it became evident that whatever he said wasn't going to stop her.

Dulcy sat back in her chair and began scanning the whopping thirty-page document, her eyes growing wider and wider with each word. It appeared that every last asset Polansky owned was detailed and appraised…and was stipulated to remain his in the event of divorce. And, since Miss Mallone would retire from her job as an exotic dancer—Dulcy raised a brow and glanced at the blonde again—and Mr. Polansky would be the couple's sole wage earner, ninety-five percent of assets acquired during the marriage would remain with Mr. Polansky for the first ten years of the marriage, then go up in increments of five percent for every ten years thereafter.

Jena had signed off on this? Dulcy looked at Mandy, who was watching her hopefully, then quickly back at the agreement.

In the event that the couple had children, it stipulated that joint custody would be awarded, and no alimony or child support allocated.

Dulcy tapped the contract. That would never stand up in a court of law, she mentally noted.

She finished reading and then leafed back to the beginning of the contract. This wasn't a prenuptial agreement; this was legal enslavement. Of course, nowhere did it limit Polansky's claim against any of Mandy's future earnings. For all anyone knew, she could design the ultimate thong underwear—a new design that didn't make you feel like you were flossing your butt—and turn into a multimillionaire overnight, and her cheapskate husband would be entitled to half her earnings. Dulcy sighed and glanced again at the last page, where it stated Mandy was to have no claim against Mr. Polansky's retirement benefits, no matter how long the couple was married. It stated the company's name: Polansky, Polansky and Polansky, Attorneys-at-Law.

Figured. She grimaced. Trust an attorney to come up with a piece of crap like this. Trust another attorney, namely one deeply in trouble Jena McCade, to let him get away with it.

She carefully put down the agreement in front of her and folded her hands on top of it. The date the agreement was supposed to go into effect was the same day she would be marrying Brad Wheeler. She only now found it intriguing that Brad hadn't asked for a prenuptial agreement, and was relieved he hadn't. Had her groom suggested she endorse the document in front of her, she would have made him eat it.

She cleared her throat and stared at both attorneys opposite her. "May I have a moment alone with my client, please?" She got up, walked to the door and opened it. "Mona, would you please see if Mr. Polansky and Mr. Saragin would like anything?" she asked the secretary.

Saragin drew even with her. "I think it would be wise for you to have a few words with Jena before you do anything rash, Dulcy."

She smiled at him, but it felt cold and unnatural. "Thanks. I'll take it under advisement." In his dreams.

She closed the door after them, then leaned against it, staring at an obviously surprised Mandy. "We have to talk."

THREE HOURS LATER Dulcy felt, well, almost herself again. Almost. She leaned back in her chair and stared out the picture window at the breathtaking view of the Sandia Mountains. She and Mandy Mallone had gone over that poor excuse for a prenuptial agreement with a thick red marker, handed it to Saragin and Polansky, then called that meeting to a close. Conveniently, Jena showed up shortly thereafter, wearing a mile-wide grin. She'd leaned against Dulcy's doorjamb, crossed her arms and asked how many pieces remained after the morning encounter.

"Figured as much," Jena had said. "Saragin called me on my cell to let me know he wasn't happy."

"Cell phone? Saragin has your personal cell phone number?"

Jena pressed her lips together and said nothing.

"Oh, Jeez, Jena. I knew something smelled fishy, but I had no idea it was because you and the tight-ass opposing attorney were getting it on behind the scenes."

"Getting it on? How crude." She'd shrugged. "For the record, we haven't even gone out. Yet. But I am intrigued by the rumors circulating about him."

"What rumors?"

"That he's hung like a horse."

Dulcy groaned. She had to ask. "Rumors likely originating from him. He probably took out ads in the paper."

Her friend laughed. "So what's the big deal?"

"The big deal is that you nearly shipped that poor girl off into shark-infested waters without a paddle to save herself."

"That 'poor girl' has made a small fortune dancing nude for a living," she said on her way out the door. "Anyway, that's exactly the reason I asked you to take the meeting. I knew you wouldn't let that piece of toilet paper fly."

Dulcy rocked slightly in her chair, feeling much better now than she had earlier this morning. She would feel even better if not for the restless awareness lurking just beneath her skin. The heat crept up on her when she least expected it, like now, when she took a moment to glance away from what she was doing and her mind hiccuped.

Truth be told, that same heat had been there for a long time—a scalding, alarming heat that one red-hot night with Quinn had only served to heighten. If not for him, and the unleashing of those needs, she might believe herself the same person she was a few days ago. The practical, sensible woman who chose corporate law over domestic cases like that she'd encountered this morning. The fiancée of a man dozens of women would kill to be marrying in six days. A woman basically satisfied with her life, who didn't spend every spare moment wondering if she'd been missing out on a whole different world of sexual wonder that she'd experienced with Quinn.

Dulcy sighed and dropped her head into her hands. Okay, two seconds and she'd basically undone three hours' worth of psychological reconstruction. She glanced at her watch and snatched up the telephone receiver, pressing the button that would put her straight through to Brad's private office line at Wheeler Industries. Four rings later she received his voice-mail announcement. She frowned, realizing it was the same one he'd recorded before leaving the office last Friday. She slowly replaced the receiver. That's funny. Brad was due back from a golf date at his country club late last night. And surely he would have been in the office this morning. In fact, she was convinced he was, because he'd told her about an important board meeting scheduled for nine. Maybe that was it. He'd gotten caught up and hadn't had a chance to update his voice-mail message.

She plucked up the receiver again and dialed the official office number, only to be told he hadn't made it in this morning.

"Is this Miss Ferris?"

Dulcy frowned into the phone. Brad's secretary had never addressed her directly in the five months since she'd started calling.

"Yes, Jenny, it is. If you could just ask him to give me a call when he gets in, I'd—"

"Well, that's just it, Miss Ferris," the woman said, lowering her voice in that gossipy way that Dulcy heard around coffee machines but never dared participate in. "You see, I don't know if Mr. Wheeler will be coming in this morning, or ever again."

Dulcy switched the phone to her other ear and pulled a file in front of her, reminding herself why she didn't participate in office gossip. So much of it resembled what was splashed across the supermarket tabloids—a sort of scandal sheet for everyday people. "What do you mean you don't know if he'll be coming in this morning? Has he called? Left a message?" She decided to ignore the "or ever" comment.

A mild ruckus came from the direction of the waiting area. Dulcy listened to Brad's secretary with half an ear as she craned her neck to get a look outside her door.

"...You see, Mr. Wheeler's missing."

The words registered just as Dulcy spotted one very coiffed, very irate Beatrix Wheeler, Brad's mother, going nose-to-nose with an equally determined Mona.

"What do you mean I need an appointment? I don't need an appointment to see my own daughter-in-law to be. Do you know who I am?" Beatrix was saying in her best born-to-be-queen voice.

The telephone receiver clattered to the desktop. Dulcy scrambled to pick it up, mumbled something incoherent into the mouthpiece, then managed to hang up. She rose from her chair and smoothed her skirt, anticipating the moment Beatrix would make her way to her office. She began to edge around the desk, her new position giving her a wider view of the waiting area and the dark, brooding man standing behind Beatrix.

Oh my God…Quinn.

Naughty, hot, erotic images slid through her mind, one after the other, setting her nerve endings on fire. Suddenly she was all too aware of the conservative cut of her business suit…and the decadent underwear Marie had given her as a wedding present underneath. Underwear she had sworn when she opened the box that she wouldn't wear, but which she didn't hesitate to put on this morning, even though it was meant for her honeymoon.

Her knees gave out. She frantically grabbed for her desk to keep from crumbling to the floor in a heap, and instead knocked her pencil holder and clock from the surface.

The racket quieted the standoff in the other room. Dulcy watched Beatrix glance her way, then swivel as if turning on the enemy. Dulcy watched her approach as she shakily ran her hands over the carpet in search of the dropped items. *Oh God, oh God, oh God. She knows. She knows. Brad knows. She knows, Brad knows, and the wedding's been called off.* Finally her fingers butted against the clock. She fumbled to pick it up, then unsteadily got to her feet, her back to the door. She briefly closed her eyes and said a little prayer, then slowly turned to face evil incarnate in the shape of Beatrix Wheeler, ignoring the devil in blue jeans standing next to her looking as shocked as she felt.

"What did you do with my son?" Beatrix demanded.

WELL, AIN'T THAT A BITCH.

Quinn Landis couldn't have felt more stunned had a fifteen-hand Appaloosa fallen from the sky and landed right on his head.

There wasn't a chance in hell…not even a remote possibility…this couldn't be…

But even as he stood outside the office and stared first at the nameplate that heralded the woman inside as Dulcy Ferris, then at the woman he knew as Dee—scrumptious, insatiable, provocative Dee—he knew that there *was* a chance that, yes, indeed, the two were one and the same.

He stepped a little more firmly into the doorway, planting his feet shoulder-width apart and sliding his hands into his jeans pockets. Dee's—Dulcy's gaze skid to him, then retreated, her cheeks fire-engine red, her hands shaking so badly she nearly dropped the crystal desk clock she held.

So, Quinn, tell me, how does it feel to know you screwed your best friend's bride-to-be? he asked himself.

"What?" Dulcy stuttered.

For a moment, Quinn was afraid he'd said the words aloud. Then he realized she hadn't direction the question at him, but rather at Beatrix Wheeler.

"I'm sorry, Miss Ferris, but the woman was quite insistent." Mona, who'd gone up against Beatrix in the waiting room seemed to indicate she was all for trying again. Especially when Beatrix glared at her and mumbled something under her breath.

Dulcy distractedly waved her hand. "It's all right, Mona."

Beatrix looked a breath away from pouncing on the pretty blonde. Then she smiled. Which was ten times worse than any frown and just as deadly. She smoothed down the front of her wool-blend jacket. "Sorry, dear, that didn't come out quite the way I intended."

Quinn grimaced, watching as the Wheeler family matriarch put on her best predatory suit of armor.

"Brad. You wouldn't happen to know where he is, would you, Dulcy?" Beatrix asked.

"If he's not at the office or at his condo…well, then, no, I don't know where he could be." Her gaze slid to Quinn's. "I haven't even seen him since Friday."

Beatrix crossed her arms over her formidable chest. At

nearly six feet, she was tall, broad, and would have been imposing, even without the wealth and power she'd been born with and wielded like a fine-edged sword.

"I don't mean to insinuate anything, dear, but, coincidentally, our information has it that that's when Brad disappeared."

Someone rammed into Quinn from behind. He shifted to allow the person to pass.

"Excuse me," a woman said, skirting him.

"What's going on in here?" Another voice, another collision. Quinn sighed and stepped off to the side in case anyone else cared to join the group.

The women he knew as Jena and Marie seemed to see him at the same time he recognized them. Marie's mouth dropped open. "Oh, my."

Jena, on the other hand, looked over the situation at hand and a decidedly devilish twinkle entered her eyes. "Well, this is interesting."

Dulcy crossed the room, passing right in front of Quinn. He told himself not to breath in her scent, to shut off his brain entirely when it came to Dulcy Ferris. But then the aroma of bananas—*bananas?*—reached his nose and he couldn't help taking a deep breath.

"No, no," Dulcy said urgently to Jena, giving her a quelling look. "Mrs. Wheeler's just told me that Brad's missing."

"What?" Marie exclaimed.

"I didn't say he was merely missing. I came to see what you did to him—" Beatrix cleared her throat. "If you knew where he might be. It's just so unlike him to be so irresponsible."

Dulcy swung on her heels so fast, she nearly toppled over. Quinn automatically reached out to steady her, his fingers hot against her cool arms left bare by her sleeveless blouse.

He didn't imagine her shiver. And he was hard-pressed to ignore his own immediate response to her. He released her so quickly she nearly fell again.

Jena made a sound of disapproval. "Do you have evidence of Dulcy's involvement in Brad's vanishing, Mrs. Wheeler? Because if you don't, you're giving me some primo evidence for a case of false accusation."

"False accusation? Why you little—"

Dulcy stepped between the two women and held her hands in a *T* shape for time-out. "Hold on a minute here. I'm not even sure what's happening and we're filing cases already?" She paced one way, then the next. "Mrs. Wheeler, why don't we all go into the conference room where we can discuss this calmly and maturely. Despite what you might be thinking right now, I did not have anything to do with Brad's disappearance. For God's sake, until five minutes ago I didn't even know he *was* missing. But if there's anything I can do to help find him, then of course I'm eager to try."

Quinn crossed his arms over his chest, ignoring Marie's frequent glances his way as if she was trying to put two and two together. He moved to shake his head, but she opened her mouth first. "*First things first.* I want to know what he's got to do with any of this."

Dulcy's gaze flew to his face and all the color that was there moments before drained from her skin.

"Don't be ridiculous. He doesn't have anything to do with this," Beatrix said. "That's Quinn Landis, Brad's best friend and the man who's going to stand up for him at his wedding."

Dulcy made a strangled sound deep in her throat, but Jena's laugh covered it. "*He's* the best man?"

Dulcy glared at her, Quinn grimaced and Beatrix raised her chin. "Yes, as much as the fact displeases me, he is."

She sighed dramatically. "Now, can we please get to the issue at hand? My son is missing and I, for one, would like to find him."

"Of course you would," Dulcy said, touching the older woman's arm. She immediately drew back when she saw the gesture was unwelcome. "Why don't we all step into the conference room?"

5

OKAY, THE FLOOR JUST MOVED—Dulcy was sure of it. Was New Mexico on a fault line? She couldn't remember ever having experienced an earthquake, but that didn't mean there couldn't be a first time, did it? She sat at the conference table and put pressure on her feet to try to stop the movement. It didn't work.

The southwestern-style conference room was jam-packed with people. In addition to Jena, Marie and Barry, Beatrix had brought in a meaty-looking guy she referred to as Bruno, the head of security at Wheeler Industries. Mona found reason to enter the room frequently, be it to deliver water, coffee, tea or pastries, aim glares in Beatrix's direction.

But it was Quinn's presence that undid Dulcy.

Somehow he'd managed to procure the chair right next to hers. Although he hadn't looked directly at her during the past forty-five-minute discussion, she was aware of his presence. She hadn't remembered him being so...large. Even sitting, he towered over her by a good half a foot. And his hands... She swallowed deeply, watching where he wrote something down in a pocket notebook. His fingers were long, thick and tanned, backs peppered with springy dark hair. The same fingers that had stroked her, teased her and slid up into her waiting slick body only a scant couple of days ago, making her say wanton things she never would have dreamed of saying.

A little sound escaped her. Quinn shifted in his chair until those rich brown eyes were staring directly into hers. Dulcy's throat closed so tight she wondered if she'd ever be able to swallow again.

Her gaze skittered away and back to the conference table. Only *she* would find a way to spend the only reckless night of her life with the one man she shouldn't: Brad's best man. Gave a whole new meaning to the term.

She reached for the water pitcher to fill her glass. Avid conversation went on around her, the participants needing very little input from her, thank God. Her hand shook so much that the pitcher of ice and water rattled. Marie reached out from her other side and took it from her, then poured water into her glass. Dulcy ignored her friend's probing gaze, then smiled her thanks as she lifted the glass to her lips with first one hand, then both.

Barry leaned forward, resting his forearms on the table. Before they'd entered the room, Barry had suggested that it might be better to let him and Jena and Marie handle the meeting, seeing as she was so close to the situation. Dulcy readily agreed, relieved that she wouldn't be facing this alone and infinitely glad she had all three of them on her side.

"So the police haven't been contacted," Barry said now.

Beatrix looked affronted. "Of course the police haven't been contacted. Do you know what the media would do if they caught a whiff of anything newsworthy going on in the Wheeler family, Mr. Lomax? We have stockholders to think about. Employees. Contracts."

Dulcy felt light-headed, barely registering that the only person Beatrix appeared to speak to civilly was Barry. The Wheeler family matriarch seemed barely able to keep herself from scratching Dulcy's eyes out, despite her carefully arranged smiles and use of endearments. Then there was

Quinn. She bestowed a steely stare on him whenever he dared ask a question or contribute to the conversation.

"We take care of our own," the meaty guy named Bruno said from where he stood behind Beatrix.

Jena rolled her eyes. "God, you sound like something out of a really bad B movie." She pulled her yellow legal pad closer to her. "Okay, enough talking. It's time to get down to business. And I think the first thing we have to do is contact the police."

Quinn's jeans-clad thigh made contact with Dulcy's leg under the table, the denim soft against her bare skin since she hadn't been able to bring herself to put on stockings that morning. Something similar to a bolt of lightning jolted through her. She pushed her chair back so quickly it nearly fell over. "Excuse me, but I need some air."

Marie appeared ready to come after her, but Jena stayed her with a hand on her arm, then continued the argument as to why they should contact the police. Dulcy stumbled out of the room and made her way to the restrooms on the other side of the waiting area. Only when she was inside the ladies' room did she stop. Actually, she did more than stop: she collapsed back against the tan-and-brown ceramic-tiled wall and gulped air.

Brad was missing. She'd had sex with his best man. Heart-pounding, breath-stealing hot sex. And if Beatrix Wheeler had her way, she'd be put behind bars for the rest of her life.

Then again, given the dim future that lay ahead of her, maybe prison gray wasn't all that unappealing.

What was going on? Three days ago she'd been a blushing bride-to-be who'd had little to worry about except whether her bridesmaids' dresses would be delivered on time and what flavor icing she wanted on her cake.

Oh boy, what a difference a reckless night could make.

She squeezed her eyes shut. She should have refused to go to that damn bar. She should have listened to Brad and insisted they take Beatrix along. If she had, then she would have known Quinn was Brad's often talked about but never met best friend and best man, and would never have given herself over to the bad-girl who'd taken possession of her body.

Think, she ordered herself. *Think. Preferably of something other than him.*

When was the last time she'd seen Brad? What had he said to her? Well, aside from suggesting she invite Beatrix to the bachelorette party? The sound of her swallowing echoed through the empty lavatory. Thursday night. Yes, that was it. She'd met him at Seasons for dinner next to Old Town. But he hadn't stayed for the entrée. In fact, she remembered thinking he looked a little edgy when their appetizers had arrived. He kept looking at his watch and smoothing his neat blond hair. She remembered this clearly because she had spent that day wondering if she was doing the right thing by marrying him. A small case of cold feet, she'd told herself. But she'd relaxed the moment she met him outside the restaurant. Brad Wheeler was, as Marie had so eloquently pointed out, one grade A hottie. It was more than just his good looks. He never smiled, he grinned. And she didn't think there was a single person out there who didn't like him on sight. He was one of those guys who dominated a room the moment he entered it and made you feel comfortable and even flattered that he would choose you to talk to.

Then there was Quinn. Her chest tightened. Where Brad was all brightness and light, Quinn was a dark, mysterious presence with his black hair and dark eyes. Like a shadow that tempted you nearer, then sucked you in entirely the instant you got too close. He had the mouth of a saint, the hands of a sinner. And, Lord help her, despite everything, she still wanted him with an intensity that made her want to whimper.

"Case of the guilts?" a deep male voice said quietly.

Dulcy jumped so high she was surprised she didn't hit her head on the ceiling. She popped open her eyes to stare at where Quinn stood inside the ladies' room, his shoulder propped against the closed door, his hands stuffed deep into the pockets of his black jeans. She hadn't heard him come in. Then again, she wouldn't have noticed if a herd of elephants had gone stampeding through the room.

Only, she suspected elephants wouldn't have the same heart-thumping, thigh-quivering effect on her.

God, but Quinn looked good. Too good. Opposite to Brad in every way.

And that was bad.

No, *she* was bad. Because despite everything going on on the other side of that door, she wanted to thrust her hands up Quinn's T-shirt and touch those fabulous abs and grind her hips against his to feel the strength of his erection against her stomach.

"You, um, needed some air, too?" she asked, wondering why there was suddenly a lack of it.

A shadow of a smile, though his eyes remained steadfastly on her face. "You could say that."

"I just did."

"I know."

Dulcy pushed away from the wall and made a beeline for one of the two stalls. She had no intention of using the bathroom while he was in there, but she figured it was the safest place for her, with him in such close proximity. She ducked inside and slid the lock home.

She instantly felt better. Contained. In control.

She sat down on the commode and wrapped her arms around herself.

Slow, easy footsteps sounded on the tiled floor, then stopped right in front of the stall. She could see his well-worn black cowboy boots and jeans up to mid-shin and wondered why it was that she found attractive even the little she could see of him.

"Here, have a look at this—"

One of those marvelously sinful hands appeared under the stall door. She reached out and took the ball of paper from it, careful not to make contact. She smoothed the paper out on her lap and her heart started hammering for an entirely different reason.

We have Bradley Wheeler III. One million for his return. You will be contacted with a time and place.

"Oh God."

She heard a long exhale, then, "You can say that again."

The boots shifted, one crossing over the other. She could envision Quinn leaning against the door. She eyed the lock. One small move and he would tumble right in and on top of her. She ran her tongue along the length of her bottom lip.

"I found it in Brad's garbage can in his office," he said.

"Garbage?" Dulcy repeated, focusing again on the paper.

"Uh-huh. Balled up like that."

"Did you find another note?"

"Nope."

She thought of Beatrix and Bruno in the next room. "What are *you* doing with it?"

"I found it. Don't worry, Beatrix has seen it."

"Ah," she said, as if his answer made perfect sense.

For several moments she sat staring at the note. Weren't

ransom notes typically spelled with letters cut out from random newspapers and magazines? This one was block-printed in blue ink. She turned the plain piece of white paper over, then back again.

"Dee—"

"Don't call me that," she whispered.

There was silence.

Dulcy balled the paper back up, then poked at the legs on the other side of the stall door. The hand appeared, and she virtually tossed the paper into the air to avoid making contact.

A soft chuckle. "This would be a lot easier if you came out of there, you know."

"Easier for whom?"

"For both of us."

The boots stepped out of sight. Dulcy leaned forward to peek underneath. God, but he looked killer in a pair of jeans. The soft, faded denim hugged his tush to perfection, the material tugging and pulling as he walked.

He turned around, and she jerked back.

"You know, the way I figure it, I have just as much to lose as you do, if anyone finds out about the other night."

Dulcy raised her brows and spoke to the door. "Oh? And how's that?"

"You mean aside from Brad being my best friend?" A pause. "The way I see it, you put the two of us together the same night Brad disappeared and, well, there's no longer one suspect but two."

"You suspect me?"

"No."

Dulcy slumped in relief.

"But Beatrix and Bruno do. And you have to admit, putting the two of us together looks worse yet." An exasperated sigh. "Do you mind coming out of there? What are you afraid of, that I'm going to maul you?"

It's not you I'm afraid of.

"I think I can manage to keep my hands to myself for five minutes," he said.

"I don't know if I can." Dulcy's eyes bulged as she realized she'd said the words aloud.

"Then, I'll make sure I don't react."

God, she was so very bad at this.

She stood up and slowly opened the stall door. Quinn stood with his arms crossed over his impressive chest, his eyes dark and unreadable. Dulcy straightened and stepped from the stall.

"That's better," he said.

Dulcy automatically walked to the sinks, switched on a faucet and began washing her hands.

"So," Quinn asked over the sound of the water. "Do you know where Brad might have gone?"

Dulcy met his gaze in the mirror. "I thought the note you found said he's been kidnapped."

He shrugged. "I'm not ruling out anything."

She swiveled to face him, hands dripping both soap and water. "Are you saying he might have gone voluntarily?"

"I'm saying it's possible Brad caught on to the kidnapping plan and is one step ahead of his captors."

Dulcy wasn't sure who made the first move, but later her best guess was that she did. One moment she was afraid he was suggesting Brad had run away from her; the next she looked at his mouth as though she wanted to devour it. The next, well, she *was* devouring it.

What was it about dark, dangerous men with full lips? Warm, wet, full lips that knew just how to move against hers. And, naturally, with the moving of mouths came the movement of other body parts. More specifically, her hands.

First they combed through all that dark hair, tugging it from the leather strap that held it back, then they trailed down his back and finally grabbed that terrific tush, tugging his hips nearer to hers.

She'd be a liar if she said she hadn't thought about doing just this every waking moment, and most of her sleeping moments, since they had parted Saturday morning. So she wasn't going to lie. Not now. Not when he was inching her skirt up to cup her bottom in his hot hands, his fingers diving toward areas that even now begged for his expert attention. He backed her against the sinks, she balked and backed him toward the stalls. He groaned, then swiveled her toward the closed bathroom door. Moments later she was flat up against it, as if in a replay of the elevator scene.

''Damn, but you feel good,'' Quinn muttered between hungry assaults on her mouth.

Dulcy wasn't even going to attempt to put into words how she felt. Like heaven. Like hell. Like she was tempting the devil himself and loving every minute of it.

There was the sound of material ripping, and Dulcy found herself without panties. Before she could think to protest, the thick tip of his finger found her damp heat. She gasped, tilting her hips forward to guide his hot hand toward her waiting threshold.

She decided the word *good* didn't begin to describe how she felt....

Quinn tugged his mouth from hers. Dulcy whimpered in response and tried to pull him back, but failed. He slid down to one knee in front of her. She nearly died when he folded up her skirt hem until her blond curls sprang free. With his knee, he edged her feet farther apart, baring more of the area to his intense gaze. Dulcy ran her hands restlessly down, then back up, skimming over her own aroused nipples. She squeezed her eyes shut as he skillfully began to part the swollen flesh between her legs, then fastened his hot, wet mouth on her most sensitive of parts.

Dulcy collapsed against the door, little more than a bone-less rag doll as he stroked her with his tongue. Quinn cupped her bottom in his hands, then urged one of her legs over his shoulder, then the other, until Dulcy was completely supported between him and the door. Ecstasy, pure and sweet and so seductive, swept over her, in her, turning her inside out as his mouth worked its magic. Wild spasms began in her stomach. Then the tip of a naughty finger found its way inside her dripping depths and the spasms became a roaring earthquake.

The door supporting her moved.

Dulcy moaned and thrust her hips more urgently against Quinn's decadent mouth. His finger slid inside her, and she clenched her slick muscles around it, Quinn drawing out her climax with the finesse of a man who not only knew what he was doing, but loved doing it.

The door moved inward again. Only, this time it was followed by an exasperated sigh. "Dulcy?" Marie's voice filtered through the wood. "Are you crying?"

Quinn's mouth still firmly attached to her delicate flesh, Dulcy's eyelids flew open and she stared into the same questioning expression on his face.

Instantly, his hot mouth was gone along with the finger, her skirt was straightened, and Quinn stood across the room from her looking like he wanted to start over again.

"Wait," he whispered, holding the door closed when she would have opened it. Then he kissed her, deeply, passionately, with the promise that what they had just begun wasn't finished, by any stretch of the imagination.

Dulcy watched him disappear into the last stall and close the door, then his boots disappeared from sight.

Dulcy took long, gulping breaths and pulled open the door.

Marie passed her. "I'm sorry to intrude. I know you probably need some time to yourself right now, but I have to use the toilet."

Dulcy grabbed her friend's arm, swinging her back toward the door. "I think we should get back."

Marie frowned at her. "I'll just be a second."

She headed for the first stall and closed the door, and soon the sound of tinkling filled the room. Dulcy nearly shrieked when Quinn's head popped up over the top of the last stall. He gave her a grin of pure wickedness. She glared at him. Then Marie was done, and Quinn's handsome head disappeared again.

"There. Happy?" Marie asked.

Dulcy tried to force air into her lungs as she watched her friend wash her hands. Paper towel still in her grasp, Dulcy maneuvered Marie toward the door and out into the hall. Only when they were almost back in the conference room did Dulcy realize she was minus a pair of panties.

QUINN HAD NEVER ONCE in the two decades he and Brad had been friends, envied a single thing his best friend had. He rubbed the silky purple material of Dulcy's panties between thumb and finger. Not until now, anyway. The way he saw it, life usually had a way of evening things out. Brad might have been born with tremendous financial resources, but was broke when it came to any true nurturing or emotional wealth. Beatrix Wheeler was as icy as they came. And so had been Brad's father before he died five years ago. No, Quinn hadn't known his own Caucasian father. But no matter how hard his mother, grandmother, aunts and uncles had had it, they never made him feel that he lacked for anything, or made him feel unwanted. And he took great pride in his

Hopi heritage, even if he didn't participate in any official way in the community.

Looking around the bathroom for a place to stash the sexy underwear, he instead stuffed them into his front jeans pocket next to the discarded ransom note. They barely made a bulge. Unlike certain parts of his anatomy that seemed forever on high alert whenever he was within breathing distance of one provocative, delicious Dulcy Ferris.

Hell, what was it about the woman that he couldn't keep his hands off her? Even after learning of her very permanent connection to his best friend, and that same best friend's recent disappearance, he'd been obsessed with the need to hear her restless whimpers. He'd gone down on her like a starving man in need of sustenance only she could provide.

Quinn clenched his fists. This train of thought wasn't going to improve his condition any.

A reasonable inner voice told him part of the appeal might be the lack of availability. Or it could even be a latent sense of wanting what Brad had, stored up over the years to spend on this one indulgence. But that didn't explain the chemistry that had existed between him and Dulcy on Friday night when he hadn't known who she was. He'd wanted her just as much then.

As a man who prided himself on his self-control when it came to the opposite sex, he was notably out of control whenever he was near Dulcy. So much so that he'd risked discovery by Beatrix Wheeler, by making out with Dulcy in the ladies' john. The old battle-ax had never liked him. She'd take great pleasure in locking him out of any search for Brad.

And that's who he should be focusing on one hundred percent right now. Brad. His friend was missing. Might be hurt. Or maybe even worse. The last thing he should be doing is lusting after Dulcy, especially now that he knew her true identity.

Cautiously opening the door, he slid a glance one way and the other, then stepped out into the hall.

What was Brad doing with a woman of Dulcy's caliber, anyway? Oh sure, she was from a wealthy family—he'd learned that much from his friend—but she was sensual and earthy and fundamental, whereas Brad's previous girlfriends had been cold as clams.

Girlfriend. Dulcy wasn't Brad's girlfriend. She was his fiancée. The woman his best friend would marry in five short days.

He strode back toward the conference room, only to find Beatrix and Dulcy's partner Barry Lomax alone in an office adjacent to the conference room. Beatrix turned on her heel and stormed from the office, while Barry grinned after her. Quinn couldn't be sure what had just passed between the two, but whatever it was had Beatrix on full throttle.

"Let's go," she said to him and Bruno, who hovered nearby. "Obviously Miss Ferris and her associates have no intention of cooperating with us. We're due at the private detective's office in twenty minutes. Maybe he'll be of more assistance."

Dulcy, Jena and Marie piled out of the conference room at the sound of Beatrix's voice. If Dulcy's cheeks looked a little too full of color, if her lips looked well kissed and if her legs seemed a little unsteady, Quinn was relatively sure he was the only one to notice.

Dulcy made a motion with her hands, indicating his hair. He reached up and smoothed it back. In the middle of his palm was a dab of bubbles. He grimaced and wiped the dampness on his jeans, then fastened his hair back into its usual leather strap.

"Call if you hear anything," he said, handing Dulcy his business card.

"Only if you promise the same," she said. She patted her jacket pocket, just before Mona popped up and handed him one of her cards.

Quinn's gaze raked her face, his mouth itching with the desire to kiss her again. He purposely looked away when Jena tilted her head slightly to give him a better once-over.

"Are you coming, Landis?" Beatrix fairly barked from the door.

Quinn followed the old hell-bitch out, promising himself he wouldn't call the very engaged Dulcy Ferris until his friend was found, and this entire mess was over and done with.

6

AN UNTOUCHED LUNCH SALAD and two hours later, Dulcy found that going on with life as usual wasn't even a remote possibility. Not when her fiancé was missing and she was sitting in her office sans panties thanks to her missing fiancé's best man.

She shut her eyes and resisted the urge to bang her forehead against the desktop. But when she closed her eyes, Quinn's very provocative mouth sprang forth. So she resisted closing her eyes.

A quick intercom call to Mona had the capable secretary canceling her late-afternoon appointment, something Dulcy didn't feel too guilty about since it was only one appointment and it was after three. Then she fished around in her middle desk drawer, looking for the key to Brad's city condo. She found it tucked between a roll of antacids and a tampon. She stared at the simple gold-colored item in the palm of her hand. Brad had given it to her two weeks ago so she could start moving her personal belongings in. She flipped the key over with a flick of her thumb. Of course, she hadn't done anything of the sort. Until they were married, she didn't feel all that comfortable with the prospect of being in Brad's condominium without him there. He might be old-fashioned when it came to sleeping together before the wedding; she was traditional when it came to claiming a spot that wasn't hers.

And the way things were progressing, it was a pretty safe bet that the condo might never be hers.

She slid the key into her skirt pocket, grabbed her suit jacket and purse and headed for the door, glad that everyone in the office had gone back to their own lives and careers and didn't question her leaving. Marie wasn't a concern. The cute little redhead hadn't a clue what had been going on in the bathroom before she entered it. And would probably die if she knew Quinn had been in there while she, um, attended to business.

Jena, on the other hand, had openly scrutinized Dulcy the instant she scrambled back into the conference room, probably noticing every hair out of place, each telltale wrinkle in her clothing, and could likely even point to the burning in her cheeks as evidence of a recent climax. Jena was a pro when it came to matters of that nature. Her powers of observations had never bothered Dulcy much before. But now that she was the unlucky focus of that observation, her opinion made a quick one-eighty.

Dulcy peeked into the waiting area to find Mona talking on the phone, more than likely rescheduling her appointment for the day. A further crane of her neck found Marie standing in front of her desk, packing her briefcase, probably heading back to the courthouse. And Jena…

Dulcy jumped when Jena slowly swung her desk chair in the direction of her door, the telephone receiver glued to her ear. Her laser-sharp gaze instantly settled on Dulcy as if that had been her intention all along. Which, of course, was ridiculous. There was no way her friend could have known she was in the waiting room.

Jena leaned forward, apparently putting her caller on hold. Dulcy quickly waggled her fingers at her, then made a mad dash for the door.

"Dulcy, wait!" she called out.

"Can't. Got to go," she responded, moving as fast as her heels would allow.

A few minutes later, her heart pounding in her chest and acutely aware of her panty-less state, Dulcy was climbing behind the wheel of her Lexus in the garage. She inserted the key into the ignition and rested her forehead against the steering wheel.

She wasn't made for this kind of clandestine existence. It just wasn't in her bones to do what she had done in that bathroom with Quinn. Not to mention what had passed between them Friday night. Well, okay, maybe it was in her bones. But the deceptive part that went along with it certainly wasn't. She'd learned over the course of her career that to some, lying came as naturally as breathing. To her, telling a telemarketer that she was in the middle of dinner so she could end the call, though she'd already eaten, made her uneasy.

Then again, maybe the trait wasn't something someone was born with, but was a learned behavior. When they were young, Jena had never been much good at hiding stuff from her and Marie. And look at her now. Not only was she the queen of deception, but she could spot it in others at ten paces. Currently, her success rate hovered between eighty and eighty-five percent. And those were only the cases of personal perjury they could *prove*.

She grimaced and lifted her forehead from the hot leather of the steering wheel to glance in the rearview mirror at her reflection. Oh, great. Now she had steering wheel head.

She started the car. Forget all that. She could sit here all day worrying about creases in her forehead and berating herself for her naughty behavior as of late. But it was Brad who needed her attention now. She tried to ignore the voice that said if she had been giving her attention to Brad all along, she wouldn't even be in the trouble she now was. And he probably wouldn't, either.

From what she understood, Barry had given Beatrix twenty-four hours to circle the wagons, so to speak, and protect the Wheeler name, and then they were calling in the police. But where did that leave Brad? None of this made any sense. If there was even a remote chance—and given that peculiar ransom note, she thought the chance was more than remote—that Brad was in trouble, had been kidnapped, why would Beatrix not want to call in the police immediately?

She ineffectually rubbed at the crease. Was it possible that Brad had taken off on his own? She remembered Quinn saying that at this point anything was possible. She shivered and drove the car out of the lot into the bright midday sunlight.

Depending on which point you entered or left Albuquerque, the city was an anomaly compared to some of the plains that surrounded the Sandia Mountains. Green, cloud-laced mountains that jutted out from the arid earth seeming to mock the nearby desert. Dulcy had spent her entire life there, even choosing to attend the University of New Mexico, rather then trekking east and doing the Ivy League bit. The view of the city itself never failed to awe and inspire her. She'd never longed to live anywhere but here. She'd been to L.A., New York, Chicago and Dallas, but, for her, this was where it was at. Aside from the fact that it's where her family and friends lived, it was the most magical place on earth.

Brad's condo was in the newer section of town where construction seemed to be at an all-time high. Dulcy forced herself to drive carefully, resisting the urge to slam the gas pedal to the floor. She had some idea of what Brad did when he wasn't with her, but she would be hard-pressed to come up with a blow-by-blow itinerary. There was the local country club, the health club, the restaurants they'd gone to together, his office at Wheeler Industries. She tightened her fingers on the steering wheel, just now finding it odd that they led such completely separate lives. They met for dinner three nights out of seven, attended social functions together, played some tennis at the club. But otherwise she lived her life, he his. Even their conversations seemed to focus on other people rather than on themselves.

Was that normal? She flicked on the blinker to turn right at the next light. She didn't know. What, exactly, was normal nowadays? The way her parents lived? Her father going off to work at the same time every morning and returning home at the same time every night, sitting down to dinner at six, exchanging vague conversation, then parting again afterward, her father to disappear into his study to read the latest political biography, her mother to nest in the kitchen, scrubbing at a spot on the ceramic tile that only she could see?

Dulcy squinted at the street signs. All her life she'd never questioned the health of her parents' marriage. That she was doing it now, so close to her own wedding and with everything else going on around her, unnerved her.

She knew the history of her family name, knew the Ferrises had been instrumental in settling Albuquerque. She could also remember a time when the gigantic tribute to European architecture that she'd grown up in had been a true showpiece inside and out, rather than just kept up for appearances' sake. She'd been five when her parents had quietly sold off the majority of their furniture and closed off most of the twenty-five rooms, leaving open only the study, the salon, the kitchen and their two bedrooms upstairs. The exterior and the salon were well maintained so that sometimes even she forgot what really existed behind the shiny red painted door and simple but manicured lawn.

She wasn't all that clear on the dynamics behind her parents' actions. Something about her uncle having sold the family business out from under her father, leaving him with nothing but a load of debt. But by then Dulcy had met Jena and Marie and started not to miss the swimming pool that had been filled in, or Benita, the saucy Latina housekeeper they'd had. And it didn't matter to her that she had to go to her friends' houses and wasn't allowed to invite them over for more than an occasional cookie set out in the stuffy salon, her mother virtually standing guard in the hall should anyone catch the wandering bug.

But while she had adjusted and achieved success in her life, moved on beyond the facade, she suspected her parents still lived like everything had happened yesterday, and were still secretly trying to find a way out of the reality that was their lives. Her mother, especially, was a pro at self-delusion. She'd never worked. Still volunteered and arranged fund-raisers as though she hadn't a financial care in the world, and acted like it was her duty to feed the under-privileged, never giving away that at times she'd been a member of that group. For Catherine Ferris, appearances meant everything. And Dulcy knew that while the outside world saw her in her old designer clothes that were kept in airtight bags, her daughter hardly saw her in anything but faded, flowered housecoats with frayed hems and crooked collars.

Her father, on the other hand, merely looked faded and frayed. If he cared about his wife's activities, he didn't show it, and certainly didn't show an interest in participating in them. He went to work every day, performing his mediocre-paying middle management job with no complaint, then came home and vegged in the study, his book propped up on his chest.

Separate lives.

Dulcy turned into the exclusive gated neighborhood where Brad lived, then flashed her identification to the attendant. Sure, she'd been there on a few occasions, but not often enough to remember exactly where the town house was located. They all looked the same. Generic. Well appointed. All with the same green lawn and flower beds. And since Brad had always been the one to drive them there, well, she hadn't paid close attention. She wondered what that, if anything, said about her relationship with Brad.

Oh, stop it, she ordered herself. Everything had been fine four days ago. Everything was fine now. Nothing had to change. Maybe Brad was just sick. She sat up straighter and pulled into the driveway for what she hoped was the right town house. Yes, that's it. Perhaps Brad had caught that nasty strain of flu virus making the rounds and was in bed trying to fight it off. He'd wanted to call the office, and her, but he'd left the cordless in the living area and didn't have the energy to reach it.

She switched the car off, amazed by her own ability to delude herself. Was it an inherited skill? She didn't know. But somehow she thought her mother would be proud.

She got out of the car and slammed the door harder than she had intended. Or maybe she had intended to slam it, if only to jolt herself from her ridiculous thoughts. She'd never been one to succumb to delusions. If Brad was in trouble, she was going to find him. An image of Quinn slid sexily through her mind. She took a deep breath. First, she'd find Brad. The rest…well, she'd deal with that when the time came.

The town house was part colonial and part southwestern. A boxy, two-story structure with white exterior, slatted wood shutters and tile roof, it wasn't all that attractive. Blooming red flowers spilled over copper pots on either side of the brown painted door.

Basically the place was what Brad referred to as his city, or in-between, pad. Up until a few months ago he'd still lived with his mother in the palatial house just outside town. He still called the Wheeler estate home. That's where his cars and the bulk of his wardrobe were kept. Unfortunately, it's also where his mother lived. Which wouldn't have been so bad in and of itself, except that Brad had talked about the two of them moving to the estate after they married. A prospect that gave her the willies. She'd instead offered up an alternative: buying their own place closer to town. Anything he wanted. Anything that didn't include a room for Beatrix Wheeler.

The sprinkler system switched on, nearly drenching her as she hurried up the stone sidewalk toward the door.

For several moments, Dulcy stood staring blankly at the glistening brown paint. What should she do? She felt she should be doing something, but couldn't quite think what. She finally decided she should ring the bell. If Brad was inside and suffering from some sort of antisocial bug or virus, she didn't want to barge in on him. She pressed the button, and the booming strains of "Beethoven's Fifth" echoed through the house. No answer. She released the breath she was holding and scanned the front. Sparkling windows with white shears and heavy, brocade curtains prevented her from seeing inside. Her gaze caught on the simple black mailbox. The lid was closed on top of a regular-size white envelope. Looking first one way down the street, then the other, she slid the envelope out, then opened the box and took out the rest of the mail. She leafed through the six envelopes. Everything was postmarked Saturday, which meant he either hadn't received any mail today, or the mailman was running late.

She looked up, startled, when she found a woman with what appeared to be gray wool for hair and steely eyes staring at her from a window next door. Dulcy forced a smile and waggled her fingers. The curtains closed and the woman disappeared from sight. What was it with nosy neighbors? Did everyone have them? She could only hope the old woman wasn't this minute calling security, or worse, the police. Dulcy sighed and felt for the key she'd put in her pocket. It fit easily into the lock, and within moments she was inside and had closed the door behind her, blinking to adjust her eyesight.

Funny, she didn't remember the place being so dark. She flicked the switch to her right, and the overhead chandelier burst to life, nearly blinding her. She switched it off, deciding she'd rather wait for her eyesight to adjust. She put the mail down on the hall table and stepped to the open doorway to the right, where the living area lay. Empty but for the dark leather furniture and heavy wood tables. Her heels clicked as she walked down the tiled hall. The kitchen, dining room and office were also empty and very, very quiet.

She started to turn from Brad's home office, then hesitated, looking back toward the heavy mahogany desk. Done in dark greens and darkly stained woods, the room was murky and forbidding. The clock ticking on the mantel didn't help matters, either. The setting could have been snipped from an old Agatha Christie novel. But no blood-stained letter opener was on the desktop. Instead, the gleaming surface was clean, the answering machine minus any blinking lights or waiting message numbers. That's funny—

A muffled sound from upstairs.

Dulcy slapped her hand to her heart and stared at the ceiling. Brad didn't believe in pets so he didn't own any.

That left only one other thing that could have made the noise. A person.

Brad?

She swallowed hard. She certainly hoped so. She strained her ears, trying to make out any other sounds. Nothing but silence greeted her.

Walking on tiptoe to avoid making too much noise on the polished tile, she backtracked to the foyer, craning her neck to see up the staircase to the hall above. It appeared as dark up there as the downstairs. No pools of sunlight flooding from an open bedroom door. Her palms clammy, she slowly ascended the steps. Could it be that Brad really *was* sick? She'd had headaches where even the slightest ray of light seemed to stab through her skull. That would explain the closed curtains, the darkness of the place.

She reached the second-floor landing and nearly tripped over something. She reached down. A book. *David Copperfield* to be precise. She looked up to where a couple of other books were teetering on the edge of the hall bureau. The source of the sound she'd heard from downstairs? She turned the book over. Seemed probable. She put the book on top of the others, then pushed them back from the edge.

She'd been upstairs only once. The day Brad had given her a tour of the place, then presented her with the key. To the left were two guest bedrooms and a bath. To the right, the master suite.

She remembered that the most. Not because of how large it was or how well appointed. But because Brad had shown it as if it was of less importance than his home office, but slightly more important than the living room. She had lingered a little longer, thinking that it was the room where they would be sharing every night together.

Now, the dark wood door stood slightly ajar. Trying to peek inside, she quietly pushed the door. She supposed she should be thankful there wasn't a squeak. Then again, why should there be? All these places had been built a little less than two years ago. There was nothing in any of them that would need oil yet.

She squinted, finding the room darker than the others. From her earlier inspection, she knew that heavy stamped brown woven curtains stretched the length of the front wall, a variation of the fabric across the bed. The rug was a rich, thick burgundy, the king-size four-poster bed imposing. She crossed to that bed now, curving her fingers around the foot post and staring down at the dark bed coverings. No Brad. Only tousled sheets and dented pillows. She stepped along the side, wrinkling her nose at an almost flowery scent.

"Fancy meeting you here."

Dulcy nearly fainted dead away.

QUINN FLICKED A SWITCH. The brass bedside lamps filled the room with a warm, yellow glow. He crossed his arms and watched where Dulcy had nearly fallen flat on her bottom. She stumbled backward, her expression confused and frightened. Her gaze fastened onto his face and that expression quickly changed. Her tongue dipped out to lick the side of her mouth. Quinn found himself wondering if she was still without panties. She wore the suit she'd had on earlier, so he'd chance a guess and say she was. He rubbed the back of his neck. Thinking such thoughts wasn't a good idea considering they stood on either side of a very big, very welcoming bed that was just the right size to use as a playground for all the naughty things he had in mind.

If only that playground didn't belong to her missing fiancé.

"What…what are you doing here?" Dulcy asked, straightening her suit jacket and tugging at her skirt though neither piece of clothing needed adjusting. Quinn, however, had some body parts that would sorely appreciate the attention.

"My best friend's missing, his mulish mother doesn't want to call the cops and his fiancée has no idea where he is. Where else would you suggest I start looking?"

Dulcy's eyes widened and she looked around the room. "Where's Beatrix?" Her voice lowered to a stage whisper. "She's not here, is she?"

Quinn felt the corners of his mouth turn up. "No. She's not."

Dulcy looked altogether panicked...and oh so sexy. Her gaze dropped to the bed and she frowned.

"Someone had to stay behind at the office in case the kidnapper calls," he pointed out.

She reached out and touched a pillow, then lifted her hand to her nose. "Do you really think there is a kidnapper?" Her voice sounded overly thoughtful, as if her mind were a thousand miles away.

Quinn shrugged and walked to the far corner of the room. He figured it was the safest place to be. Dulcy standing next to that bed was growing all too inviting. "I don't know." He opened the drawers to a tallboy. "But we want to make sure all the bases are covered if there is. Beatrix has already been in contact with her accountant to secure the money."

Dulcy's brows rose. "One million dollars?"

"That's the amount on the note."

She nodded slowly, seeming preoccupied with the bed. Quinn got the impression it was not for the same reason he was preoccupied with it. She reached out and fluffed, then straightened the comforter, the action looking suddenly domestic. Quinn turned his back to her and groaned. Of course it was domestic. How many nights had she spent in that bed with Brad? His best friend? His *missing* best friend?

"So tell me, Dulcy, how is it we hadn't met until...now."

Her head snapped up to meet his gaze. She let go of the bedspread, then rubbed her palms on her skirt as if ridding them of something she would have preferred not to touch. That was odd.

"I don't know, really. I mean, Brad talked about you and all, but he said that you lived outside of town and only came in every now and again."

He nodded.

A shadow of a smile. "He also said that he wanted to wait until right before we were married to introduce me to you. Said you had this, um, way with women he couldn't compete with."

Quinn grimaced. Way with women? Brad had never had a problem with women.

She pointedly looked away and cleared her throat. "He, um, said you were one of those tall, dark and handsome loners that women loved to try to domesticate."

"Makes me sound like an animal."

Her pupils widened, nearly taking over the hazel of her eyes. "Is it so far from the truth?"

Quinn closed the bureau drawers. He supposed that for all intents and purposes it wasn't. Only one woman had come close to taming him, although even now he questioned whether it had been the sex with Yolanda, rather than the beginnings of love, that had made him think they had a future. He rubbed his chin with his forefinger, realizing that he was staring at Dulcy. And that his attention was making her hot and bothered.

She turned from the bed and switched on the light in the master bath. "How about me? What did Brad say about me?"

"Nothing."

She swiveled to face him. "Nothing?"

He shrugged and crossed his arms over his chest. He'd

already gone through the master bathroom. He'd found it strange that there weren't any women's toiletries in there, not even an extra toothbrush. Strange for a man about to get married. Yolanda had basically taken over his house the instant he let her into it. Why hadn't Dulcy done the same with Brad?

"He told me he was getting married."

"That's it?"

"Yeah, that's about the extent of it." He shrugged again. "We haven't really had a chance to get together lately. You know, talk things out man to man. That's why I came into town a week before the wedding. So we could do that."

Dulcy gripped the side of the doorjamb. "Didn't you think it unusual that he didn't say anything about me?"

He hadn't been completely honest. Brad had said one additional thing to him. That Dulcy's family was loaded. But considering the situation, he wasn't about to impart that bit of info to Dulcy.

"Why the name Dee?" he found himself asking out of nowhere.

She froze in the doorway, looking everywhere but into his face. She hadn't buttoned her suit jacket. It hung open to reveal the way the white silky material of her blouse clung to her breasts. Even from here he could tell the tips were engorged, pressing against the confining material, begging for release. His gaze trailed down to her bare legs and the way she held them tightly together. If he'd had any doubts before about whether she'd replaced her missing panties, he didn't now. Only a woman turned on and bare under her skirt would squeeze her thighs together so tightly she could have cracked a walnut.

"Um, Jena and Marie used to call me Dee when we were kids." A small laugh. "I used to hate my name. Dee...well,

Dee could have been the short form of any name. Deborah. Denise. Deedee.''

Just like the woman in front of him could be any woman. ''Dulcy's a pretty name.''

She crossed her arms over her chest. He didn't miss her small shiver. But whether it was from the cold of the air-conditioning, or from his presence, he couldn't be sure. And it was better that he didn't find out.

''Would you have known who I was if I told you my real name?'' Her eyes blinked and looked directly into his.

He didn't know what she was looking for. Absolution, maybe? Or perhaps simple understanding. Whatever the motivation for the question, the answer appeared important to her.

''It's an unusual name, Dulcy.'' He grinned. ''But I don't think it would have made a difference. That night…well, you could have told me you were Julia Roberts and I wouldn't have put the name together with the actress.''

She stared at him for a moment, color rising high on her cheeks before she looked away. Her gaze fell on the bed. Quinn's gaze followed. How easy it would be just to back her up against the mattress, slide up that skirt of hers and re-create certain scenes from Friday night.

The strains of Beethoven wound through the house. Quinn grimaced and looked toward the hallway.

''Expecting someone?'' Dulcy asked.

He shook his head. ''Just Brad. But I don't think he'd use the doorbell.'' He looked back at her. ''Do you?''

''No.''

He crossed to the closed curtains. The suite overlooked the well-manicured street. He immediately spotted a white van with some sort of lettering on the side parked right behind a silver SUV in the driveway. Dulcy's more than likely. Quinn had parked outside the compound and gained access via a more private route, in case someone was watching the place.

He glanced over his shoulder at her. "Looks like a delivery."

"A delivery?" She came to stand next to him, and tried to make out the lettering. "A florist?"

Quinn grimaced. "Maybe he has fresh flowers delivered once a week?" Lord knows, that's the way Beatrix operated. The Wheeler estate on the outskirts of Albuquerque smelled like a funeral home, which was fitting, since the majority of the inhabitants were emotionally dead, anyway.

Dulcy shook her head, the movement pushing the sweet scent of oranges his way. What was it with her and smelling like fruit? And never the same fruit. This morning she'd smelled like bananas. Quinn resisted the urge to breath the new scent in as his gaze scanned her. All he had to do was reach out a hand...

"Well, do you think we should get it?" she asked.

"I assumed you would answer the door. You are Brad's fiancée. The one with the key to let herself in."

She winced. He frowned. He took no true enjoyment out of taunting her that way. Although he had no idea why the idea of being engaged to Brad would make Dulcy wince, he could count off at least half a dozen reasons why he wished she wasn't.

She left behind the scent of oranges as she left the room for downstairs.

QUINN WAS GOING TO BE the death of her. She knew it already. Dulcy tightly gripped the stair handrail to keep herself from toppling to the floor below. Not just because of the height of her heels. But because Quinn had virtually turned her knees to Jell-O. Jell-O he would use that decadent mouth of his to eat off.

She stood before the front door and took a deep breath, then pulled open the door.

The deliveryman swiveled from where he'd had his back to her, a vase full of water lilies in his arms. In his mid to late thirties, he looked too big, too beefy, too swarthy to be a flower delivery guy.

"Yeah, I got a delivery for Wheeler."

"I'm Dulcy Ferris, Mr. Wheeler's fiancée." She stretched out her hands. "I'll be happy to accept."

The guy made no secret of trying to look around her into the house. "I got express instructions to give these to no one but Mr. Wheeler."

"I'm sorry," Dulcy said slowly, automatically moving to prevent further inspection of the house. "Mr. Wheeler is…unavailable at the moment. You're going to have to leave them with me."

The guy took a step back. "Sorry, ma'am, but that ain't gonna happen."

Ma'am? Had he just called her 'ma'am'?

"I've got to deliver these directly to Wheeler myself. Is he around? Where is he?"

Dulcy swallowed. Well, that was the question of the hour, wasn't it. Where *was* Brad?

"Is he here?"

Dulcy squinted at him, for the second time thinking that he didn't look like any kind of flower deliveryman she'd ever seen. Furniture mover, maybe. Or someone in construction. He looked like an ex-con who had spent the past five years lifting nothing but iron. Which might very well be why he was delivering flowers. Jena dealt with these kinds of guys all the time. They were sprung from jail and had to do a brief stint in a regular paying job as part of their parole agreement. And the fact was that many ex-cons had never held a regular job in their lives, leaving them with myriad minimum-wage positions to choose from. She supposed delivering flowers was more attractive than flipping burgers at a fast-food joint.

She glanced over her shoulder to where Quinn stood at the top of the stairs, looking on. She felt safe enough saying, "No, unfortunately Mr. Wheeler's not home at the moment." She reached for the flowers again. "But I'd be more than happy—"

"When will he be home?"

Dulcy sputtered, "I—I don't know."

The guy practically ripped the vase from her hands. "I'll come back, then."

Dulcy stood staring after him in unveiled shock as he made his way back to the van.

"What was that about?" Quinn asked, coming to stand next to her.

"I'm not sure." The van marked Manny's Flowers backed out of the driveway, then drove toward the security gates. "He had a flower delivery for Brad but refused to leave them with me."

"Strange."

"That's what I thought."

He narrowed his eyes. "Could he have been one of those singing telegram performers?"

Dulcy grimaced at him. "I don't think so."

"Yeah, I don't think so, either."

As Dulcy watched the van disappear from sight down the winding street, she remembered she was supposed to meet with the upscale florist she'd chosen to outfit her wedding. She glanced at her watch. An hour overdue. But the question wasn't whether she should call and reschedule. It was whether there was going to be a wedding at all.

She stepped to the hall table and picked up her purse. Moments later she was on her cell phone with Mona, asking the secretary to reschedule the florist appointment. She watched in the gilt-edged wall mirror as Quinn stepped into the dining room behind her, giving her a clean view of his backside in his soft black jeans. Saliva gathered at the back of her throat. What she wouldn't give to be that denim, hugging his tush to perfection.

"Is that it?" Mona asked.

Dulcy cleared her throat and tore her gaze from the mirror. "Yes, that will do, Mona. Thank you."

She pressed the disconnect button and returned the phone to her purse. Her gaze caught on the mail she'd laid on the table. She picked it up again and leafed through it. Four pieces of junk mail and two bills. Nothing ground-shaking there. She had moved to put the envelopes back down, when a business card caught her eye. The glossy black rectangle blended nicely against the swirled black marble tabletop. But it was the neon pink lettering that stood out. *Pink Lady Lounge.*

"Well, there's nothing here. I'm going to head out."

Dulcy started, then turned to face Quinn where he stood in the open doorway. She calmly slipped the card into the front pocket of her purse. "Yes. I, um, better get going, too."

He held open the door and motioned for her to precede him. Dulcy did, trying not to notice the fresh tang of his cologne, the heat of his body. God, but were guys like him born with that incredible magnetic quality? She shivered despite the bright midday sun as she hurried for her car.

"Dulcy?"

She swiveled to stare at him.

"Don't worry. We'll find Brad."

Her throat completely closed up. Simply because just now that had been the last thing on her mind.

She nodded and climbed into her car.

7

QUINN HADN'T THOUGHT that Brad had it in him. He claimed one of the stools at the black linoleum-topped bar that stretched the length of the Pink Lady Lounge. Sweat, cigarette smoke and beer choked the air, while the square tile mirrors on the wall behind the bar reflected the liquor bottles set in front of them and the colored flashing lights focused on the stage behind him. As he ordered up a brew, he tried to imagine one proper-heeled, well-groomed Bradley Wheeler III in a seedy joint like this. A black stripper had her bare bottom turned to a customer and was doing a grind only strippers knew how to do, her white G-string leaving very little to the imagination. Not that the customer had a problem with it. Probably a salesman, Quinn decided, eyeing the guy's cheap green polyester suit, balding pate and personal beer keg around his middle. A beefy hand tucked a crumpled, sweaty bill into the stripper's string and tried to cop a feel. The stripper easily swayed away from his grope and focused her attention on a customer on the other side of the stage. The base-heavy, pulsating music made conversation all but impossible. Which was the point. The owner only wanted the customers buying the overpriced drinks and food and keeping their attention on the girls working the floor in their fringed shorts and pasties. Of course, if the girls also did a little something on the side…

Quinn took a slug of beer and motioned for the bartender—a woman he guessed had probably been up on that stage herself until a few years ago. Her longish red hair was too brassy to be real as she tilted her head nearer so she could hear him.

"I'm looking for somebody," he said.

She pulled back and smiled, drying a beer glass with a white towel. "Aren't we all, honey."

"Yes, but I'm interested in one person in particular. Maybe you know him." He fished in his pocket for the picture Beatrix's henchman Bruno had given him at the Wheeler offices earlier that morning. The photo was of the specially commissioned oil portrait of Brad that was displayed in the Wheeler Industries lobby. He flashed the five-by-seven at the tender. She frowned.

"Figures. The first interesting guy in weeks that comes into the joint is interested in playing for the other guys."

Quinn chuckled. "Trust me. It's not like that."

"Sure it isn't." She sighed and set the clean glass down on the counter behind the bar. She'd barely given the photo a glance. "You seen how dark this place is? I couldn't tell you if Clinton himself had been in here."

"Uh-huh." Quinn glanced at the photo, folded it and put it back in his pocket.

The outer door opened to his left, letting in a shaft of dim, early evening light. He was aware of someone walking up to stand next to him, and the bartender looked in that direction. He reached for his wallet, wondering how much he had there and how much it would take to get her to talk.

"Well, la-de-da. A little fancy for these parts, aren't you, sweetie?" The bartender said to the new arrival, a smirk on her face. "Open auditions are at eight every Thursday."

"I'm…I'm not here to audition," a familiar female voice said with obvious hesitation.

The bartender rolled her eyes. "Another switch-hitter," she said and put her hands on her hips. "What'll it be?"

"Be? Oh. To drink. Just give me an iced tea."

The bartender raised a penciled-in brow.

Quinn tossed a couple of bills onto the bar. "Get her a double shot of tequila."

The bartender moved to fill the order. Quinn looked at the woman next to him. "You saw the card, too, huh?" he asked one very antsy-looking Dulcy.

She pulled at her suit jacket so tightly she probably cut off circulation. Her eyes bulged as she stared at the gyrating stripper on the oval stage. Quinn glanced in the mirror to find the black woman doing interesting things with the metal pole that stretched from stage to ceiling. Dulcy stood transfixed for several minutes, until the announcer, a thickset guy off stage right, said, "Let's have a big hand for Ebony, everybody."

Half of the ten or so men around the stage applauded, and the girl sashayed toward the pink fringe curtains at the back.

Dulcy was so pale that Quinn was afraid she might pass out. He pulled out the stool next to him. She immediately took it, her eyes practically ready to pop out onto the bar in front of her. The bartender put her drink in front of her, and Dulcy downed it. Her coughing fit told him she had forgotten what he'd ordered. She dragged the back of her hand across her mouth, then stared at the limb in horror.

"First time at a strip joint?" Quinn asked.

She nodded emphatically and asked the bartender to bring her a glass of water. Quinn upgraded it to a cola, knowing the water would never appear, then asked for a refill of Dulcy's shot glass.

"Oh, no, thank you," she said.

Quinn nodded for the bartender to bring the drink. Whether Dulcy drank it or not was her decision, but you couldn't stay in a place like this unless you had a drink in front of you.

The instant her shot glass was refilled, Dulcy touched the bartender's arm and launched into what he'd done right before she entered, although the picture of Brad she had was a shot of her and him on what looked like a golf course. He grimaced and drank more beer than he had intended.

Dulcy sighed when she didn't get any further than he had with the brassy redhead. And he was coming to think no amount of money would improve her memory. Dulcy slowly slid the photo back into her purse, then looked around the seedy interior of the bar, taking in the men seated around small dented tables, the empty stage. "Do you really think Brad came here?" she practically croaked.

Quinn eyed her pale face. "Shocking, huh?"

Her gaze finally rested on him, but only briefly. She licked her lips, then re-routed her hand from where it automatically reached for the shot and picked up the cola instead. "I didn't think he was, um, that type of guy."

Quinn paid for the additional drink. "He and I have been friends for more than twenty years and I didn't have a clue, either."

Dulcy paid extra-close attention to her cola glass, probably to guarantee she didn't accidentally down the other tequila. "Funny. I was just thinking you looked at home here."

"Oh?" he asked with a raised brow.

She nodded, glancing down at his jeans and T-shirt, then up again. Her gaze was almost like a caress, causing heat to rise in Quinn's groin. "You know, bad-boy goes to bad-boy places."

He grinned. "Who said I was a bad-boy?"

Her eyes bulged again.

He took a swig from his beer bottle. "Anyway, I said I was surprised Brad came to such a place."

"You mean you didn't come together?"

"To places like this?" He shook his head. "No."

Sure, Quinn had spent his share of time in joints like this. At sixteen he'd looked twenty-five. It had been more than his physical characteristics that made him look older, although putting in twelve-hour workdays on his uncle's ranch hadn't hurt in that department. By sixteen he'd seen much more than other kids his age, not that he knew that at the time. His grandmother used to tell him he had the soul of a shaman. Now he rationalized his hanging out in bars by saying, What sixteen-year-old wouldn't want to see a few strippers expose their wares? What he had really been doing was making up for not having his buddy Brad to hang with. As his friend attended upscale parties, balls and events that required a wardrobe Quinn's tiny closet could never hold, Quinn himself had taken other roads to adulthood. While Brad's first sexual experience had come as the result of some adolescent groping in an upstairs bedroom while at a party, Quinn had been shown the ropes by a stripper nearly twice his age in the back room of a place just like this.

No, he'd never thought Brad would come to a place like the Pink Lady. But the past few days had offered up a lot of surprises.

He felt Dulcy's gaze on him as he took another swallow of beer. "You know, when Brad told me you were a bit of a bad-boy, I…"

Quinn looked at her, wondering how close Dulcy had ever come to a man like him before last Friday. He'd guess never. Then again, he'd questioned his observation skills the minute he entered this place and realized Brad had been there.

"…I, well, thought he was speaking relatively. You

know, you liked to play sophomoric pranks at the fraternity, drink until you puked your guts out, that kind of thing.''

Quinn's grin was decidedly dark. ''I've never been inside a fraternity, babe. A few sororities maybe, but never a fraternity.''

Her long, elegant throat convulsed as she swallowed. ''I guessed that.'' She nursed her cola some more. ''How, exactly, did you and Brad become friends, then?''

He squinted at her.

She grimaced and crossed her arms on the bar. ''Don't look at me like that. It's a valid question. Just as I didn't expect Brad would ever come into a place like this—'' she waved around the bar ''—I don't think there would have been a lot of opportunity for your path and Brad's to cross when you were younger. And you two did meet when you were young, right?''

Quinn nodded. ''We were nine.''

''Nine. That's a long time. Almost as long as Jena, Marie and I have been friends.'' She gave a visible shudder. ''I'd hate to consider what I don't know about them.''

Quinn skimmed her shapely body, vividly recalling how each curve and dip had felt in his hands.

''So, how did you meet?''

He motioned the bartender for another beer. ''I think that's something you should ask Brad.''

She shifted in her stool. ''I would do exactly that but, strangely, Brad's not around to ask right now.''

The music notched up again, nearly drowning out the last of her comment. Quinn's gaze snagged hers and held.

''Gentlemen—and I see we have a lady in the house— give it up for Miss Candy!'' the announcer shouted.

There went her bulging eyes again. Quinn nearly grinned at Dulcy's discomfort. During their conversation she seemed to have forgotten where they were. Only, there was no ignoring it now. He turned to lazily watch the young, curvy blonde stepping out onto the stage. If he squinted just right, she was a double for Dulcy. He slanted a gaze toward the woman next to him, finding her doing an *Exorcist* like move. Her body was facing the bar, but her attention was very definitely glued to the stage.

"She's like Candeeeee," the singer of the song crooned, followed by a deeper male voice offering up dialogue on the title woman's generous assets.

Quinn recognized the song from the mid-eighties or so. High on bass, low on content, the song seemed the perfect score for the experienced stripper who stopped in the middle of the stage oval, feet shoulder-width apart. She slid her thumbs inside the tiny straps of her top, mocking herself by tugging the fabric out for a peek and then releasing it.

"Oh my God," Dulcy croaked next to him. "Where do they get bodies like that?"

Quinn resisted the urge to glance at her. She didn't seem to have a clue that the stripper's body didn't even compare to her own toned curves. Dulcy's breasts were natural, perfect globes with the pinkest tips he'd ever seen on a woman. Unlike the stripper's, whose breasts were obviously chosen from a catalog and whose dark nipples hinted that she wasn't a real blonde at all. The stripper swung around the pole, then offered her bottom to the audience, doing the string-tugging thing again.

Dulcy's quick intake of breath drew Quinn's gaze to her. Her mouth was open in a soft *O*. She had finally given in to temptation and had swiveled her stool to face the stage. Her long, long legs were crossed at the knees and her throat worked around a swallow she couldn't quite seem to get down. A silky wisp of blond hair had escaped the twist at the back of her head and teased the corner of her pink lips.

He resisted the urge to push it back from her cheek, afraid if he touched her, he wouldn't be able to stop.

As he watched her mouth, her wet tongue dipped out and nervously ran the length of her lower lip. He gave a hearty mental groan. She had no idea that just watching her like this turned him on in a way that a dozen strippers never could. And knowing she was indulging in decadent behavior while he watched notched the heat factor up even farther. He'd lay ten-to-one odds that Dulcy had never seen another woman completely nude, much less offering up that nudity in an uninhibited, titillating way designed to turn men on.

He leaned closer to her, discreetly blowing on her hair near her ear. Her shiver was exactly what he'd been after. "You could put those women to shame, Dulcy."

"Me?" she whispered, and glanced around as if he had just suggested she engage in group sex.

He grinned. "Yes, you."

"You mean, like, up on the stage?"

He nodded.

"Never. I…I could never do that."

He hiked a brow. "Not even for the man you love?"

Color flooded her cheeks and it was obvious she was having a hard time imagining herself doing the things the stripper on the stage was doing. "Not even for the man I, um, love."

Had she ever stripped for Brad back in that dark, cold bedroom at the condo? The thought caused his gut to tighten. Then he remembered their time together at the hotel, her initial hesitancy, her hungry awkwardness, her complete discomfort in the lounge—and he hazarded a no. While she wore naughty underwear under all that designer clothing, he suspected that Dulcy believed stripping was something best left to professionals. His gaze slid down the front of her blouse to where the first few buttons were undone, revealing a stretch of pale silken flesh that rapidly moved in and out as she tried to control her breathing. He made out the hard, bunched tips of her nipples through the material and wondered if she was slightly turned on by the new experience. He knew she was when she re-crossed her legs. Then did so again.

Quinn thought of the scrap of lace he had in his pocket, panties that Dulcy would now be wearing if he hadn't stripped them from her earlier. His gaze slid up her bare legs to where her skirt hiked farther up with every leg crossing. He nearly groaned at the thought that if he were positioned just right, he'd be able to catch a peek of her own priceless wares.

The place was just dark enough, the long bar positioned in such a way, that Quinn suspected if a person had something…naughty in mind, no one would notice. The bartender was at the other end of the bar talking to a customer. The remainder of the clientele had their gazes riveted to Candy. And that left the very hot Dulcy completely at his mercy.

And at his mercy was exactly where he wanted her.

When they'd met, all he'd wanted was a quick roll in the hay. Then this morning had happened and he'd discovered she was his best friend's fiancée. Now…well, now he wanted to show her all the things that Brad never could. Wanted her to taste what it was really like to be with a bad-boy. Make her beg for him in a way that made her question her choice in men.

Leaning back against the bar, he covertly swiveled her stool so that she was facing him as much as she was the stage. She blinked at him as if in a trance. Her pupils enlarged to claim nearly all the color in her irises, her eyelids half closed, giving her a sleepy, provocative look. Quinn swallowed hard as her attention slid back to the stage.

He leaned slightly forward, pretending an interest in the peanut bowl behind her, then rested his hand on her bare knee. She tensed beneath his touch, her gasp telling of her surprise. But she didn't remove his hand. Didn't ask him to remove it. So Quinn slid his fingers up a couple of inches, until his fingertips brushed the hem of her skirt. His nose was nearly buried in her hair. He breathed deeply, restraining the desire to press his lips to the delicate shell of her ear. Her own breathing came in shallow gasps, then stopped altogether when his thumb crept the remainder of the way up her leg and flicked against the tight bud of her womanhood.

"I've always admired women who are comfortable in their own skin," he murmured, stirring her hair with his breath. "Who feel as comfortable in their clothes as out of them."

Her shudder seemed to ripple straight to the core of him.

"Tell me, Dulcy. Would you strip for me?"

She blinked at him, her eyes swimming with desire and confusion. Her lips parted as if awaiting his kiss.

Quinn gave in to the urge to groan. She hadn't put panties on after their ladies' room encounter. The thought of her walking around in public for the past three hours, naked under her skirt, air caressing her soft flesh, made him rock hard. He drew his thumb down the length of her crevice, then dipped it inside, pleased with her dampness.

He didn't know how he would pull it off, but he had to have Dulcy again.

DULCY KNEW she should be ashamed. That instead of thrusting her hips into Quinn's sinful touch, she should have pulled away, asked him to stop. But she had been powerless to do either. The truth was that his touching her felt so, so good. Made her want him so, so bad.

Strip for him? She restlessly licked her lips. Never. No matter how titillating the thought of baring her skin to Quinn's hungry gaze, even as she gave in to the sheer need surging through her body, she knew that she could never, ever do what the woman on the stage was doing. Could never put herself on display in such a provocative, public manner. Just thinking about it made her feel panicky, out of control. And control was so very, very important to her. Especially given how much of it she had lost recently.

"No...never," she murmured.

His dark eyes seemed to stare straight into her, uncovering her fears. "Never?"

Her breath caught. "Never."

Dimly she noted a shaft of artificial light from the street penetrate the bar. She saw Quinn's glance flick to the door, but her focus was on pressing herself farther into Quinn's hand...only to have his hot, stroking fingers disappear. She was afraid he'd stopped because of what she'd said. Then his breath caressed her ear, making her shiver.

"Let's get out of here."

She gazed at him and slowly nodded. She carefully tugged her skirt back down, then stood. But instead of leading her toward the door, he led her to the back of the club down the hall to the rest rooms. Remembering that morning, she questioned whether he planned to finish what had started in a similar environment earlier. The prospect excited and shocked her at the same time. Her palm dampened where it rasped against his. He opened first the ladies' room door, then the men's room. He tugged her into the men's room. Dulcy leaned against the closed wood, her breathing growing ragged, her thighs moist in anticipation. But rather than kissing her, he motioned her toward one of the stalls. She hurried after him, only to find herself being boosted by two hands on her bottom through a window over the alley.

Dulcy landed flat on that bottom and stared wide-eyed at Quinn as he followed her through the window. Before she knew it, he was pulling her up to stand next to him.

"Sorry about that," he murmured, his gaze raking her face. "Remember the flower guy?"

Dulcy blinked at him. "What?"

"The flower deliveryman at Brad's place."

She licked her parched lips and nodded. "Sure. But what's he got—"

"He just walked into the club."

"Oh," she said dully. Then the importance of what he'd said slowly sank in. "Oh!"

Grabbing her hand again, he led her down the alley toward the parking lot. Sure enough, sitting under a light pole, was the white van with the flower shop's logo on the side.

"No phone number," she said to herself, finding him holding her hand disconcertingly comfortable. Strangely, she didn't try to remove it.

"I'm guessing it's a front. That there is no Manny's Flowers within a hundred-mile radius of Albuquerque."

"How could you know something like that?"

He stared at her, his dark features and eyes looking dangerously handsome in the dim light of the alley. She guessed he knew all sorts of ways of doing things that she preferred not to know about.

"Oh." She seemed to be saying that all too often lately.

"Come on," Quinn said, looking toward the closed door to the club. "Get in your car and leave. I'll stick around and make sure he doesn't follow you."

Dulcy didn't move.

"What?" he asked.

"We need to talk."

Even when he gave her a shadow of a smile it came off as a grin. "I don't think now's the time, Dulc."

She swallowed hard. "I'm not talking about…that." She finally gathered the courage to tug her hand out of his. "Where are you going next?"

"I don't get what you mean."

"In your search for Brad."

He didn't say anything for a moment, merely stared at her unblinkingly. "Go home, Dulcy."

She crossed her arms. "And do what? Continue to work as if today was any other day? Or plan my wedding as if my fiancé isn't missing?"

He winced, and she took far too much satisfaction in the reaction.

"Look, Quinn, I want—no need—to find Brad as urgently as you do. And since we've both ended up in the same place twice now, don't you think it would be a good idea to work together on this?"

"Together…" he asked, putting his index finger to his lips.

Her gaze caught on the gesture. He seemed to grow aware of her attention and ran the pad of the digit across the length of his bottom lip.

"Normally that would sound like a good idea…"

She forced her gaze away from his decadent mouth.

"But nothing seems to turn out normal when we're together, Dulcy."

He had a point there. But she couldn't stand the thought of going back to the office, jumping every time the phone rang, passively hoping for some sort of news on Brad. On her life.

She uncrossed her arms and smoothed down her skirt. "Well, since you won't tell me where you're going, I'll share where I'm heading—to Brad's country club a couple of hours outside of town, near Socorro. He had a golf appointment yesterday. I plan to see if he kept it."

"Dulcy—"

She raised her hand. "There is no way I'm just going to sit back like a good little girl and wait for all this to work itself out. It's not what I'm made of. Not what I'm about."

The grin returned along with a good dose of sexual suggestion. "Oh, I would never mistake you for a good little girl, Dee. You forget, I know how very bad you can be."

Dulcy's cheeks blazed but she held his gaze. "Then, we're in agreement."

"No."

She shrugged. "Fine. See you at the country club."

He grasped her arm. "Tomorrow."

She suddenly found the simple act of swallowing difficult. "Tomorrow?"

He nodded. "I'm going to head out to the Wheeler estate. See what Beatrix, Bruno and the greasy detective they hired earlier have unearthed." He released her. "You're welcome to come."

She rubbed the skin he'd touched. "I don't think that would be a very good idea."

"That's how I thought you'd feel."

She searched his eyes, finding them unreadable. "You'll call me at home if you find out anything?"

He nodded once.

8

DULCY FELT she had chugged down ten coffees instead of the half she was still sipping. She made a face at the cooling liquid in the cup sitting on the edge of her desk and automatically reached for the phone. She pulled her arm back. There was absolutely no one else for her to call.

No sleep the night before wasn't helping matters any. But she supposed she'd be more worried had she slept like the dead. She shuddered at her unfortunate choice of words and worried her engagement ring around and around her finger, then glanced at her watch. Only five minutes later than the last time she'd looked. Which meant the group visit to the police station was still a good two hours away at noon. They planned to meet with Barry's contact there to report Brad's disappearance.

She turned the page of the legal brief in front of her and sighed, resting her forehead against her palm. She'd talked to Beatrix for a full two minutes first thing this morning. Up until yesterday, Brad's mother had been suspiciously solicitous with her, warmly welcoming her into the family and going out of her way to try to bond with her. Now with Brad's disappearance, she came off as a female Jeckyl and Hyde, one moment kind to her, the next oozing a dislike that made the hairs on the back of Dulcy's neck go prickly.

Beatrix had taken what appeared to be an equal amount of pleasure and displeasure in telling her that no progress had been made in locating Brad on any front.

Then there was Quinn…

Dulcy refused to admit that he had a thing to do with her not getting any sleep last night. Her mind had been on Brad and his whereabouts and safety only. Nothing else. And if she drifted off for a couple minutes and woke up with the sheets twisted around her legs and pulled tight between her thighs, Quinn's name on her lips…well, that was because she was an anxious bride four days away from her wedding night.

A no-good bride who had done some very naughty things with her groom's best man.

Dulcy groaned. What was she going to do?

She reached for the phone to put in another call to Quinn, although she hadn't left a message the past ten times she'd tried him. The moment her hand met with the receiver, the phone rang.

Slapping her other hand to her chest, she answered the phone mid-ring. "Hello?"

"Dulcy?"

She swallowed and nodded, the female voice on the other end of the line unfamiliar. "This is she."

"Thank God, I got through to you. That dragon lady of a receptionist refused to let my call through until now."

Dulcy leaned forward. Mona was away from her desk, which meant the caller was given voice-mail instructions on how to reach the attorney of her choice. "Mandy? Is that you?"

She recalled the young blond stripper bride, and the prenuptial agreement from hell, of the day before. "Yes. Yes, it is. And, oh boy, do I ever need your help." There was a relieved sigh on the other end of the line. On Dulcy's end, discomfort reigned. She remembered the night before and the women at the Pink Lady. She clamped her eyes shut, not wanting to think of her client in that light. Not wanting to think of life, period, in that light.

Dulcy swiveled her chair, trying to see across the waiting area to Jena's office. Her friend was dictating into a hand-held tape recorder while reading a document in front of her. "Mandy, hold on a minute. I'm going to put your call through to Jena McCade."

"No!"

"Why not?"

"Because I want you as my attorney, that's why not." She hesitated. "What you did for me yesterday...well, not many people would have stepped up to the plate the way you did. I can't thank you enough. I think."

I think? Dulcy glanced at her watch again. "You're welcome. I think. And I'm flattered, Mandy. But I really—"

"I received a document this morning. Do you want me to read it to you? No, wait a minute, I'll read it to you. It was delivered by messenger. Or a server. I think he said his name was. Okay, here it is. It says Motion of Intent."

"From your groom?" Dulcy asked, raising her brows.

"Yes. I'm not sure what it all means, but I think Jason wants to sue me for...let me find it...breach of contract. But I don't understand. I never signed a contract. How can I be in breach of one?"

Dulcy grabbed a pen and wrote a couple of notes. "When was the last time you saw Polansky, Mandy?"

"Two hours ago. He spent the night."

Dulcy nearly choked on the coffee she was swallowing and grabbed for a nearby napkin. "You're kidding."

"No. He even left his suit jacket behind. I just put a call in to his office a little while ago, telling his secretary I was going to drop it off there when I go out for lunch."

"Don't you dare."

"Why not?"

"Tell me what else the document says, Mandy."

"I don't know. It's something legal, so I thought I should call you about it. I haven't read it all the way through yet."

"It should have been delivered to me. Or at least to Jena, since she's your attorney of record." She sighed, tapping her pen on her blotter. A moot point, since the document had been served and the ink wouldn't change regardless of who had it in hand. "Okay, read it and tell me what it says, Mandy."

"Okay." Silence.

Dulcy waited five full minutes while the blonde read it, ready to bang her forehead against the desktop.

"Oh my God," said Mandy.

"What?" Dulcy perked up.

"He wants the ring back."

Figured.

"He also wants me to assume, let me read it, 'all financial responsibility for nonrefundable deposits made thus far for the wedding.'"

Dulcy didn't say anything.

"So...?" Mandy prompted.

"So..." Dulcy repeated, not knowing quite what to say. She didn't think 'I told you so' was very professional. And it definitely wouldn't make Mandy very happy. "When will you be seeing Jason again?"

"At lunch, of course. When I drop off his jacket at his office."

Dulcy rolled her eyes. "Scratch that. Keep the jacket. When is the next time you'd usually see him?"

"Tonight. When he gets off work. We have reservations."

Well, that made it all right then, didn't it? Forget being sued, they had reservations. "When did you make the reservations?"

"He asked me to call in and make them this morning."

Boy, this just kept getting better and better. "Cancel them. Does Jason have a key to your place? Forget I asked. Of course he has a key, right?" She quickly made several notes in succession. "Change the locks, Mandy."

"What?"

"Call a locksmith the instant we get off the phone. Change the locks. As soon as possible. This morning."

"But I don't—"

"Do you understand what that document you're holding means, Mandy?" Obviously she didn't. And Dulcy didn't blame her. How did one take a document of that nature when the man behind it was acting like nothing was wrong? Make reservations, indeed. "It means Jason says your engagement is at an end. He's not marrying you. And he's making it look like you're the one who broke it off because of your refusal to sign that piece of crap he and his attorney called a prenuptial agreement."

"Yes, but we revised it."

"Yes, well, I'd say what you're holding means they rejected it."

"You're kidding."

"No, I'm not."

A series of curse words that nearly singed Dulcy's eyebrows off sounded through the phone. "I've got to go."

"Oh, and Mandy? Don't—"

The dial tone sounded in her ear. Dulcy finished her thought. "Don't call, see or otherwise contact that slime Mr. Jason Polansky, except through me." She sighed and hung up the phone. Mandy was probably already halfway out the door on her way to see him.

QUINN STOOD OUTSIDE the open glass door, the office of the Albuquerque police chief already filled to overflowing.

There were Beatrix and Bruno, and Dulcy's partners Barry Lomax and Jena McCade. Then there was Dulcy herself. He realized his fingers were coiled into fists and forced himself to open them. Of course the Albuquerque sports forum wouldn't have been a large enough space to hold him and Dulcy without his wanting to pull her blond hair out of that damn twist and watch the ends of it tease her naked breasts.

From what he understood, the chief was an old friend of Lomax's from law school. Quinn glanced around the large, bustling war room behind him, catching the curious glances of plainclothes detectives and uniformed officers alike. From an urgency standpoint, you couldn't have paid for a better connection in the department. Who better than the chief of police to cut through all the red tape involved in a missing person case?

On the downside, if Beatrix hoped to keep things hush-hush, their combined and obvious presence inside and outside the chief's office was not going to help matters. He watched a detective pick up a phone, his gaze glued to Beatrix's back as he spoke. He'd allow five minutes before the whole of the department knew what was going on. And five minutes after that before the media got hold of the information.

He absently rubbed his chin. Of course, public attention might help in their search for Brad. Then again, it might hinder it. If the crumpled ransom note in the middle of the chief's desk was authentic, there was a risk that the kidnappers might get spooked. And without knowing who they were, there was no telling what their reaction might be.

Quinn took out his notepad and wrote something on it, then tore off the top sheet.

"Thank you, Jim," Barry Lomax was saying, actively pumping the chief's hand. "I owe you one."

"You owe me two." The chief chuckled. "Don't worry. I'll find some way to make you pay up."

Quinn watched everyone else get up from their chairs—except for Bruno, who, of course, had been standing behind Beatrix's chair—and follow Barry's lead as they thanked the chief.

"You can rest assured that I'll put my best men on the case," the chief said, checking to make sure his shirt was properly tucked into his pants. "I'll let you know the minute I hear anything."

Quinn leaned against the door, watching as everyone filed out one by one. As he'd hoped, Dulcy was at the tail end. Unfortunately, Jena was smack-dab next to her.

Dulcy gave him a look full of fear and warning. He nodded at her friend. "Jena. Dulcy."

He hadn't gotten a chance to address either of them before the meeting simply because they had already been in the chief's office with Barry when he arrived with Beatrix and Bruno.

He walked on the other side of Dulcy, and she instantly picked up her step. He brushed his hand against hers, finding her palm damp. She gasped and stared at him. Then she sensed the piece of paper he placed in her palm and grasped it.

Quinn passed them. "Until next time."

Jena slowed and crossed her arms, watching him. Quinn winked at her. He had no doubt Dulcy was going to get an earful from her—if she hadn't already.

"YOUR APARTMENT. THREE."

Dulcy stared at the note she carefully shielded in her hand, as Jena openly appreciated the view. She glanced up to see Quinn turning the corner to take the stairs, rather than heading for the elevator with the rest of the group. She sighed gustily.

"You can say that again." Jena pursed her lips, then turned her gaze on Dulcy. "So, what did he give you?"

"What?" Dulcy tried to act as if she didn't have a clue what her friend was referring to, as she casually caught up with the others. Even though being anywhere near Beatrix was not high on her list of choices, being left alone with Jena was virtual suicide.

"You know *what*," Jena said quietly, leaning closer to her, her expression determined.

"Just something I dropped."

"Uh-huh. I'll tell you what I'd like to drop every time I see that hunk of man. My panties."

Dulcy stared at her.

Jena laughed.

The elevator doors slid open and Jena excused herself so that she could enter first and stand in the back, then dragged Dulcy along with her. Beatrix, Barry and Bruno entered last and turned to face the doors. Jena made no secret of checking out Bruno's assets. Which, given his minimal contribution to conversation, lay strictly in his physique. The absence of a neck didn't seem to bother her friend one iota.

Dulcy elbowed Jena…hard.

"What?" she said for Dulcy's ears only. "Trust me, right now you are exactly the wrong person to be admonishing anyone."

Dulcy stared at her and hoped her jaw wasn't about to drop to the elevator floor.

Jena smiled. "If I didn't know before, I certainly do now, sweet cheeks." She curved her arm over Dulcy's shoulders. "Way to go."

Dulcy shrugged her off. "This is not the time or the place."

"I know. But trust me, soon you and I will come across both. And then you're going to tell me everything. And I mean *everything*."

Barry cleared his throat and slid them a warning glance. Dulcy would have dived through the escape hatch, if only she could find one.

Beatrix turned her head and fastened a smiling glare on her. "I hope you're satisfied, Dulcy."

Dulcy cleared her throat and resisted the urge to straighten her jacket. "I'm sure I don't know what you mean, Mrs. Wheeler."

"The police. You do realize that now that they're involved, we lose our anonymity. You're not going to be able to step out of the house or your office without some third-rate reporter trying to get a scoop. Forget about trying to find Bradley on our own. We'll have to worry about which shot of us is going to be featured on the front page in the morning paper. Or what clip they're going to run on the evening TV news."

Dulcy was afraid she was going to revisit her morning coffee right then and there.

Jena coughed. "Police and media involvement might also lead to Brad's rapid recovery. You know—in case you weren't going to mention that little aspect of this whole fiasco."

"Fiasco, Ms. McCade? I find your choice of words very interesting. And I'm sure my attorney will, too."

Dulcy raised her brows. She had to admit, she found Jena's statement a little odd herself. By *fiasco* did she mean that she believed Brad had taken off on his own? And what of the ransom note?

Barry's quiet chuckle filled the interior of the elevator. "Trixie, what's say you and I go get some lunch. I know a great café nearby."

Trixie? Dulcy nearly tripped over her own feet. And she wasn't even moving.

Beatrix added to her shock by beaming at Barry. Surprisingly, ten years seemed to drop from her features. "I'd love to." The expression vanished and she glanced at Bruno. "You, of course, will have to wait in the car, Bruno. Your presence will only serve as more fodder for gossip."

Jena leaned closer to Dulcy. "Oh, happy day."

9

"NO, MR. WHEELER didn't make his golf date the day before yesterday," the private club manager, one very stuffy Mr. Jones, said some five hours later. "If you need to know anything further, I suggest you speak to the Albuquerque police department. I've already told them everything I know." If his nose had been any higher, Dulcy swore she could have counted the hairs in there. She glanced to find Quinn's jaw tight, his eyes glittering dangerously. Personally, if she were Mr. Jones she'd have headed for the hills five minutes ago.

Three o'clock on the button outside her apartment she'd found Quinn pulling up to the curb in a black Jeep. He'd said very little. Merely opened the door for her to climb in and nodded when she asked if they were heading to the exclusive golf club of which Brad was a member.

That was nearly three hours ago. And it seemed Quinn hadn't weathered the tension that had stretched between them in the narrow confines of his Jeep any better than she had during the drive southwest of Socorro. She felt hot and bothered, and suspected that if she were a man, she'd have wanted to hit something. Or, even better, someone. Too bad Mr. Jones seemed to be unwittingly offering himself up for that honor.

She swallowed, considering the undercurrents traveling between the two men. Apparently the manager thought himself skimmed from the cream while he considered Quinn in his black jeans and T-shirt to have been dredged from the muddy bottom of society.

Quinn stepped menacingly closer to Mr. Jones. Dulcy laid a restraining hand on his chest, then wished she hadn't. The muscles beneath her itchy fingers were hard and hot, setting her skin to tingling. She quickly snatched her hand away.

"Thank you, Mr. Jones," she said, trying to diffuse the situation.

"We'd like to check in for the night," Quinn said darkly.

The manager seemed to grow a foot taller as he practically bounced on his toes. "We're not a hotel, sir. We're an exclusive club with a very restricted membership policy."

Dulcy glanced at her watch. Just after six.

Quinn was right. By the time they got back to the city, the possibility of following up on any leads would be moot—that is, if they had any additional leads to follow up on. She didn't have any. And she suspected that if Quinn did, he wasn't about to share that information with her.

Moreover, aside from getting some much-needed rest, sticking around the club would give them an opportunity to see if anyone knew anything more about Brad and his whereabouts. Who had he planned to meet? Were they still in residence? How could they be contacted?

Dulcy turned her best smile on Mr. Jones, which probably wasn't much given the circumstances. He instantly looked repentant. "I don't believe I introduced myself. I'm Dulcy Ferris, Mr. Wheeler's fiancée."

He raised his brows, but her pronouncement didn't seem to make a difference. Not when coupled with the fact that she had come in looking for her errant fiancé.

Quinn pulled his wallet from the back pocket of his jeans and took out a card, practically flinging it at the manager. "Check your records, dickhead. I'm a member."

Dulcy raised her brows. Quinn was a member of the club?

Mr. Jones didn't seem to know what to do as he caught the card between hand and chest. He mumbled something that sounded like "I'll be right back," then practically scurried from the room.

Dulcy turned and looked around the well-appointed lobby of the resort. Gleaming marble floors, carved columns and antiques made it appear more home than hotel. A very wealthy home. She cleared her throat and glanced at Quinn, who stood watching her closely.

"You could have saved us a lot of trouble by telling Mr. Jones you were a member from the onset," she said quietly.

His grin wasn't all that warm. "What? And miss all the fun?" He slid his wallet back into his pocket. "That's the only reason I belong. To watch men like him trip all over themselves to make up for their bad behavior."

Dulcy tucked a strand of escaped hair behind her ear. She wondered why she felt as though *she* suddenly had something to make up for. Okay, so, no, she hadn't even considered that Quinn might be a member of the club. Not because of his choice of clothes and hairstyle, but rather his down-to-earth character. He didn't strike her as the sort who got into a round of golf with a bunch of work associates. The calluses on his hands hinted at a life that entailed more than palming a few golf irons.

She was not being a snob.

Telling herself that didn't make her feel any better.

It was bad enough that they had ridden out to the resort in Quinn's Jeep. The two-hour drive down Route 25 had been one of the longest of her life. She usually enjoyed watching the Sandia Mountains give way to endless desert dotted with breathtaking mesas and small rolling hills, but today all she'd been able to think about was how close Quinn was. And how much she'd wanted to hike up her skirt and straddle him while he was driving, taking up where they'd left off at the strip club the night before.

Now he was looking at her as if he expected something. And it wasn't what she wanted to give him.

"Admit it, Dulcy. You were as surprised as Jones was to find out I belonged to the club."

"I was not."

His grin widened.

She grimaced. "Okay, maybe I was little surprised," she grudgingly admitted.

Mr. Jones's reappearance saved her further embarrassment. He couldn't have hurried over to Quinn fast enough, his about-face enough to make Dulcy do a double take. Quinn crossed his arms, standing silently as the manager blathered on and on, offering up one apology, then another, and even extending a free night's stay for the, er, confusion.

"Of course, we're talking for both the lady and me," Quinn stated rather than asked.

"Of course, Mr. Landis. I'll personally see to it you have one of the finest suites."

"We'll need two," Dulcy interjected, feeling suddenly jittery. "We'll need two rooms."

"With connecting doors," Quinn added.

She practically gawked at his audacity. Didn't he realize that news of connecting rooms between a bride and the groom's best man would make the gossip circuit before they even inserted their card keys into the door locks? She quickly looked away, judging by his expression that he did know that. And he appeared to like knowing that she did, too.

Dulcy shivered. She tried to tell herself it wasn't in anticipation, but her body wasn't having any of it.

Within minutes she and Quinn were not only being led to their suites, but also promised that a fresh set of bed and day clothes from the exclusive boutique in the lobby would be delivered to each of them posthaste. Mr. Jones himself escorted them up. At the end of a long hall, he opened the door to a room and gestured for her to enter.

Dulcy hesitated, glancing at Quinn as if waiting for answers. He didn't offer any as he scanned the hallway. She offered a weak smile in Mr. Jones's general direction, then stepped inside. The door whooshed closed behind her.

Done in pale blue and white stripes, muted florals and tasteful antique replicas, the room was impeccably designed with the utmost comfort and visual appeal in mind. Only Dulcy wasn't feeling very comfortable. She paced from one side of the spacious room to the other, pressing her ear against the connecting door to seek out any sounds in the next room. Even after the clothes and toiletries were delivered, she felt like a caged animal waiting for the trainer to feed her. Speaking of food, she hadn't eaten since a quick bagel that morning and her stomach was making sure she knew about it.

Another trip to the connecting door. The metal cut to resemble carved wood yielded nothing. She knew there was another door behind the door she was trying to listen through, but she was afraid that if she opened hers, she'd find the other one open as well. And then where would she be?

Instead, she plucked up the phone and asked to be put through to Mr. Landis's room. No one answered. She slowly replaced the receiver. That's odd. Could he be taking a shower? She went into her bathroom and listened through the wall in there, but she couldn't make out a sound. Sighing, she went back to the phone and put a call through to Mr. Jones, who was all too happy to tell her that Mr. Landis had requested a list of Mr. Wheeler's golf companions and had already arranged to meet with the sole member that remained on the premises for an extended weekend visit.

He'd gone without her.

Dulcy forgot to thank the man as she slowly hung up the phone a second time.

Oh, this was ridiculous. She refused to sit around moping because Quinn thought he could do a better job without her. If he found out anything that might lead them to Brad, he'd tell her.

Speaking of Brad...

A moment and a quick dial later she was listening to the incessant ring of his cell phone. Ever since getting the news yesterday, she'd tried his wireless countless times and had gotten his service provider's message just as many times, telling her to try again later.

She hung up the phone for a third time. What would she do if Brad did pick up?

Slipping off her shoes and suit, she headed for the marble-tiled shower. A half hour later she was freshly scrubbed, wearing the simple white cotton panties that had come with the rest of the clothing, and the hotel robe. This time when she went to the connecting door, she opened it, only to stare at the closed one behind it. She tried the knob, finding it locked. So she knocked quietly. She wasn't surprised when there was no answer.

She stood there for a minute considering her options. Only, there didn't appear to be many. Sitting down on the bed, she put the phone down on the spread in front of her folded knees and leafed through her address book, then she put a call through to Mona at home. While Barry and Jena never thought twice about contacting the secretary after hours, it was the first time Dulcy had ever done it. She didn't feel comfortable with it. Mona answered on the second ring with the same efficiency she did at work.

Without giving away too much information, Dulcy asked for her messages, told Mona she'd be late getting to the office the following day, and asked Mona to track down Barry for her. Mona hesitated, then told her that Barry hadn't returned to the office after their appointment with the police chief. He'd called later in the afternoon and said he'd be gone the following day as well. No itinerary, no number to be reached, he was just simply going to be gone.

She thanked Mona and pressed the disconnect button, still holding the receiver in her hand.

On the surface, she supposed that Barry and Beatrix made an obvious couple. Both were from the wealthier part of town and were around the same age and still relatively good-looking. If, in Beatrix's case, you found cannibalism attractive. Still, Dulcy had been surprised when Barry had called Brad's mother Trixie in the elevator earlier. Even more surprising, Beatrix had never batted an eyelash.

She knew given Barry's three failed marriages that the legal community at large believed him to be a terrible flirt at best, a philanderer at worse. But they didn't know what she did, mostly because Barry had kept the information close to his chest.

Two of his three ill-fated marriages had come later in his life. His first wife, to whom he'd been married for over twenty-five years, had died by her own hand.

Dulcy rubbed the skin between her brows and sighed. Of course, their problems had begun long before Janice Lomax had convinced a male nurse to fiddle with the valve on her morphine tube. More specifically, they had started ten years into their marriage, when Janice was involved in a car accident that left her a quadriplegic.

Dulcy had met Janice once. And had never really been the same afterward. While the unconditional, overwhelming love between her and her husband had been palpable, so had the tone of impending tragedy. Simply, Janice had had enough of life as it had become for her, and Barry could do nothing to change her mind.

The receiver in her hand began to beep, telling her to hang up, and the noise pierced Dulcy's thoughts. The mere idea of dear, sweet, wounded Barry with that…barracuda made her stomach upset.

She slowly depressed the disconnect button again, then dialed information, wanting to empty her mind of Barry and Trixie. A couple of minutes later she learned that there was no Manny's Flowers listed in Albuquerque, or all of New Mexico for that matter.

She lay back against the pillows. That's strange. First the deliveryman had refused to give the flowers to anyone but Brad. Then he had coincidentally shown up at the same strip club, even though it was on the other side of town from Brad's town house. She fingered the black and neon-pink card from the club. Maybe she'd gotten the name of the flower shop wrong. She got up from the bed, stepped to the connecting door, then returned to the bed when she received no answer to her knock. She pushed the card aside and scanned her shorthand notes of the messages Mona had passed on. Exasperating bride-to-be Mandy Mallone had left no fewer than ten messages for Dulcy to call her. No specifics. Just call her.

Despite the little voice screaming not to, she dialed Mandy's number, then settled against the pillows. The ex-stripper picked up in the middle of the second ring.

"Thank God!" There was urgency in the response. "I was going crazy over here wondering what I should do. Crazy? Did I say crazy? Yes, I did. What I meant is that I'm going out of my mind."

"That's all right. There's nothing wrong with feeling a

little crazy considering what you're going through,'' Dulcy said.

''Yes, there is,'' Mandy nearly whispered. ''When your mother is carted off in a straitjacket right in front of you when you're six… Never mind.''

Dulcy briefly closed her eyes. Damn. ''Tell me what's happening, Mandy. Did you change the locks?''

''Yes. And Jason wasn't very happy about it, either. Wait a minute while I sit down. No, I can't sit.''

Dulcy heard the phone being juggled as Mandy presumably began pacing. ''That was the whole point.''

''What was?''

''To make Jason think about what he'd done.''

''Well, then it worked. Not only did he think about it, he sent the police a-knockin'. They left like an hour ago.''

''Police?'' Dulcy sat up.

''Yeah. Since you told me not to take his jacket to him, I had it messengered over to his office. In pieces. Along with everything else he ever left in my apartment.''

Dulcy cringed. ''You didn't.''

''I did. And I was very happy about doing it, too. Until the police showed up, that is.''

She made a sound and the phone was juggled again. Dulcy guessed she was pacing up a storm and moving the receiver from ear to ear.

''Jason told them he felt physically threatened.''

Dulcy thought of the short, slender, stacked blonde, then Jason Polansky with his ex-college football player physique.

''The police, um, pointed out that what I'd done to his boxers was proof of Jason's claim.''

Dulcy didn't ask. Instead, she berated herself for ever having spoken up at the meeting the day before. For having suggested Mandy change her locks. For telling the jittery bride-to-be that her fiancé was playing her for a fool.

But how was she supposed to know all this would happen?

"Dulcy? Are you there?" Mandy asked.

She blew out a long breath. "Yes, I'm still here."

"Good, I was afraid you'd hung up."

Which is exactly what she should do, she thought. Tell Mandy to sign the damn prenuptial agreement, marry Jason and go on with life as usual.

She shifted uncomfortably. "I'm just trying to figure out where I should go with this." She wrote a couple of notes on her pad, then tapped her pen against it. "Tell you what, Mandy, why don't I give Jason's attorney a call?" She knew just where to get his personal contact information. "I'll get back to you the minute I'm done, okay?"

"Okay."

"Oh, and Mandy?" she said quickly, before the girl had a chance to hang up. "No more mangling of Jason's personal belongings. And if he calls, or if his attorney tries to contact you, you refer them to me." She gave Mandy her contact information at the hotel, even though she quietly wondered at the wisdom of doing so.

She hung up the phone and sat silently for a moment. She'd known there was a reason she stayed away from family law. There was something orderly and manageable about corporate law. In that area, you knew going in that all the participants were interested in their own bottom lines and that the name of the game was compromise. Unemotional. Logical. In family law, that entire schematic was turned on its ear.

Which, as luck would have it, appeared to be the sum total of her life right about now, as well.

She picked up the phone and dialed Jena's number, only to replace the receiver the instant the line began ringing. She closed her eyes. Okay, so, yes, she was a coward. Facts were facts, and the facts in this case were that she would have a hell of a time explaining where she was and who, exactly, she was with. She bit her bottom lip and glanced toward the closed connecting door. Then she called Jason's attorney's office, relieved to find Steve Saragin still in.

In, but completely unreasonable.

It seemed Mandy's skills with a straight razor had tipped the scales in Jason's direction.

"Come on, Steve. You know we wouldn't even be having this conversation if you'd met me halfway on that prenup."

"She was going to sign it as is."

"Key word being *was*."

"Speaking of keys, did you advise Mandy to change the locks to her apartment?"

"I plead the fifth."

"You know my client pays for that place."

No, she hadn't. "Whose name is on the lease?"

He sighed. "You and I know that doesn't matter."

Mandy's name was. Good. At least her client wouldn't end up homeless. Not for the foreseeable future, anyway.

Dulcy crossed her legs and moved the body of the phone to the side. "So where do things stand with the prenup?"

"They don't."

"So your client isn't even willing to consider revising it?"

"I'm advising him not to."

"Well, then, I hope he likes the prospect of *going without*. Because that's exactly what he's facing if he doesn't come around." Dulcy smiled to herself, proud at having adopted one of Jena's sayings.

"Define *going without*."

"You should know, Steve. I'm guessing *going without* is a permanent state with you."

"Shows what you know."

"Shows what I'd prefer not to know."

"What's that supposed to mean?"

Dulcy bit her tongue to stop right there. Was this really her talking to a professional colleague? She cleared her throat, trying to get a grip on her runaway emotions. "It means that you shouldn't call me, and your client shouldn't try to contact Miss Mallone, until that prenuptial agreement looks…more agreeable. Have a nice night, Steve."

She slowly hung up the phone and savored the moment. There was something about standing in a courtroom after having just won a case, but having just bested one of Albuquerque's better attorneys felt equally satisfying. She put in a quick call to Mandy, told her to sit tight, then sat drumming her fingers against the phone.

Placing it back on the table, she decided to deal with the rest of her messages in the morning. It was after eight. She pushed from the bed, resisted the urge to check the connecting door again, and instead stepped toward the French doors that led to the balcony. Swinging them open, she was immediately aware of the scent of cigarette smoke. She blinked into the growing darkness and found Quinn leaning against the marble railing connecting their balconies.

Dulcy's heart teeter-tottered in her chest, and just like that she forgot about Mandy, Steve, Mona, Barry, and all the reasons why she shouldn't want the guy stubbing a cigarette out in the soil of a planter. He glanced her way. She crossed her arms over her chest.

"You went information hunting without me," she said.

"That I did."

"And?"

"I came up a little short on the information end."

"Tell me."

He was silent as he crossed his own arms over his broad chest. His dark hair was held back in the usual leather strap.

"Only one of the men Brad was supposed to meet yesterday is still in residence. Nathan Armstrong."

"And?"

"And he has no idea where Brad might be. Brad didn't call to cancel or apologize. The last time he spoke with Brad he didn't seem distracted or nervous." He glanced at his watch. "And right about now Brad's old college bud is probably hightailing it home in his Beemer to cover for the platinum blonde he had draped over his arm."

"Nathan's having an affair?" Dulcy nearly croaked.

"It would appear so."

She backed up, nearly collapsing into the ironwork chair positioned beside a matching table.

She knew Nathan and his wife Nancy. She and Brad had gone out to dinner with them on a couple of occasions and had even attended a party at their house. Dulcy had played with their three kids. They all had seemed so...close. So happy. So in love. The model family.

So then, what was Nathan doing at the resort with another woman?

She noticed movement on the next balcony, and suddenly Quinn was standing next to her chair. She stared at the three feet that separated his balcony from hers, but couldn't seem to add the two and two involved to get him from there to here.

"You okay?" he asked quietly.

Dulcy pressed her fingertips against her closed eyelids, thinking of her most recent case, Brad, and everything else in between. "Yes. I guess so. It's just that I feel like I fell asleep and woke up in the middle of *Ally McBeal.* And it's not even a particularly good episode."

Quinn's chuckle was so quiet she nearly didn't hear it. She grimaced. "You know, I never thought of myself as gullible. As naive. But after today I wonder how long I've had my head buried in the sand.'' She looked at him. ''Have you seen a lot of that?''

''A lot of what? Gullible women?''

''No. Men engaged in extramarital activities.''

''It's not limited to men.''

She sighed. ''You would have to tell me that, wouldn't you.'' She sat back, feeling the robe slip down over her shoulder. She absently pushed it back up, only to have it flop down again. ''This is a new millennium, for Christ's sake. No more obligatory sex or arranged marriages.'' She pushed the robe up. ''There are…diseases.''

Quinn watched the soft Turkish terry cloth skim down over her arm, and resisted the urge to cover the bare flesh back up. The one-size-fits-all robe all but swallowed her slender frame in a sea of white foam. From where he stood beside her, he had an unhindered view of the deep V between the flaps of the robe and the pink, clean skin it revealed. Dulcy covered her shoulder and the material bowed, the tightly cinched belt the only thing preventing the robe from falling off altogether.

He swallowed hard.

''Given what's, um, happened between us…well, I must sound like an idiot,'' she said.

''No.''

She turned her head to stare up at him, her mouth soft and inviting. ''You don't think…I mean, do most of the men here… Is the resort known for such activity? Could Brad…''

The robe dipped again. Quinn reached out and fingered the soft material, then drew it up, his knuckles grazing her hot, soft skin. ''No.''

He was not sure why he lied to her. Maybe because he didn't trust the source the information had come from. But once Mr. Jones had learned he was a member with large amounts of cash, the snobbish man had all too willingly told Quinn about a dark-haired woman Brad had met at the resort a time or two in the past few months. No, he didn't know the woman's name. No, he couldn't even give an accurate description, for both times the woman had been wearing a wide-brimmed hat and large sunglasses. All he could share was that, on those two occasions, Mr. Wheeler hadn't set foot outside his suite the entire night.

Dulcy relaxed again, turning her head to stare out at the lush resort grounds. Quinn skimmed her soft blond hair with the back of his knuckles, merely the lightest of touches. Not hard enough so that she'd notice, but enough to satisfy some of the desire that had been with him ever since he'd met the woman next to him. She shivered.

"Are you cold?" Temperatures dipped low at night in the desert.

She shook her head.

"Have you eaten?"

She shook her head again.

"Me, neither. Why don't I go catch a shower while you order us up something from room service?"

She glanced up at him, opening her mouth as if to say something, then snapping it shut again.

Quinn rested his hand against her shoulder, finding the material had dropped again and left him with skin-on-skin contact. The simple touch seemed to set his nerve endings on fire, shooting flames straight to his groin.

"Don't worry, Dulc. We'll find him."

That, he was sure of. But what they would find Brad doing was something he wouldn't even guess at.

THE TENSION WAS SO THICK in the room she could have tripped over it. Dulcy pushed her asparagus around her delicate china plate, peeking at where Quinn sat across the table from her. How was it that one man could be so sexy? So completely irresistible? Especially since he was the last man on earth she should desire.

She tugged at her robe, wishing she had thought to put something on. But she had been so preoccupied with what Quinn had told her out on the balcony, it had taken all her powers of concentration to order up food from the kitchen. It had taken even more willpower to ignore that Quinn had left the connecting doors open, allowing the sound of the shower to waft into her room.

Even now he wore nothing but a snug pair of faded jeans, leaving his sculpted abs open to her perusal, his skin enticing her more than the food on her plate.

She abruptly pushed from the table, causing the clattering of silverware. "I'm suddenly not very hungry. I think I'm going to go for a swim instead," she murmured. "You know, before I turn in."

Quinn narrowed his gaze on her, the surprise on his face evident. "I thought you hadn't eaten."

She smiled. "I haven't. But my appetite isn't what it used to be lately." At least, not for what the kitchen had offered up.

He wiped his mouth with the white linen napkin, then draped it across his plate. A plate he'd cleaned down to the last drop of cranberry sauce that had been dribbled over the thinly sliced beef.

Then again, a man like him was probably used to being in the same room as a female who wanted him so badly she could scream. She imagined he'd never lacked for companionship. But it had to take great restraint to ignore the strong current that seemed to tangle the two of them together whenever they were less than ten feet apart.

Dulcy started for the bedroom.

Quinn's quiet voice stopped her. "What time do you want to head back in the morning?"

She swallowed hard. "I was, um, thinking it might be better if I took a cab," she said. "Or perhaps Mr. Jones would be willing to see to my transportation back into town. You don't have to wait for me."

That damnable grin tugged at his mouth. "I see."

She pulled the sash tighter around her waist. "I don't think I'm going to get much sleep, so I thought, you know, that I'd head back early." Very early. Say, three o'clock. Or maybe even sooner, depending on how well she could keep her hormones in check.

He casually pushed from the table and stood. "I thought you wanted us to work together."

The way he said "together" made her nipples harden beneath the soft Turkish terry cloth. She shrugged and turned away. "This club was my last lead. Unless you can think of anything else, I think our short-lived partnership has reached the end."

"Shame."

Yes, "shameful" about summed up how she was feeling now. She gestured toward the connecting doors. "Well, then...good night."

His gaze languidly raked her from bare feet to forehead. "Good night."

Dulcy thought she couldn't have run out of the room faster had the floor been on fire.

Fifteen minutes later she stood beside the long, kidney-shaped pool. A dip of her toe told her the water was kept at just the right temperature. There had been few suits in the cabana in her size. The black bikini that hugged her curves wouldn't have been her first choice, but it would do the job. Besides, there was no one in the pool to notice what she was barely wearing.

She slowly stepped into the water, her goal to do as many laps as it took to chase the very provocative Quinn Landis from her head. Or at least exhaust herself until the thought of doing anything more than dropping into her bed, alone, was impossible.

She dove into the cool water and began swimming the length. Never in her life had she felt so…mesmerized by a man. So obsessed with the thought of having sex with him. Of feeling him between her legs, his hands branding her flesh. Sure, she'd wanted men before. But usually she wanted them most powerfully while they were kissing. With Quinn, she felt breathless and needy just thinking about him. She quivered with a lust the others couldn't have elicited with ten hours of foreplay. And he didn't even have to touch her.

She realized her frenzied pace would result in a side cramp so she evened out her strokes. Concentrating on her swimming also kept her too busy to compare her attraction to Quinn to the lack of any true fire between her and Brad.

That wasn't fair. She and Brad had never really been intimate. No hot and bothered necking as they said goodbye at her apartment door. No casual touches that left her wanting more.

She crushed her eyes closed, seeking the end of the pool with her outstretched fingers, rather than visually. But when she should have touched cold concrete, she brushed against skin instead.

Dulcy caught herself up short, swallowing a mouthful of pool water as she treaded water and stared at the man who had thrown her world into a tailspin a few days ago.

"I thought a swim sounded like a good idea," Quinn said.

Dulcy nearly didn't hear him over the thud of her heartbeat. Instantly her mind was filled with images related to everything but swimming. She smoothed her wet hair from her face, envisioning gyrating pelvises, jutting breasts, spread legs. Looking at Quinn now somehow made her think of the strippers from the night before. Their sexual prowess. Their completely uninhibited nature. Their skill at knowing how to evoke the reaction they wanted with a simple shake of their bottom, a peek of forbidden flesh.

The complete opposite to how she'd spent the first thirty years of her life and would likely spend the next thirty.

Funny, but being this close to Quinn made her rethink all that. Especially considering she wore a suit that was just as revealing as the costumes the strippers had worn.

His dark eyes caught and held on something at water level. Dulcy looked down to find her nipples bunched and hard and very visible through the thin black material of her top. She shivered, and goose bumps immediately appeared across her bare skin. She slowed her kicking so that she sank a little lower in the water. Quinn's grin told her he knew what she was up to, and that it didn't make one iota of difference.

She turned in the water to continue her lap, then pushed off the side of the pool near Quinn's waist. She didn't know what she expected. For him to stop her? Join her? But she was surprised that when she returned to the spot where she'd left him, he was still there, his gaze glued to her body.

She pushed from the side again and quickly swam in the other direction, ignoring the burning of her lungs.

There was something uniquely erotic about sliding through the water, knowing he was watching her. Her back seemed to arch farther, her bottom breaking the water, offering him a view that pretended to be innocent but was anything but. And when she reached the opposite side of the pool, she slid over onto her back, her sensitive breasts jutting from the water. She, of course, pretended not to notice. At least, until she met his gaze from across the pool and knew that he was aware of what she was doing. And that he was open to doing anything she wanted. As much or as little.

He dove into the water and began swimming for her. Dulcy's breath caught in her throat. This end of the pool was shallower. She put her feet down and stood, the water coming to just below her breasts as she watched Quinn. At midpoint, he dove beneath the surface. Dulcy anxiously tried to follow his progress, but the dim lights in the trees surrounding the pool area reflected off the small waves, making her effort impossible.

Something pressed against the crotch of her bikini bottoms. She gasped and looked down, realizing it was Quinn's mouth. His fingers grasped her hips and his teeth nibbled at the bud just beneath the wet material. Then he broke the water's surface and shook his head, sending his loose hair in every direction. Dulcy's knees threatened to give out from under her.

So much for allowing her to set the pace.

"You look incredible in this suit," he murmured, pressing his mouth to her bare stomach, then dragging his tongue across the length of it.

Dulcy hadn't thought she looked incredible in the suit when she put it on and stood staring at herself in the cabana mirror, but Quinn's quiet statement made her feel incredible.

Now he stood so that she had to look up to see into his face. Her breath came in quick, quiet gasps, bringing the tips of her nipples in contact with the hard, wet expanse of his chest every time she took a breath. She held his gaze as steadily as he held hers.

"Damn it, Dulcy," he said hoarsely, his eyes black in the shadows. "I don't know if this is a good idea, but damn if I can stop myself."

She hadn't even been aware of his moving until she felt a finger work its way under the elastic of her suit, seeking the area he had nipped moments before. Dulcy grabbed his arms for balance as he flicked the tight button of her desire, the movement of water making her feel weak. Dear Lord, she was on the verge of losing it and they hadn't even done anything yet.

He caught her pulsing flesh between thumb and forefinger and squeezed. Dulcy collapsed against him, pressing her cheek against his damp chest. She flicked her tongue out, licking the beads of moisture from his skin as he worked his fingers along the length of her aperture. She felt hot where her body touched his, cold where the night air brushed against her damp skin. The combination was heady and exciting, as was the very public place in which they were conducting their underwater activities. While trees shielded the pool, she knew that if she had seen the pool from her balcony, others could see it as well. And while she couldn't see anyone, it didn't mean that someone wasn't this instant watching them.

Quinn crouched down and drew her legs around his hips. She crossed her ankles behind him, reveling in the feel of his erection pulsating against her swollen flesh. Dear Lord, but he felt so very, very good. Lowering his head, he worked his index finger inside the scrap of material covering her right nipple, then tilted the distended flesh up and out of it. She made a move to protest, but then his hot mouth covered the aching tip and her protest came out a quiet moan. She ran her fingers through his damp hair as he hungrily laved her breast and then he thrust his manhood between her legs.

The water sloshed around their waists as Dulcy frantically worked her hand between them, seeking the long, hard, throbbing organ that could bring her so much pleasure. Finally her fingertips were inside the front of his swim trunks and were touching the knob of his arousal. He gently bit down on her nipple, and she cried out.

Quinn chuckled and leaned his forehead against hers. "Unless you want Mr. Jones bearing down on us, you might want to be quiet."

She restlessly licked her lips, eyeing his mouth with rapt attention. "He's probably already in the bushes with his binoculars."

He slowly curved his hands over her bottom and brought her more fully against him, trapping her hand between them. "I'd laugh, but I'm afraid you're right."

She drew back and smiled at him. "Well, we wouldn't want to disappoint him, would we?"

Quinn's jaw tightened, giving him an almost savage appearance. Then his mouth was crushing hers, devouring it. Dulcy gave as good as she got, sliding her tongue along his, afraid she might never get enough of his taste, his feel, his essence. She tilted her hips so that she moved against his length. He quietly groaned, further fueling her need. Covertly, she worked his erection free from his trunks, then directed the tip inside the elastic of her bikini bottoms. When the hot, throbbing end contacted with her flesh, she shuddered, climaxing immediately.

Moments later, she was spent, gasping for breath against his shoulder. Quinn kissed the top of her head, then her exposed neck, nudging her hand from between them even as he inserted his own. Dulcy instantly snapped upright as he thrust forward, until she sandwiched the thick length of his arousal in her heated flesh. Reignited flames licked over her damp body. She grasped his shoulders to balance herself, then drew her own hips back, seeking to have him inside her. Deep inside her.

Quinn gripped her hips. "Don't." He pressed his lips

against her temple, his breathing ragged. "I don't have…anything on me."

Condoms. Dulcy bit down hard on her bottom lip. Equal parts fear and disappointment rushed through her veins. Fear that she'd forgotten about protection. Disappointment that the renewed fire within her had no hope of being extinguished.

Quinn rested the tip of his erection against her entrance. Dulcy tensed, half wishing his self-control would snap and he'd enter her. Then he thrust forward again, along her flesh, leaving her breathless and wanting him inside her even more than before. Desire spiraled within her, leaving her shivering uncontrollably as she rocked him. Just when she was afraid she'd never be satisfied, a climax crashed over her, Quinn's low groan only intensifying it as he grasped her bottom and held her tight against his arousal.

His mouth sought and found her ear. "I want you. Now."

10

QUINN DREW HIS HAND DOWN the length of Dulcy's leg, then back up again. When he'd awakened with the sun slanting across the stark white sheets he'd been momentarily disoriented. Then he glimpsed the naked woman lying with her blond head toward the end of the bed, her feet next to his head, and he knew exactly where he was...and exactly what he'd been doing all night long after leaving the pool and returning to their suites. He drew his fingertips up her inner thigh to find the dripping enclave at the top. Dulcy moaned something and automatically arched her bottom into his touch. As he caressed her silken flesh, he was amazed that even in sleep she was the most responsive woman he'd ever known.

He glanced down to find the top sheet draped across his hips, his erection pressing against the lightweight fabric. They were in his suite, but that's not where they had begun. He couldn't put his finger on exactly what it was about Dulcy Ferris, but even knowing who she was, he couldn't get enough of her. One minute he would be experiencing the most fantastic orgasm of his life, the next he'd want her twice as much.

The smell of her sex, their sex, filled his nose and he groaned, cupping her swollen flesh. Her hips ground against his palm, and he couldn't resist dipping a finger into her slick wetness. Her low moan made him want to cover her body with his and start all over again.

The only problem was that they were no longer under cover of night, when following up on Brad's whereabouts were limited, and it was all too easy to let passions burn out of control. The ringing telephone on the nightstand next to him served as an unwelcome reminder of that.

Dulcy's head snapped up and she peered at him from beneath a tangle of blond curls, her hazel eyes unfocused. Quinn quickly snatched up the receiver. "Landis."

Even before he could remove his hand from where it rested between Dulcy's legs, she was up and out of the bed, taking the top sheet with her. Quinn ignored that that left him completely uncovered. He'd never been ashamed of his nudity before; he certainly wasn't going to start now, even with Dulcy staring at his erection with wide eyes.

Mr. Jones spoke nonstop into his ear. "Hold up, man. Take a breath. Who's doing what?"

"Mrs. Wheeler is on the line for you, sir."

Quinn grimaced.

"What?" Dulcy asked. "What is it?"

She was making a mess out of trying to wrap the sheet around herself and searching the floor for anything she could put on. Only, they'd left the little they'd been wearing the night before in her room.

"Beatrix is on the line."

Dulcy's eyes bulged again. But strippers weren't the reason this time around.

"Quinn, where in the hell are you?" Brad's mother practically screamed over the line.

"You're the one who called me, Beatrix, so clearly you know."

A long-suffering sigh. "You know what I mean. What are you doing lollygagging about when my son is still missing."

"I'm looking for your son."

"At the club?"

"Yes."

Dulcy tossed the bedspread over his nude form. While he didn't seem to have a problem talking to Beatrix *sans* clothes, Dulcy apparently had a problem with him doing so. He watched her shuffle through the connecting door to her suite, her actions jerky and anxious. He frowned, then rasped a hand over his unshaven face.

"Brad had a golf appointment here on Sunday with a few buddies. He never made it."

"What else do you have?"

"Not much. You?"

"I didn't call to share what I have. I want to see what you got."

"Well, then our conversation's over, isn't it."

Beatrix hung up on him.

Quinn sighed and dropped the receiver back in its cradle. "Old hellbitch."

Dulcy's head popped back into the open doorway along with a flash of bare shoulder. Apparently she was getting dressed. "Are you referring to Mrs. Wheeler?"

"Yes." He threw off the bedspread and swung his feet to the floor.

"Has she…?"

Quinn met Dulcy's gaze, trying to read the emotion in her eyes. "Found Brad? No."

Guilt. That's what it was. He pinpointed it the instant before her head disappeared again. A moment later all of her reappeared wearing the hotel robe.

"So what now?" she asked.

"Do you really want to hear my answer to that?"

Dulcy's gaze strayed to the destroyed bed he sat on, then back to his face. "I mean, where do we go now to find Brad?"

He raked a hand through his tousled hair. "That's what I was afraid you meant."

She disappeared again. This time he pushed from the bed and strode to the door, watching her pluck their wet suits from the floor and gather together her clothing from the day before. He leaned his shoulder against the jamb and considered her. She looked about ready to jump out of her skin. Far from the woman who had been all over his skin only a short time ago.

"Dulcy?"

"Hmm?" She glanced his way, but when her gaze landed on an area she apparently wanted to think about least, she looked away again, her cheeks blazing red.

"Are you okay?"

She froze at his words, although her fingers continued plucking at the suits she held. "Okay? Yes, I suppose I'm all right."

"I know you're all right physically. But what about otherwise?"

"You mean, how am I feeling about having just slept with my fiancé's best man?" She closed her eyes. "Not just once, but twice?"

"The first time doesn't count."

She blinked at him.

"You didn't know who I was then. And I had no idea who you were, remember?"

She moved toward the table and draped the suits over the back of the chair. "Oh, that makes me feel better."

Quinn came up behind her and rubbed her arms through the thick terry cloth. "Look, Dulc, I'm not saying there's a way to justify any of this. I'm merely suggesting that there are elements at work here that not even you and I know about yet."

She was as stiff as a telephone pole. Unfortunately, so was another certain area of his anatomy.

"The flower shop doesn't exist."

He frowned and released his grip. "What?"

She stepped away from him and continued her housekeeping efforts by putting her bed back together. "The delivery van at Brad's condo yesterday? I called information. There is no such flower shop."

"I know."

She stared at him.

"I called, too." He crossed his arms over his chest. "I also called a friend of mine over at the DMV. The plates came up as belonging to a Honda Civic reported stolen a month ago."

They stood like that for several moments. Then Dulcy's gaze dropped to his waist and lower, and her flush returned—along with a very revealing flick of her tongue over her provocative lips.

"Don't do that," he warned.

"Do what?"

"Lick your lips that way."

She quickly turned away. "I think it would be better if you put on some clothes."

Quinn could describe the things he'd like to do in intimate detail, and not a one of them included clothing.

"I'm going to take a shower," she said. "Shall we meet downstairs in, say, twenty minutes?"

"I thought you were going back to town."

She swallowed. "I take that to mean that you're not."

He shook his head.

"Then, I'm coming with you."

"Dulcy—"

She held up a hand. "Don't try to talk me out of it. I'll borrow one of the club's cars and follow you if I have to."

He nodded. He understood her need to find Brad. But he questioned what her actions would be once her missing fiancé did show up as a blip on the radar. "Fine. I'll meet you out front in an hour and a half. I have some things I need to pick up first."

ONLY WHEN THERE WAS NOTHING left to do did Dulcy take a good long look at herself in the mirror. And that only happened by accident when she was reaching for the suite door to go downstairs and wait for Quinn to return from whatever errand he'd had to run.

She dropped her hand to her side and turned more fully toward the gilt-edged hall mirror. Aside from the unfamiliar clothing of white casual blouse, cargo shorts and sandals that had been provided by the club, for all intents and purposes she looked like the same woman she'd been a few days ago. But she knew that aside from the mark Quinn had left on her right shoulder, the one that peeked out from inside her collar when she turned just so, there were no visible changes. No, the transformation she'd undergone had happened on the inside. Imperceptible to all but herself. Turning, she dropped into the iron chair next to the mirror and stared at the opposite wall.

It felt as if the sun itself had completely changed directions, rising from the west instead of the east. If only the explanation for the way she felt could be that simple. There, just beneath her skin, rolled a chaos, a hectic urgency, that she couldn't begin to comprehend. She knew that sex with Quinn was a contributing factor. But she wasn't all that convinced it was the sole factor. The frenzied emotions had roots deep down inside her. It was as though they'd been lurking there all along, just waiting for the right moment to spring out and throw her life into turmoil.

With a shaking hand, she smoothed back her already

smoothed hair, resisting the urge to muss it all up again. The truth was, she was having a difficult time trying to push herself back into the neat lifetime role she'd spent thirty years creating. Even her hair didn't want to cooperate, curls springing up after she'd moussed them to death. She touched her mouth, noticing that there seemed to be new poutiness to her lips. Or had they always been like that and she hadn't noticed?

But above and beyond everything, there was a sexuality…a neediness…an awareness that sizzled along her nerve endings, making her take a look at the world with a whole new prospective. It hadn't been so long ago that she'd stopped in the middle of a very important deposition, wondering what she would think thirty years from now, looking back at her life. Would she remember this deposition, the claimant in the case, or even the case itself? Or would she look back and realize she'd missed the point altogether?

It had been that day that she'd decided to stop saying no to her mother's wish that she not only marry, but marry well, and said yes to Brad's surprising proposal.

And now? Now that she couldn't move without an aching muscle reminding her of her time with Quinn? How about thirty years from now? Would she look back and see this time as a horrendous mistake? Or the most fantastic time of her life?

Dulcy absently rubbed her hands over her exposed arms and stood. None of that mattered this instant. What did was finding Brad, if only to make sure he was all right. The rest…well, the rest she hoped would come to her when she saw him again.

She gripped the door handle and nearly ran straight into Mr. Jones, who seemed to have been leaning against the closed door.

"Oh! My apologies, Miss Ferris." He straightened his

jacket. "I was just checking to see if you needed anything further this morning."

Dulcy eyeballed him. Did the man ever let up? She remembered her and Quinn's activities in the pool last night and wondered if Mr. Jones had been aware of the little get-together. And whether or not he had a camera or if they sold disposable ones in the gift shop.

"That's kind of you, Mr. Jones, but I won't be needing anything more. Thank you very much for your hospitality."

She moved to pass him.

"Miss Ferris? I thought you might be interested in this—"

He held out something to her. Dulcy slowly opened her palm, and he dropped a single key into it.

"It's against club policy, but I thought my doing a little snooping in Mr. Wheeler's on-site locker wouldn't be out of the question. You know, given the circumstances surrounding his disappearance. I found this inside."

Dulcy swallowed hard. "Thank you."

It was only when she was halfway down the hall that she realized Jones had had his hand extended, expecting a tip.

QUINN SAT BACK in the Jeep, his appearance relaxed by design. Only he knew that relaxed was the last thing he felt. He watched Dulcy step down the curved club walkway, her long legs turning the head of an older gentleman just entering the establishment, her hair pulled back severely. She tugged on the collar of her blouse, spotted him, then started in his direction.

He resisted the urge to fidget.

What was it about this one woman that got to him so? He'd been with countless women, some more beautiful, others oozing wit, but not a one of them could hold a candle to the enigmatically provocative Dulcy Ferris. She affected him on a level he couldn't begin to comprehend.

In his mind's eye he saw his wizened Hopi grandmother smiling at him. "I'll never fall in love," he'd told her. He'd been all of eight, and the night before, he'd caught his mother crying over his long-gone father, not for the first time. His grandmother had patted his head with her gnarled fingers and laughed. "Love is not something you fall into, or find, little one. Love is something that finds you, no matter how carefully you hide."

Quinn had forgotten about that conversation, even though for weeks after his grandmother had said it, he'd tried his hardest not to fall asleep at night, afraid love would sneak in under his door and grab a-hold of him, hurt him the way it had hurt his mother.

Of course, he'd long since learned that it hadn't been love that had hurt his mother, but his father. And nothing he could do had been capable of tipping the scales in that regard. Not even when he was fifteen, and sought out his father where he was living in Arizona with his second of what would be three families, and demanded answers where there were none to be had. Yes, feeling the solid connection of his young fist against his father's jaw had brought some satisfaction. But that satisfaction had long since vanished, leaving him with little more than bittersweet memories of what his mother's hopes had been. Hopes he feared she still lived with, residing in his grandmother's old house near White Sands where she insisted on spending her days. Alone. Her face full of wistful dreams when she heard the sound of a vehicle approaching.

Quinn ran his hand over his face, then punched the button to switch on the air conditioner. It was only ten-thirty, but already the strong desert sun was promising another scorcher. Dulcy hesitated outside the passenger door. He reached across the seat and opened it for her. He forced himself not to watch when she climbed in and stowed a bag in the back, presumably her clothes. He put the Jeep into gear then pulled away.

Five minutes into the drive, he finally looked her way, only to find her staring at something in her hand. The object reflected the sunlight, and he squinted. "What's that?"

Dulcy lifted her head as if deep in thought. "Hmm? Oh. Jones caught up with me as I was leaving. He said that he had poked around in Brad's locker and came up with this." She handed it to him.

He considered the key.

"It doesn't match the one I have to his condo, so that's out."

Quinn gave it back to her. "How about to his office?"

"He has a card key."

He nodded. He already knew that.

"It's too big to be for a desk drawer, or even a filing cabinet." She sighed and slid the key into her purse.

Quinn pulled the Jeep to a stop. Looking for traffic, he made a U-turn, heading back the way they'd come.

"Where are you going?" she asked.

"Brad has a cabin in Colorado, just outside Aspen."

Dulcy frowned. "He never said anything to me about it."

"He never said anything to anyone about it, aside from me. Not even Beatrix knows of it."

"I don't understand."

Quinn glanced at her confused expression. "Try his cell phone again."

He watched her pull out her own portable and punch the redial. After a few minutes, she closed it again. "Nothing."

"There's no phone at the cabin. He just had electricity installed last year, but still no major appliances or television.

It's where he used to go when he needed some time to himself."

"Then, why didn't we just check there first instead of going through all this?"

"Because he always let me know when he was going there. You know, in case something happened and someone needed to get in contact with him." He checked his rearview mirror. "And he always had his cell phone with him."

He watched her cross her arms beneath her breasts and give a little shiver. "Isn't there a caretaker or someone we could call?"

"No."

Her eyes widened as she looked at him. "You're not proposing we drive all the way to Colorado?"

He shook his head. "No. I'm proposing we go to my place, about forty-five minutes northeast of here, and make a few phone calls. Brad's secretary would be a good start. I've never been to the cabin, but if anyone would know where it is, she would."

"Wouldn't she tell Beatrix about it?"

"Beatrix would be the last person she'd tell." He gave in to a grin. "The top reason Brad hired her is because Beatrix had fired her. She hates the woman."

She nodded. She could certainly relate to that.

Quinn stared out at the two-lane highway that split the desert in half for as far as the eye could see. Not a word passed between him and Dulcy for a full thirty minutes. The silence was slowly grating on his nerves. Why didn't she say something? Tell him he was every bit the cad Brad told her he was? That last night was a mistake not to be repeated?

That the instant they found Brad she was calling off the wedding?

He glanced over to find her twirling her engagement ring

around and around her ring finger. Quite a task, considering the size of the rock. Three carats at least, he guessed. Brad had never been one to do things by half measures. He grimaced and slipped a CD into the player. A moment later strains of vintage Santana filtered through the speakers. But rather than diminishing his tension, the sultry Latin guitar licks served to increase it.

"So tell me, Dulcy...what do you plan to do once we find him?" Quinn asked.

He wasn't positive he had asked the question aloud until she turned to stare at him, her sexy mouth working around an answer though no sound came out. Finally, she turned her head back toward the passenger window. "I don't know," she whispered.

"Do you love him?"

Quinn winced. Was he really asking his best friend's fiancée these questions? And what about his own thoughts on love? On its fickleness? Its impermanence? Surely the past few days only served to prove his beliefs. If love was forever, why had Dulcy slept with him a mere week before her wedding?

Her response finally came. "Do you really want to know the answer to that question?"

"No." And he didn't. Mostly because an answer either way wouldn't tell him what he wanted to know. And what he wanted to know was how she felt about Quinn himself.

"You live out here?" she asked, staring at a large mesa off to the left, tumbleweeds to the right.

"It's where my people are from."

"So you *are* Native American."

He glanced at her.

"Jena thought you might be."

"Half. My father was Caucasian."

"Are you close with your parents?"

"With my mother."

He felt her gaze on his profile, but refused to look at her. If she found his answers evasive, so be it. Until he knew where she stood, he didn't think revealing too much of himself was wise. In fact, he'd never felt comfortable enough around a woman to reveal any more than he already had to Dulcy.

"My father left when I was two. My mother, grandmother and maternal uncle were my family."

Quinn rubbed the back of his neck. What was it about this woman that found him thinking one thing, and saying the complete opposite?

"My parents have been married thirty-three years." She straightened her skirt. "I don't know that that's any better. Then again, it's all relative, isn't it. I think part of the reason I waited so long to get engaged was that I couldn't figure out what made my parents' marriage work. Love? Convenience?" She shook her head. "I still can't figure it out. I can tell you it wasn't because they were or are blissfully happy."

"Is anyone?"

She stared at him. "No. I guess not. There's always a catch, isn't there?"

Quinn grimaced. In their case the catch was in the shape of one wealthy missing fiancé, Bradley Wheeler.

"My grandmother used to tell me that things that come easily are never appreciated."

Dulcy turned back toward the window. "I wonder how that philosophy will apply when we find Brad."

"That's not what I meant."

"I know."

About a mile up the road loomed bright orange cones indicating roadwork. The sight never failed to strike Quinn as odd. He always associated roadwork with cities. Yet here was a self-contained crew out in the middle of nowhere. It stood to reason that someone had to look after the roads. It just seemed odd somehow. He glanced in his rearview mirror. Where the road had snaked off endlessly empty a few minutes earlier, now other cars dotted the landscape. Figures. Even out here road construction backed up traffic where usually there was none.

"Do you live alone?"

Quinn glanced at Dulcy. "No."

She blinked to meet his gaze. "Oh."

"There's the housekeeper, Esmerelda. She's the only one who stays in the main house. A dozen ranch hands stay in a bunkhouse out back."

"Ranch?"

"Horse."

She nodded, then returned her attention to the road.

"Have you always wanted to be an attorney?"

"Yes."

She didn't offer more and he didn't ask.

Quinn eased his foot from the gas pedal to avoid plowing into the five or so cars slowed to a crawl ahead of him, automatically glancing behind him to make sure the others were doing the same. A flash of white caught his eye. He squinted into the mirror. What appeared to be a white van was coming up quickly, two cars back. He reached out and adjusted the mirror. It was a familiar white van with familiar lettering on the side.

"What is it?" Dulcy asked.

Quinn grasped her arm, preventing her from turning to take a look. "Don't. We wouldn't want our new friend to know we're on to him."

"Friend?" Realization seemed to dawn. "Are you talking about the delivery guy?"

"Uh-huh."

Quinn took stock of the construction ahead of him. Cones blocked the left lane for about half a mile, leaving two highway patrolmen to alternate traffic in both directions. He pulled the Jeep to a stop. Cars drove in a steady stream from the other direction. He covertly glanced behind him, to find the van hemmed in by cars. With the White Sands Missile Range a few miles to the west, it was reasonable to think that the traffic was due to military employees coming and going, traffic usually unnoticed unless there was roadwork.

Quinn reached for the door handle.

"Where are you going?" Dulcy quickly grasped his arm, giving in to the urge to look behind them.

"I'm going to find out just what, exactly, this guy knows about Brad's disappearance."

She released him and grasped her own door handle. "Then, I'm coming with you."

Quinn stared at her. "Stay put, Dulcy."

"Forget it. I'm not going to stay in here like some sitting duck. Wherever you go, I go. I thought I made that clear."

He reached across the seat and grasped her wrist, tugging her back onto the seat. "Stay here, Dulcy."

Quinn could feel the steady thrum of her pulse beneath his thumb and noted the rise of color in her cheeks. But whether it was due to anger or his touch, he couldn't be sure. Whatever the reason, he was glad when she sighed and voiced reluctant agreement.

Quinn climbed out, his boots thudding against the hot road. Nearby, a truck churned its contents and a steamroller was evening out the freshly laid asphalt. The sharp smell of tar coated his nose as he set his path straight for the van. He was nearly on top of it when the door opened and the driver stumbled out. It was the same guy.

And he started running in the other direction.

A LINE OF SWEAT trickled down Dulcy's back, making her shiver as she swiped at curls that had escaped her twist. She turned in the seat to watch Quinn bearing down on the van, his dark hair back, his entire posture full of purpose and determination. She made a soft sound in the back of her throat, then reached again for the door handle. There was no way she was going to stay in the Jeep. She needed to know where Brad was just as badly as Quinn did. Even more so. And if the delivery guy could give her that information, then, by God, she was going to get it.

The coolness of the Jeep had masked how very hot the day had become. The asphalt beneath her feet felt soft, the short wood heels of her new sandals seeming to sink into it. She quietly closed the door so as not to catch Quinn's attention, then stalked toward the passenger side of the van. She was halfway there when she saw the deliveryman bolt from the van and make a run for it. But rather than heading for open road, he turned toward the roadwork.

Damn. Dulcy watched Quinn give chase. She issued orders to her feet to do the same. Skin-scorching heat pressed in on her from all sides, making it nearly impossible to breathe and weighing down her muscles. Quinn was right behind the guy, while she remained separated from them by a line of cars. She began to question the futility of such a chase. Boy, she really needed to start working out more. Who knew she was so out of shape?

The row of cars was now behind them and roadwork lay straight ahead, along with big, heavy machinery that seemed to waver in the heat. Sweat rushed down Dulcy's forehead and she wiped it from her eyes even as she kept pace. Then the guy cut in front of her. She reached out, grabbing for his shirt. She managed to get a handful, but if he noticed, she couldn't tell, because he kept running, towing her along with him—

Then Quinn plowed into him from behind. Dulcy tried to extract her hand, but it was caught firmly between their bodies. All three of them flew toward a section of freshly laid blacktop.

Dulcy wasn't sure what hurt the most. The stones that bit into her bare knees, the hot tar, or her throbbing hand where Quinn lay on top of it.

Quinn quickly got up. She freed her hand and sat, watching as he swung the deliveryman around, his fists twisted into the front of the guy's T-shirt. Dulcy cradled her aching hand in her other one.

"Who the hell are you and where's Brad?" Quinn demanded through gritted teeth.

The heat against her bottom seemed to seep right through the material of her shorts. She scrambled to stand, the sweat that had slithered down her back earlier now a stream.

"Let go of me, man! I don't know what the hell you're talking about."

"I think you do," Quinn disagreed. "Let me make this easy for you by asking the first question again. Who the hell are you?"

"What do you mean, who the hell am I? You know who I am. I...I deliver flowers."

"Wrong answer." Quinn tightened the fabric around the guy's neck. "Try again."

The guy coughed. "I'm telling you the truth, man. Check the back of the van."

Dulcy hadn't been sure Quinn knew she was behind him until he looked at her. He nodded to her and pushed the guy in the direction of the van. When they finally reached it, he said, "Check it out."

Dulcy quickly rounded the van and peeked in the back window. It was empty but for a tarp and some tools. She moved to tell Quinn the same, only to see the guy working his arms in between Quinn's and knocking them outward. Quinn had a hold on the guy's torn shirt. Before he could drop it and grab the guy again, he took a sucker punch to the solar plexus that left him flat on his back.

"Quinn!" Dulcy ran for him, putting herself directly in the path of the delivery guy. He plowed into her, knocking the breath from her lungs. She saw Quinn scrambling to his feet, so rather than continuing toward him, she ran after the guy.

Horns honks as she wove between cars. She didn't know where the guy thought he was going. Even if he did manage to get away, where would he go? Aside from the White Sands Missile Range, which wasn't open to the public, nothing but desert stretched for miles in any direction.

He was widening the gap between them. And with only one car left in the line, she was facing an all-out chase in open road.

"Stop!" she shouted, as if the order would instantly result in his halting in the middle of the road with his hands up.

She caught the gaze of the driver of the last car. The deliveryman drew even with the door and the driver swung it open, catching the runner across the waist. Quinn passed Dulcy and grabbed the guy.

"I think it's time you and I had a little talk with local law enforcement, don't you?"

11

"ALL RIGHT...OKAY. If you want to know the truth, I *was* following you." The guy finally 'fessed up from where he sat in the back of a highway patrolman's car, his hands cuffed behind his back. Quinn knew all the enforcement officers by their first names out here. He also knew the names of their wives and their kids and sometimes the nicknames of their pets. That's why it wasn't surprising when the running man's claims of harassment fell on deaf ears and he found himself the property of the State of New Mexico for however long it took Quinn to get the answers he wanted.

Jerry Rimmer, a rookie patrolman, was looking through the guy's wallet. He came up with a California driver's license. "Michelangelo Tucci." He flicked it over. "And he's an organ donor, too."

"Yeah, well, there are people out there who need his organs more than he does," Quinn said.

Dulcy nearly choked on the water she'd sipped from a bottle one of the guys on the construction crew had given her.

Jerry bent toward Tucci in the back seat, his mirrored glasses reflecting his image back at him. "Is that your real name, sir?"

The deliveryman rolled his eyes. "Do you think that's something I'd make up?"

He slid the license back into the wallet and tossed it into

his lap. "So, Mr. Tucci, do you mind telling us what your involvement is in the disappearance of Mr. Bradley Wheeler?"

"Disappearance?" His eyes grew large and sweat drew lines down his soot-covered face. "What in the hell are you talking about? Wheeler owes me money. That's where this begins and ends."

Quinn hiked a brow. "Ends?"

Michelangelo sighed and made an exasperated face. "You know what I mean."

Dulcy stepped up beside Quinn. "He's lying. There's no reason to believe Brad would have anything to do with this man, much less borrow money from him."

"Borrow? Who in the hell said anything about his borrowing?" The guy shrugged, trying to get more comfortable despite his hands being bound behind his back. "The guy placed a few bad bets. He's gotta pay up."

Quinn met Dulcy's gaze, careful to keep his own thoughts from showing. Shock, however, was written all over her face.

"That's impossible," Dulcy said. "Brad doesn't gamble."

"Yeah, well, try telling that to someone who's listening, babe. Me and Wheeler have been doing business for the past eight years. But this is the first time he's welshed on a debt."

Quinn crossed his arms tightly over his chest. The two patrolmen nearby caught the personal tone of the exchange and made themselves scarce, moving to stand near the front of the car, well out of earshot. "How much are we talking about here?"

Michelangelo shrugged again. "Twenty big ones. Give or take a thou."

"Twenty thousand dollars?" Dulcy whispered. She began

shaking her head. "He's lying. He's got to be..." Her words drifted off.

"So why were you following us?" Quinn asked, suspecting he already knew the answer but wanting to verify it just the same.

"I thought you'd take me to him, you know? I haven't been able to find the guy all weekend. You two were my last bet."

Quinn leaned his hands on the door and pushed as if to close it with deliberate casualness. The bottom caught Michelangelo's legs, and he gave an unmanly yelp.

"Tell me, Tucci. Are you really looking for Brad? Or have you already found him?"

"I don't know—" Another yell. "Hey, knock it off with the door! Or else I'm going to file brutality charges."

The patrolmen near the front of the car gave a pointed glance, then turned purposefully in the other direction.

"Give it to me straight, Michelangelo," Quinn said, holding the door steady against his legs. "Do you or do you not know anything about the possible kidnapping of Brad Wheeler?"

"Kidnapping? Oh man, do you ever got the wrong guy." He yelped again, then leaned forward to ward off the door with his upper body. "Hey, I'm just a small fish, you know? If Wheeler was kidnapped, someone higher up the ladder would have to see to it. And I would have been told. Got it?"

Quinn stared him down. He had no proof that the guy was telling him anything other than the truth.

He released the door. Tucci groaned and lay back flat on the seat, raising his legs inside the car. Quinn turned toward Dulcy, who looked far too pale in the bright midday sun. He thanked the patrolmen.

"That's it?" Dulcy asked.

"Unless you can think of something else to ask him."

She remained still for a moment, then silently shook her head.

Jerry called out, "What do you want us to do with this guy?"

"Give us a half hour, then turn him loose."

"I FEEL LIKE I've just run a marathon, then ended it with a nice long dip in a tar pit," Dulcy said quietly, looking down at her ruined shorts and blouse. She picked at a spot on her leg but only made it worse.

Quinn turned the Jeep into a long, winding driveway, the entrance to which was flanked by two tall flowering cacti. She froze where she was bending down in front of the air-conditioning vent; the view outside the windshield was breathtaking. A long, one-story adobe-style ranch sat atop a low rise, the color rich in the bright sunlight and blending into the red of the surrounding desert. A rough-hewn wood swing sat on the narrow front porch, covered with a colorful Indian weave rug faded by years of sitting in the sun. Bleached cattle skulls decorated either side of the front door, while multicolored paper lanterns were strung the length of the house. Behind the house, about five hundred feet back, sat a long mesa, a small, isolated flat-topped hill, the perfect counterpoint to the flatness of the rest of the land. Off to the right Dulcy made out several low-lying buildings, probably the bunkhouse and stables. At this time of day, nothing moved. Not one lick of evidence to prove that there was life within miles.

Quinn parked the Jeep and got out. She followed, trying to take in everything as she walked.

Quinn seemed right at home in the rugged environment. His swagger just right. The leather strap holding back his black hair perfect. He opened the front door and held it for her, his gaze steady on hers, watchful. Dulcy returned his gaze, somehow sensing the moment an important one, but unable to pinpoint why.

Once inside, the temperature instantly dropped, making her shiver. Her eyesight slowly adjusted to the dim interior. The rough adobe walls were continued inside, decorated with southwestern tapestries and more Indian rugs and earthenware. But where she might have found the effect stale and artificial in someone else's home, here it all felt…right.

"The bathroom's down the hall and to the right," Quinn said. "Feel free to use the shower."

Dulcy finally found her voice. "Where will you be?"

His gaze flicked over her face, then up to her eyes. "Out back. I'll get a shower at the bunkhouse, then catch up with the ranch hands. I'll meet you in the kitchen when I'm done."

A half hour later, Dulcy stood in the tiled shower, scrubbing tar spots from her skin and wringing the desert dust from her hair. She watched the red-tinted water swirl down the drain at her feet. There was something decidedly decadent about being completely nude in Quinn's house. After he had gone, she'd taken her time getting to the bathroom, running her fingertips along the unvarnished tops of tables, picking up frames displaying old and cracked sepia prints of Native Americans she guessed were Quinn's family. Nowhere had she caught a hint of a feminine presence. And everywhere she had felt him. She could see him choosing every last item in the place, which left her feeling both comforted and uncomfortable.

Funny, two minutes inside Quinn's ranch house and she felt more at home than she ever had visiting Brad's condo.

She pushed the unwelcome thought from her mind and again picked up the soap in the wall dish. Sandalwood— purely male and one-hundred-percent Quinn. Lathering up, she ran the bar over her exposed skin, reveling in the satiny feel of the cool water and drinking in the pure recklessness of her actions. She'd never even taken a shower at Jena or Marie's place, yet here she was making herself right at home. What did that mean?

Nothing. It meant nothing. The past few days were far outside anything she'd consider normal, which meant normal reactions would be just as out of whack.

The shower curtain was suddenly ripped open. Dulcy gasped and turned to face a small, wrinkled old woman staring at her accusingly.

"You're Dulcy?" she demanded.

Dulcy was sure there was a time and a place for such a question, but it definitely wasn't while she was buck naked in a strange shower facing a woman who could have been fifty or a hundred.

She strategically placed her hands to cover herself and tried to grab the shower curtain.

"I'm...yes, I'm Dulcy."

The woman's black eyes held amusement. And just as quickly as she'd ripped open the shower curtain, she closed it.

Dulcy collapsed against the tiled wall. What was that? An inner voice told her the woman had to be the Esmerelda whom Quinn had mentioned. She'd automatically assumed the housekeeper would be a young, lush-bodied Latina. Instead she was a tiny, wiry Native American with long braided hair, wearing a gold lamé jogging suit.

With hurried movements, Dulcy squeezed the last of the soap from her hair and body, then switched off the water. The shower curtain was again ripped open and the woman stood holding a thick cotton towel. Grabbing the shower curtain to cover herself, Dulcy reached for the towel. "Thank you."

Esmerelda refused to relinquish control. She motioned Dulcy from the shower. "Out."

"But—"

"Out."

Dulcy swallowed hard. She'd never been completely nude in front of another woman—unless she counted her mother, but mothers were supposed to see their children naked.

She cautiously stepped out, her hands covering herself. Amusement returned to Esmerelda's eyes as she skillfully nudged her hands out of the way and began roughly drying her off. Dulcy gasped. Was this the Native American way? Somehow she thought it important that she know. The old woman lifted her breasts up as she dried them, making a small sound that appeared to be approval. Then the cotton was between her legs. Dulcy snapped her thighs together and grabbed the towel.

"Please...I can do it."

The woman made no secret of her perusal as she reluctantly gave up the fight. A slow smile creased her wrinkled face and she seemed to come to a conclusion Dulcy could only guess at. She felt like...a horse who had just been given thoroughbred status.

"Thank you for your help. I think I can take it from here." Dulcy held the towel to her breasts, then opened the door to find Quinn standing there, his hand raised in a knock.

He dropped his hand. "Everything all right?"

Dulcy considered her options. Either make a further fool of herself by forcing Esmerelda from the room with Quinn looking on, or bear the woman's open curiosity.

She slammed the door.

There was something decidedly weird about doing something so intimate in front of a stranger. But Dulcy also found the experience oddly liberating. She'd never considered herself a prude. Okay, maybe she had. In high school, she'd always found some way to get out of showering with her classmates. In college, her roommate seemed comfortable with nudity, but Dulcy had always been sure to cover herself decently.

After making quick work of drying herself, she reached for the clothes she'd stripped out of, only to find them gone. Esmerelda held out a short silk robe.

Dulcy shook her head. The robe was much too short. "My clothes. Where are they?"

"In the garbage."

Dulcy quirked a brow. "All of them?"

"The bag I put in the wash."

Sighing, she dropped the towel and held herself as proudly as she could, as Esmerelda helped her into the scrap of material. She got that feeling of being perused again, until she finally cinched the belt at her waist. She turned to face the old woman, her chin held high. Esmerelda smoothed a hand over Dulcy's abdomen.

"Good breeding stock."

Dulcy nearly choked. Before she could respond, Esmerelda opened the door and left.

Peeking into the hall, Dulcy looked around. No Quinn. No nosy old woman. Biting her lip, she ducked into the first bedroom she came to. Decidedly masculine—it had to be Quinn's. A quick inventory of his drawers left her with a pair of black sweatpants she had to roll up and a T-shirt that covered her far better than the skimpy robe.

She flopped down on the mattress. For God's sake. If this is what the women Quinn brought home went through, no wonder he was still single.

Who was Esmerelda and what was her relationship to Quinn? Dulcy felt violated beyond description. Yet a small part of her was proud that she had made the grade, whatever grade that was.

QUINN EYED ESMERELDA where she skillfully put together a light lunch of taco salad at the terra-cotta tiled counter. She was humming an old Native tune usually sung at fertility ceremonies. He grimaced and glanced at his watch. Dulcy had yet to make an appearance, and at least fifteen minutes had passed since his housekeeper had come into the kitchen.

"Okay, Ezzie, what did you do to her?"

The humming stopped but the old woman didn't say anything.

Quinn stepped beside her and tossed a couple of pieces of diced tomatoes that had dropped to the counter into the bowl. He didn't miss the wide grin on her face. An answering grin tugged on his own mouth.

The last woman Quinn had brought home had inspired a bone-deep frown from Ezzie, so her reaction to Dulcy was a surprise—and a welcome one, albeit an inappropriate one.

"She's engaged to Brad, Ezzie."

The old woman shrugged.

Quinn rubbed the back of his neck, then turned to lean his hips against the counter next to her. "Maybe that doesn't mean much to you, but it means everything to me. Brad's...well, he's my best friend." He gripped the counter edge tightly. "I can't tell you how guilty I feel. Brad's missing—and what do I do? I bang his fiancée."

Ezzie raised an eyebrow. Quinn didn't kid himself into thinking she didn't know the saying. She'd spent her entire life around ranch hands, and their "language" was one she had long since mastered—and been known to use.

She wiped her hands on a towel, then poked a bony finger

into his chest. "In life, Brad may be the one Sunflower is promised to, but it is not who her soul calls out for."

Quinn grimaced. The last thing he needed was some hokey Indian soul-seeking. Lord knows, he'd had a lifetime of it from his grandmother before she passed on and then his mother.

"And who does your soul call out for, Ez?" he asked.

The light instantly vanished from her dark eyes.

Quinn felt a stab of remorse for having turned the tables on her, but he'd had to do something to knock her from her current path. Dulcy was not his for the taking, no matter whom her soul called out for.

He glanced up to find Dulcy standing in the doorway. He slowly crossed his arms over his chest and watched her look over the room, her gaze skittering past his. If he'd needed any proof that Dulcy wasn't his, this was it. Rather than wearing the robe he'd seen Esmerelda take into the bathroom with her, she'd donned a pair of his black sweatpants and a matching T-shirt. Even in the too-big clothing, she looked elegant and out of reach.

Ezzie hadn't turned around, but she must have sensed Dulcy's presence. Her voice dropped as she leaned toward Quinn. "Listen with your heart, not with your ears."

He pushed from the counter lest Ez think he was in need of further counsel. He motioned toward the rough-hewn table and chairs on the other side of the cooking island. "Have a seat."

Dulcy drew her shoulders straight. "Where are my clothes?"

Quinn stared at Ezzie, who had gone back to humming the Native tune. "I'm sure they'll be done soon. Until then, why don't we enjoy the meal Esmerelda is preparing for us?"

Dulcy finally moved to the table. Quinn caught the way

she caressed the back of the chair before pulling it out and sitting down. He seated himself across from her.

Esmerelda appeared immediately, rearranging the place settings she'd put out side by side, then distributing the serving bowls between them.

Then, suddenly, she was gone, and Quinn felt ill at ease.

There had been only one other time a woman had been in his home. And given the way that had turned out, he wasn't sure how he felt about Dulcy's presence, especially under the circumstances.

Still, he couldn't help a secret smile at Ezzie's reaction to Dulcy. The old woman had been so opposed to his last girlfriend, Yolanda Sanchez, he had wondered whether Ez would ever approve of any woman for him. Ironically, Yolanda had been part Pueblo on her mother's side, although mostly of Hispanic heritage, while Dulcy's veins very obviously didn't contain a drop of Native blood.

He eyed Dulcy, wondering why Esmerelda thought her compatible to him. For all intents and purposes, they were as different as night and day—in looks and background and interests.

"Do you think he was lying?"

Quinn slowed his chewing, considering Dulcy's quiet words. There was no doubt she was talking about Tucci, the would-be flower deliveryman who claimed Brad owed him money. He put down his fork and took a long sip of cold herbal tea. "I don't know. Do you think he was?"

She seemed to go out of her way not to look at him. "I don't know what to think anymore. First there was the strip joint. Then I find out about the things that take place at the club. Now there's...this." She wasn't eating much, merely pushing the food around her plate. "You think you know someone..."

Quinn narrowed his gaze on her, trying to decipher what

she was trying to say. Which could have been no more than what she was actually saying.

Damn Ezzie and her cryptic words.

"Dulcy…do you still plan to marry him?"

There it was—the question he'd been avoiding asking for the past few days. The words he'd wanted to say when they first met and he'd surmised that she was engaged.

Her cheeks colored and she nervously tucked her hair behind her ear.

"Forget it," he said roughly, hating himself for asking the question and her for not answering quickly. "It doesn't matter, anyway."

She blinked at him. "It doesn't?"

Quinn forced himself to focus on his food, shoveling it in though he couldn't taste a single bite. "No. It doesn't." His fork clattered to his plate. "Facts are facts. And the facts are that even if you decided not to marry Brad, you and I…well, there could never be a you and I."

"Why?" she whispered.

Quinn caught and held her gaze. In her eyes he read uncertainty, guilt and another fathomless emotion.

"Because Brad's my best friend. Closer than that. He's my brother." He pushed from the table. "And brothers don't go around stealing each other's women."

He started for the door, surprised when she was on his heels and pulling him to face her.

"This isn't exactly a picnic for me, either, you know."

He glanced down at where her hand rested against his forearm, left bare by his white T-shirt. She removed it, but it seemed to take her a moment to figure out what to do with it. She finally dropped her hand to her side.

"You don't understand," Quinn growled, not sure whom he was angry with, although pretty sure it was himself. "Brad saved my life."

Dulcy's eyes widened as she stared at him.

He sighed and restlessly ran his hands through his hair, then refastened the strap at the back. "I was nine. It was back when my father's family occasionally felt they had to make up for my father's absence. Either that, or the novelty of my being Hopi made them…" He cursed. "One of my white cousins invited me to stay for a week at her house in Albuquerque that summer. While I was there, she attended a birthday party of one of her friends. A pool party." He stared at the opposite wall but didn't see it. Instead he pictured an upscale house with an upscale in-ground pool in the backyard and dozens of laughing kids. Already, he was taller than them, and thin. And his cousin Heather's habit of introducing him by blood first, then name, was growing old quick.

"The boys had jumped into the water first. All the boys but me." He hated that his throat tightened just thinking about it, despite how many years had passed. "The girls started teasing me. Why didn't I get in the water? And the boys started calling me a fag, even though I didn't know what that meant then and I don't think they did, either." He met Dulcy's gaze head-on. "So I jumped in the water. The deep end. And I couldn't swim."

A shadow of horror passed over her eyes. "Oh, Quinn, no."

"I sank like a rock straight to the bottom. I knew that was it. The end. Because of stupid pride, I was going to die." He cursed again and paced a short way away, his back to Dulcy. "It was Brad who realized what was going on and dove in to drag my ass out."

He paused, remembering how much the smaller boy had had to tug at him and kick at the water to pull him up to the surface. "Everyone was deathly silent. But I wasn't humiliated. Instead I was grateful. Then Brad cracked a joke and erased all the uneasiness.'' He smiled. ''He enrolled me in swimming courses at his family's country club the next day. We've been friends ever since. And he's never introduced me as his 'Indian' friend. To anyone, ever. To him I was just a friend. His best friend.''

Silence reigned in the room as Quinn closed his eyes and pulled his thoughts together, trying to douse the guilt twisting in his gut like razor wire. He owed Brad. Not because he'd once saved his life, but because he was the one man, the one friend, who had never judged, belittled or competed with him.

He opened his eyes.

''Despite what you might think, I did not go out last Friday looking to get laid by the first handsome stranger I crossed paths with.''

Dulcy's words only served to make him feel worse. Quinn turned to face her, the anguished expression on her face killing him all over again.

''And once I…did discover who you were, I didn't think to myself, 'Hey, this just gets better and better. Who better to fool around with while my fiancé is gone than his best man? After all, if you can't have the groom, the best man isn't called that for nothing, is he?'''

Quinn grabbed her wrist so quickly he surprised himself. ''Stop it,'' he ordered.

Her hazel eyes glittered with gathering tears. ''No, you stop it.'' She thrust her face within millimeters of his. ''Isn't it bad enough that I'm beating myself up over all of this? Do you have to add your two jabs, as well?''

Quinn found his gaze drawn to her mouth. Her moist, succulent mouth still open from having spoken.

''Don't,'' she whispered.

But when that pink tongue of hers peeked out and dragged across her bottom lip, Quinn knew he was a goner.

He lowered his mouth to hers and gently, slowly drank from it. He tasted tears. Tears she must have shed during the time it took her to get from the bathroom to the kitchen. Tears that told both of them just how important Brad's disappearance was. Tears that he had had a hand in creating.

Quinn thrust both of his hands into her freshly washed hair, holding her still as he slid his mouth first one way, then the next. She moaned quietly but stood completely motionless, allowing him control over the direction of the kiss. He reveled in the texture of her tongue against his. Drank in the sweet taste of her mouth and her desire for him.

Dear God, what was he doing? With every lick, every nibble, he felt himself falling for her more and more. And there wasn't a damn thing he could do to stop it from happening. He looked into her eyes and found her watching him. Her half-closed eyelids gave her a sleepy, sensual look he was hard-pressed to look away from.

She stepped closer, bringing her hips against his, her softness against his hardness. He groaned, then ripped his mouth from hers so violently he was afraid he hurt her.

"This is crazy," he said, stepping back from her.

Dulcy's lips were trembling.

"I've got to get out of here." He started for the door, then stopped, dragging in deep breaths. Fingers twisted around the door handle, he spoke to the inanimate wood instead of to Dulcy. If he looked at her, he wouldn't be able to leave. "My office is the last door to the left. Feel free to use it. And if you need anything, Ezzie's around."

He yanked the door open and headed for the ranch beyond. Despite his best intentions, he did glance back once, to see Dulcy still standing in the same spot, looking well kissed and like she wanted more. The problem was, he wanted to give it to her.

12

DULCY SAT BACK at the mammoth desk Quinn directed her to. She stared at the notes she'd made. Three hours had passed since Quinn had kissed her senseless, shared his heartbreaking connection to Brad, then left her standing alone in the kitchen with no explanation of where he was going or when he might be back. She glanced at her watch, then pushed her hair back from her face, only then realizing that she hadn't fastened the curly strands in her usual twist at the nape of her neck. She felt reckless, wild, leaving it loose like that.

Aesthetically speaking, Quinn's office was as simple in design as the rest of the house. Technologically speaking, it was better appointed than Dulcy's office. Top-of-the-line computer, laptop, Palm Pilot, fax, scanner, printer and color copier were just a few of the items she'd admired when she first ventured inside the room. That the computer had a direct satellite feed made responding to e-mail a flash, and a general check of the LexisNexis research site only took up a few minutes of her time rather than the hour she generally allotted for periodic updates.

Getting up from the chair, she paced to the window overlooking the mesa and low-lying stables out back. Earlier she'd watched, transfixed, as Quinn had worked a bay Appaloosa up into a lather. He'd stripped off his shirt and skillfully guided the animal, his muscles rippling and moving with the same grace as the horse he trained. She'd been mesmerized by the sight of man and beast, the two complementing the other, working in harmony. Each one silently challenging the other. The stallion might not have had a clue who was going to win in the beginning, but Dulcy never had a doubt that Quinn would ultimately dominate. It seemed his skill with people extended to animals, as well. There was a powerful magnetic quality about him, an enigmatic pull. His strength extended beyond his physical attributes. It went all the way to the bone, and shone in his dark eyes like a single star in the midnight sky.

When Quinn finished, Dulcy had cupped her hands over her eyes to watch the same man cool down the horse with nearly as much attention to detail and thoroughness as when he touched her.

Now, he was nowhere in sight. Not that she expected him to be. She'd watched him put on chaps, then ride off, his dark, unbound black hair flying behind him as he pointed a black Arabian stallion toward a point unknown.

Dulcy looked down at her hands, which absently twisted her solitaire engagement ring around her finger. She bit on her bottom lip, wondering why it was called a solitaire when it was supposed to symbolize togetherness. Shouldn't there be two diamonds of equal size, positioned side-by-side, to reflect the significance of the coming union? She couldn't help thinking the single stone looked…single. Alone. Isolated, somehow.

Then again, it seemed appropriate that her ring would mirror exactly what she was going through.

She turned from the window. Discarded ransom note aside, it was becoming clearer that Brad hadn't been kidnapped or taken against his will, but rather had disappeared voluntarily. To escape the coming wedding? It was looking more and more likely.

She twisted the ring from her finger and held it up, admiring the way the slant of sunlight entered the diamond and splintered off in a thousand different directions. She crossed to pick up her cell phone from the desk. A call to Brad's cell phone number brought no results, so she dialed another familiar number. Two rings, then she heard her mother answer.

"Mom?"

"Dulcy, is that you?" Catherine Ferris asked, genuine concern in her voice. "We've been wondering why we haven't heard from you. Where are you? Is everything ready for the wedding? I've been calling the office constantly, but that Mona person is of no help at all. And you know how awful I am with the number to that wireless phone you have. Do you need help? Is there something we can do?"

Dulcy curved her fingers around the back of the desk chair and closed her eyes. She was relieved by the worry in her mother's voice. Maybe it would make telling her about Brad that much easier.

She remembered the day Brad had proposed, and the three days it had taken her to accept. How happy her parents had been when she'd told them. She swallowed. Actually her father had been silent about the matter. It was her mother who had been ecstatic. She supposed there lived a small part within all mothers that longed to see and manage their daughter's wedding—that one day when her little girl would be a princess meeting her prince at the altar, then riding away on a gleaming black stallion. She glanced toward the window, recalling Quinn riding away alone.

She dropped into the chair and assured her mother that she was fine. Everything was fine. Then she listened as Catherine told her all that had been happening on her end of the line—from the travel arrangements of extended family arriving Thursday night for Saturday's wedding to all the food she planned on catering to see them through the week-end.

"Mom?" Dulcy tried to interrupt.

"It's been years since I've seen your father so excited."

Her father excited? She couldn't imagine that.

"Look, Mom—"

"I can't tell you how happy you're making us, Dulcy. You're achieving everything and more than we ever dreamed for you."

Dulcy rested her elbow on the desktop and planted her palm against her forehead. Obviously it hadn't gotten out that Brad was missing. Which had been Beatrix's intention all along, hadn't it? Don't go to the police for fear the media would get hold of the news. While Dulcy didn't consider herself a news junkie, she was sure she would have heard something by now had Brad's disappearance made the news. No news is good news definitely applied here, especially considering that she suspected Brad was behind his own little vanishing act.

"Mom," Dulcy said a little more forcefully, her agitation level growing with every word her mother said.

"What is it, Dulcy?"

Now that there was silence, she felt as if her throat might close around what she had to say.

"Nothing," she finally said, staring at the diamond ring one last time. She slipped it onto the finger of her right hand and twisted the diamond to the inside. "I...I have to go."

She wasn't entirely sure why she hadn't said the words. They'd been right there, on the tip of her tongue. *Mom, Brad's gone. There isn't going to be a wedding.* But she couldn't stomp all over her mother's dream. Not just yet. There were three days to go until the wedding. Let Catherine Ferris bask for as long as she possibly could.

And what of her own dreams?

She gave her mother her cell phone number again, then disconnected the line. The phone lay lifeless in her hand.

Had she ever had a dream?

Her attention again wandered to the window and the ranch beyond. When she'd accepted Brad's proposal, she'd done so with no visions of puffy white wedding gowns or doves or even children. Looking back, she saw the incident as a merger of sorts. Hey, don't we get along well, and wouldn't life be grand if we put our two households together and became a family, since that's what every other normal person does?

She slumped down in the chair. She couldn't blame herself. Not really. Because up until that point she'd experienced nothing to compare with her relationship to Brad.

And now that she had?

Now she saw how very shallow and selfish and compromising her engagement had been.

Two THINGS MATTERED MOST to Quinn. His relationship to nature. And his connection to those he loved.

His black stallion Ewtoto snorted. The Arabian seemed to be telling him to make up his mind. Go home, or head back out into the wide-open nothing from which they'd just returned.

If only Quinn knew which was the right decision.

He squeezed his thighs to let Ewtoto know that he'd heard him, then looked back over the horizon. It wasn't so long ago that the view could calm the worst of his disquiet. Provide him with the answers he sought. Now he couldn't find a lick of peace in the view.

Ewtoto snorted again, living up to his namesake as the chief and spiritual leader of all *katsinam*. Quinn slowly climbed from the stallion's back and draped his reins over a low branch of a cactus. Scooping a bowl into the hard earth, he poured water from his canteen, then sat down on a boulder and watched as Ewtoto drank. And tried like hell not to think of the woman back at the house waiting for him.

Brad's woman.

He ran the back of his hand across his forehead, then squinted at the cloudless afternoon sky. He knew all too well that life made a habit of throwing you for a loop every now and again, letting you know how little control you had over it. But in the past few days he'd been knocked over so many times he'd lost count.

He dug his boot heel into the dry earth and gazed out at the ranch house. He had thought he knew Brad like the back of his hand. But every piece of information he and Dulcy uncovered made him wonder if he'd really known his friend at all.

Ewtoto finished with his water, then slid his cold snout against Quinn's forearm. He absently stroked the horse.

Of course, knowing—as he now did—that Wheeler Industries was virtually broke, facing bankruptcy, wasn't helping his mind-set, either.

He really wished he hadn't stumbled across that scrap of information. But he couldn't exactly do a thorough search for Brad if he didn't examine all possibilities. So he'd placed a call to a buddy he'd gone through Desert Storm with, asked him to get what he could on the company and get back to him. Four hours later, the guy had told him that in the past six months Wheeler Industries had suffered a serious blow to their stock worth. A couple of bad managerial moves—for which Brad had been directly responsible—had placed the company in danger of being taken over by a bigger company. Or worse, closing down.

Quinn didn't know how Bugler—ironically nicknamed such because of his silence—had gotten the information. But he knew he didn't have to question it. If Bugler said the company was in trouble, then it was in trouble.

And it was likely the motivation behind the crumpled ransom note in Brad's garbage can. A discarded, half-baked plan Brad had come up with to get the needed funds from his mother, who it was rumored had her king-size mattress stuffed with all the money Wheeler Industries had made over the years.

Ewtoto thrust his nose against Quinn's shoulder. "What would you tell me if you could speak, Toto?"

Ewtoto neighed, causing Quinn to smile.

"Sorry, buddy, but I didn't quite catch that."

The horse caught his reins between his teeth and gave a tug, shuffling his hooves as if ready to head home.

Quinn squinted at the house again. Yes. Maybe the horse was right. Maybe it was time for him to stop running and head back to face the music. Lord knew, sitting out here wasn't doing him a damn bit of good.

AT SOME POINT Dulcy felt her head would explode with all the thoughts swirling around in it, so she'd made her way to Quinn's bedroom and stretched across the mattress, intending only to lie down for a little while. Two hours later she opened her eyes to find the sun low in the sky and her business suit and blouse neatly laid out next to her.

She pushed up onto her elbows and glanced around nervously. The thought of Esmerelda anywhere near her while she was asleep was frightening. She could only imagine what the odd, wrinkled old woman had been up to while she wasn't looking. Had she gauged her snores? Graded her on her prone position? Measured her fat-to-muscle ratio? Taken a blood sample?

Sighing, she gathered her clothes together and went into the connecting bathroom, careful to lock the door behind her. She washed her face and attempted to run a comb through her hair. Without all her hair products, the blond curls were combative and refused to give in to her attempts to tame them. So she gave up and changed into her skirt and blouse, then eyed the jacket she'd hung on the back of the door. The silk blend was marked Dry Clean Only, as was her blouse. And since she hadn't spotted any one-hour cleaners on the drive out, she could only wonder how Quinn's housekeeper had managed to clean them.

Leaving the jacket where it was, she quietly left the bedroom. The house was silent, but the smell of something cooking beckoned her to the kitchen. She stopped in the doorway, staring at Esmerelda's stooped back where she sat on a stool, doing something on the cooking island. A gnarled hand patted the stool beside her. Dulcy swallowed and walked to the stool, then cautiously climbed up on it.

Esmerelda was sorting through beans. All sorts of beans. Black-speckled ones, brown ones, green ones. Fingering them like discs on an abacus, she kept a few, then pushed a couple of shriveled ones off to the side to join the small pile of others that hadn't made the grade.

Dulcy's immediate desire was to ask if she could help, but she was afraid to make a mistake in front of the curious woman. She jumped when Esmerelda elbowed the huge bowl of mixed beans in front of her and nodded her head, indicating Dulcy should sort, too.

Following her lead, Dulcy poured out a portion of the beans and slowly began sorting through them, keeping like-size beans and pushing aside the small ones and particles that could have been stones.

She felt the old woman's gaze on her. She lifted her chin and found Esmerelda smiling. Her mouth was closed, and she didn't say a word. But that one gesture was enough to make Dulcy grin stupidly.

Finally the bowl was empty, the hill of keepers large, and Esmerelda pushed from the stool and carried the beans to a large pan. Dulcy combined the two small piles of discarded beans and threw them away in a nearby trash container.

"Quinn is a good man."

Dulcy slowed her movements where she was washing her hands at the sink. She looked at Esmerelda, startled she had said anything. "Yes. Yes, he is." She cleared her throat. "So is Brad."

The old woman made a disgruntled sound.

Dulcy decided not to pursue that line of conversation. She didn't think she was up to defending Brad's qualities right about now.

"How long have you worked for Quinn?" she asked instead.

"I don't work for Quinn."

Dulcy frowned at her. "I don't understand. Are you family?"

"Not by blood."

Dulcy lifted the lid on a boiling pot and was immediately shooed away.

"Do you live here?" she asked, finding conversation with the woman like pulling teeth.

"No."

Dulcy crossed her arms and leaned against the counter. "So let me get this straight. You're not related to Quinn. You don't get a paycheck. You just come by and cook for him—"

"And clean."

"And clean for him, out of the goodness of your heart."

Esmerelda shook a finger at Dulcy even as her attention was on her cooking. "Because of the goodness of *his* heart."

Dulcy made her way around the cooking island and settled back onto her stool. The view outside the window over the sink was breath-stealing. The deep blue of the sky clashed with the dusty horizon, jagged, flat-topped mesas breaking the monotony.

"Our Quinn hasn't always had what he has now," Esmerelda said quietly, as if to herself. "His father ran out before Quinn even got a chance to know him. His mother...well, love she's always had. Money she hasn't."

Dulcy shivered. "How did she raise Quinn, then?"

Esmerelda looked at her over her shoulder. "We raised him. All of us. The community." She returned her attention to her cooking. "Not that any of us could do any better money-wise. But we managed." She paused as she stirred the contents of a pot. "This ranch belonged to Quinn's uncle. Stubborn old mule, he was. Never paid a man his worth. Worked young Quinn's hands to the bone and sent him off with pocket change."

She shook her head. "But even pennies add up. That's what he used to tell his mother every night when he got home." She pointed at a spot outside the window. "They lived in a small house out there. One room. Dirt floor." She wiped her hands on a towel. "Don't know why Quinn keeps it up. Should have been torn down years ago when he and his mother moved out."

"How...how did Quinn come by all of this? Did his uncle leave it to him?"

"His uncle wouldn't have given a dying man a drink of water. Before he died, he sold Quinn the ranch at an inflated price."

Dulcy opened her mouth to ask how he possibly could have afforded it, but didn't dare.

"Those pennies," Esmerelda said as if she had asked, a twinkle in her eyes. "Started working when he was twelve."

Dulcy sat up straighter. "And his education?"

She shook her head. "Did you see any schools on your way out?"

No, she hadn't.

"We all taught him what we could." She turned to face Dulcy. "It was very satisfying when he got his GED, then went into the Marines. After his discharge, he attended university. Graduated top of his class and opened his own computer company." She waved a hand. "Service provider or something along those lines. Sold the place a few years back when he bought the ranch."

Dulcy fidgeted. She wasn't sure she wanted to know this. Her body already yearned for Quinn in a way she couldn't control. To allow Esmerelda to open up a spot for him in her heart was inviting trouble.

"Women?" she asked quietly.

Esmerelda made a sound. "There was one. About a year ago. Brought her out here, he did. Not that it mattered. I knew from the instant I saw her she wasn't going to stay."

"Why?"

"Because she was taking inventory of Quinn's belongings even as she cradled him between her legs."

Dulcy winced, at both the imagery and the thought that someone had tried to take advantage of Quinn's generosity and all he had worked so hard for.

She absently traced the stencil on the tiles in front of her. "I'm curious...you haven't asked anything about me. Why is that?"

Esmerelda got that odd look on her face again. The same expression she'd had when she sized her up after the shower. "All I need to know I see in your eyes, and in Quinn's."

Dulcy quickly looked away. She'd never put much stock in what others saw. She told herself not to start now. Even if the idea that Quinn felt something more than desire for her appealed greatly.

Resisting the urge to question Esmerelda further on the subject, she said instead, "I'm engaged to Brad."

"Are you?"

Dulcy followed the woman's gaze to her naked ring finger and the light tan line there. She instantly covered the hand with her other one.

The thundering sound of an approaching horse made Dulcy's stomach dip to her ankles. Before she could think of the wisdom of such an action, she got up from the stool and hurried to the back door. Pushing aside the curtain there, she watched Quinn pull his black stallion to a stop. It wasn't possible: somehow their brief time apart made her even hungrier for him. He'd peeled off his white T-shirt and tucked it into his belt. Dark denim hugged his thighs. His black hair hung loose and tangled around his tanned, sculpted shoulders. He looked like a fierce Native warrior just back from battle, his expression intense and full of passion. Goose bumps covered every inch of Dulcy's skin.

"Go," Esmerelda said, touching her shoulder. "He waits for you."

The old woman's words shimmied straight down her spine.

"Dinner can wait."

With trembling fingers, Dulcy reached for the door handle and was outside before the voice inside her head could tell her that what she was doing was wrong. She knew one awful second of hesitation. Then Quinn reached out one long, tanned, muscled arm for her. She took it. He hauled her up to sit behind him. She slid her hands around to rest against his washboard stomach—and then the horse was off again.

LIKE COMING HOME. That's what it felt like to have Dulcy flush against his back, her cheek pressing against his shoulder. Quinn slid his hand on top of hers where they rested against his stomach, and tipped his face toward the sky. Ewtoto and his own land beneath him, Dulcy behind him, the limitless sky above him and the magical New Mexican horizon in front of him...in that single moment, he had it all. No matter how fleeting that moment might be.

Dulcy shifted her head and pressed her lips to his bare skin. His grip on her hands tightened. "I want you," she whispered, then took his earlobe between her teeth.

The hands beneath his moved, inching down to the crotch of his jeans. If she was surprised to find him fully aroused, she didn't show it. Instead, she worked her fingers inside his waistband, stroking the tip of his erection almost reverently as Ewtoto slowly walked beneath them. Curiously, the stallion had balked at returning to the stables, but instead had led him to the ranch house. Quinn was glad.

Quinn removed Dulcy's hand from his jeans, then grasped her bare knee, pulling her leg around him. He tugged her hand, indicating what he had in mind. With a few awkward moves, she was sitting in front of him, her legs hugging his hips, her skirt hiking up to show him a peek of plain white cotton panties.

He grinned. "Oh, no. We can't have this."

He slid his finger inside the damp crotch of the panties and pulled, taking great satisfaction in the ripping of material. She gasped and dug her fingers into his shoulders as he released the panties into the air, the dry desert wind catching them and carrying them away.

Then he looked at her—really looked at her for the first time since riding back to the ranch. The sight of her took his breath away. The setting sun set her blond hair aglow from behind, her hazel eyes were nearly black, her lips were smooth and parted, ready for whatever he choose to give to her.

He watched the expression on her face change. The waiting vanished, replaced by want. Her hands moved from his shoulders and into his hair, then she planted her mouth against his, slipping her tongue inside. Her breath fanned his cheeks as she restlessly moved from one side of his mouth to the other.

Quinn grasped her bare thighs and hauled her swollen flesh flush against the fly of his jeans. She moaned and broke contact with his mouth, but only briefly. When she returned, she was twice as hungry, her movements urgent. She fumbled for the button to his jeans. He caught her hands.

"I don't have anything with me, Dulcy."

She blinked at him. "I don't care."

He swallowed hard. "I do. I...want to protect you."

"I haven't been intimate with anyone but you for three years," she rasped, her hands sliding down his back and into the waist of his jeans.

Quinn stretched his neck and closed his eyes. Dear Lord, help him. "I've never had unprotected sex."

"Then that means we don't have anything to worry about, doesn't it?" The tip of her tongue flicked against one corner of his mouth, then the other. "I want to feel you, Quinn. All of you. Flesh in flesh."

He caught and held her gaze, Ewtoto's trot slowing even further as though he sensed what was going on on his back. "And the risk of pregnancy?"

Her smile challenged the brightness of the setting sun and won. "What of it?"

On a normal day, words like that would have sent him running full speed in the other direction. Hadn't it been an unexpected pregnancy that caught his mother up short at seventeen?

A groan caught in his throat as she circled her fingers around to the front of his waistband, then slowly undid the remainder of the buttons there. The feel of the hot desert air against the sensitive skin of his erection sent jolts of heat spiraling through his bloodstream. As soon as he was completely free, he grasped her bottom and hauled her up on top of him, his gaze glued to hers, searching, waiting for any sign that she'd changed her mind. Then, for the first time in his life, he felt the pure, slick heat of a woman surrounding him. Of Dulcy taking him inside her. No thin layer of latex separating them.

He closed his eyes against the headiness of the moment. The weightiness. She was heaven.

Her shiver told of her own exciting reaction. As she balanced herself, he unbuttoned her blouse and pushed it back on her shoulders, gazing down on the soft crests of flesh spilling out of her bra. He swept his palms down over the front, then cupped her breasts in his hands.

She slid down to the hilt, and Quinn grasped her hips, held her aloft, then thrust upward, breathing in her sharp gasp.

Ewtoto made a soft neigh, but Quinn was too far gone to consider the stallion. In and out, he moved inside Dulcy's sweet flesh, thrusting in time to Ewtoto's steps. Dulcy wound her arms around his neck as if holding on for dear life. Then he felt her crisis hit. Her stomach shuddered, her flesh tightened around him, and an instant later he followed.

Hot...hard...full. That's how Quinn felt deep inside her. He filled her unlike any man before him. Physically. Spiritually. Needfully.

Dulcy fought to catch her breath, her fingers digging into

his sweat-coated back, her tongue dipping out to taste the salty residue covering his right shoulder. Somewhere over the past few minutes, she'd forgotten about her fear of falling from the horse and lost herself in the moment. Lost herself in Quinn's embrace. His kiss. His lovemaking.

She closed her eyes and rested her cheek against his shoulder. When she blinked, she caught the view of the sun sliding down over the horizon, vivid steaks of red, purple and blue painting the sky.

Quinn shifted her slightly but didn't pull out. She steadied herself and drew back to look at him. It was there, staring deep into his dark eyes, his flesh still deeply imbedded in hers, evidence of his desire trickling down her thighs, that she felt she might burst from the emotion filling her.

"I love you." Dulcy's throat tightened. Thinking the words was one thing, enough to scare her half to death. Having said them aloud…

"Dulcy, I…" Quinn grasped her hips, as if caught between wanting to continue their lovemaking and ending it.

"Shh," she said, pressing her sensitive fingertip against his lips. Even the horse seemed to sense the gravity of the conversation as he drew to a stop beneath them. "I don't want you to respond. I didn't even mean to say it." She swallowed hard. "I didn't even realize until this moment that that's how I felt." She tucked her chin into her exposed chest. "I know this is such a mess. Everything. Brad. Me. You." She shook her head. "This is the worst possible time for this to happen." She blinked up at him. "But nothing will change that it has happened."

Quinn didn't say anything. The sun had totally set, casting his face in shadow. "Dulcy, Brad is my best friend."

"I know," she whispered.

What more was there to say?

Making up his mind for him, she pulled back, forcing his

withdrawal. He let her. Which made the tiny ache in her chest blow up into a full-octane pain. She drew in a ragged breath. "This is all so crazy."

She moved to get off the horse. Quinn caught her forearm just before she fell and helped ease her down. In that moment she realized she trusted him more than anyone. Could she ever have said that about Brad? Even in the beginning when she'd been told he was gone, a part of her suspected his vanishing had been voluntary. In five months they hadn't come near to making the connection that she and Quinn had forged in mere days.

But in the end did any of that matter? Quinn was a man true to his word and true to his family and friends. And his and Brad's friendship transcended any woman. Especially if that woman was her.

The ground beneath her bare feet was hot, while the air around her seemed suddenly cold. She shivered and rubbed her hands against her bare arms, then began rebuttoning her blouse. Quinn climbed down to stand next to her, helping when her trembling fingers appeared incapable of the simple task.

He tapped her under the chin until she was looking up at him. Once again she was struck by how very tall he was. How magnificent.

"There will be time to figure this all out later, Dulcy."

She rested her palm against his chest. "Will there?" Cotton met her touch instead of bare, hot skin. He'd put his T-shirt on after she'd slid to the ground.

"And what if we don't find Brad?" she whispered, tears stinging her eyes. She forced her gaze away and looked toward the horizon. "What happens then, Quinn? Do I continue on as if I'm still engaged to a man if I don't know whether he's dead or alive? Do you stay true to a friend?"

He tucked her hair behind her ear. "I don't know."

She turned in the direction she thought was the way back to the ranch house. "I do. We both live in limbo, waiting for what tomorrow will bring. Wishing for it all to be over. Forever calling into question each other's loyalty. To your friend. To my fiancé." She glanced briefly at him. "To each other." She shivered again. "I don't know if you believe me, Quinn. There's really no reason for you to believe me. But I've never done anything like this in my life. Given my word to one man, then slept with another. Much less his best friend."

She turned quickly to walk away.

Quinn caught her hand, stopping her. She didn't face him. He didn't force her to. His voice, when he spoke, was deep and full of emotion. "Have I ever given you reason to believe I think less of you because of your connection to Brad? Because of what's happened between us?"

Dulcy could barely make him out through the tears in her eyes.

"If I'm hesitant, it has nothing to do with you, Dulcy. Not one damn thing."

"Wait—"

"No. You need to hear this." He took a deep breath and released it. "Actually, I'm wrong. My hesitancy is completely due to you. Not because I think less of you. But because I think so much." His voice lowered. "Don't you see? I have had women in my life who have tried to make me do things I don't want to do. Asked me to turn my back on my family. To give up everything I love about ranching and move to the city." He shook his head. "But you…you ask for nothing. Not one single thing. You tell me you love me, but you don't want me to respond. You give yourself to me freely, with no conditions, with no thought to the emotional cost." He skimmed a finger over her cheek. "And it all makes me want to give you everything."

Dulcy made a soft choking sound. It was the sweetest thing anyone had ever said to her. And that it had come from Quinn made it all the sweeter. All the more meaningful.

"Did I want all this to happen? Did you? No. But it doesn't change that it has happened." He paused, curving his hand around the side of her neck. "Brad...Brad was the first friend I ever knew. I owe him a lot, my life. But my heart...my heart is mine. Mine to decide what to do with." He smiled. "Well, at least it was until one very wild, sexy attorney stole it right out from under my nose."

Dulcy lunged into his embrace, listening to the quick thud of his heart beneath her ear, helpless to stop the tears from gliding down her cheeks.

"Come on," Quinn said after a long while, his hands softly stroking her back. "There's a house on the ranch not too far from here. There's water there where we can clean up." He gestured to the horse, still standing where they'd left him. "And Ewtoto would probably appreciate a rest and a drink."

The stallion neighed, and Dulcy smiled and wiped the tears from her cheeks.

Quinn held out his hand and Dulcy slid hers in it, as if they were made to fit together.

13

___

QUINN FORCED HIMSELF not to hold on too tightly to Dulcy's hand as they walked the short way to the tiny pueblo where his mother had managed to raise him. They'd survived on the limited income she'd received as a housekeeper for a cattle ranch three miles up the road—on a tract of land he'd since bought. As he led Dulcy to his childhood home, he tried to define what he was feeling and came up short. Raw. Exposed. Warm. Trusted. Trustworthy. Each swirled around in his head and chest, and grew more complicated with each step.

Dulcy loved him....

She squeezed his hand, and he realized he was squeezing hers. He lifted it to his lips and kissed the back, then dropped their joined hands back to his side.

By the light of a luminous quarter moon he led the way to the house, although he could have found the place in the dark. He'd done it enough times when he was a kid after a long day spent working on his uncle's—now his—ranch. The adobe house was little more than a fifteen-by-ten room with three windows—two in the front on either side of the door, one in the back—both the east and west walls solid, cutting down on direct sunlight to combat the desert heat. He'd kept it exactly the way it had been the day he'd come home from his first real job off the ranch and told his mother to come with him to Albuquerque, taking little more with them than the personal mementos and their clothes.

The only person he'd ever brought out here was Brad. And that was only once, back when they were younger and he hadn't had a choice. Brad had just gotten his first car and insisted on driving him all the way home instead of leaving him off at the road near the ranch, more than likely because he'd wanted his friend's company for a little longer rather than because of any real curiosity about Quinn's upbringing.

Quinn remembered the queasy feeling in the pit of his stomach as he wondered what Brad would think, if the new information would affect their friendship, change it. Strangely, he didn't feel that way now with Dulcy. It was as though he knew instinctively that he could trust her with the truth about his background. That she wouldn't use it against him, make him feel inferior.

A small well powered by an old windmill was about thirty feet behind the house. He led Ewtoto there and pumped him a good portion of water. He removed his saddle and blankets, then splashed a bit of water over the horse's back and hindquarters, then washed his own face. He stepped aside and watched as Dulcy did the same.

"This is where you were raised?" she asked quietly.

Quinn smiled at her. "Ezzie must like you."

"Why do you say that?"

"Because the only person who could have told you that is Ezzie. And she never talks to anyone." He took her hand again, finding her skin cool from the water. "Come on."

Within moments they were standing before the front door. Quinn found it remarkable that every time he visited, the place seemed to grow smaller and smaller. Or perhaps it was he who had grown bigger.

It had been some time since he'd been out there. He felt for the key hidden in the loose adobe on the left side of the door opposite the lock. It wasn't there. He frowned and wrapped his fingers around the knob. It turned easily.

Strange...

And he found out just how strange things could get when he opened the door and in the dim light from the moon saw two figures scramble from the bed in the middle of the room.

"What in the hell?" a man called out.

Dulcy gasped and grabbed Quinn's arm. "Brad!"

DULCY DIDN'T KNOW whether to scream or bolt, so she decided doing neither would be a good bet. Her heart thundered against her rib cage. Her fingernails were deeply imbedded in the flesh of Quinn's arm.

She supposed the surprise of finding anyone at all in the tiny house would have been enough to startle her. But to see Brad there, with another woman no less, was enough to send her stomach pitching to her feet.

Fast on the heels of surprise came another emotion. Relief. Full, profound, muscle-robbing relief. He wasn't lying dead in a ditch somewhere, the victim of a car-jacking gone wrong. He wasn't tied up in a dank, dark basement undergoing torture while his kidnappers decided what to do next. No. He was okay.

The words wove through her mind a second time. *He was okay.*

She gasped as Quinn did what she suddenly itched to. He hauled off and hit Brad right in the jaw.

"Ow!" Brad toppled back onto the mattress, the sheet he held in front of him nearly falling away. "What the hell did you go and do that for?"

Quinn looked as if he wanted to do much more than hit Brad. His body seemed to vibrate with a suppressed energy that made her shiver, and Dulcy wrapped her arms around herself. Someone lit a gas lantern, and she realized that someone was a woman. A very naked, very attractive Hispanic woman who didn't seem to care that she was completely nude.

Quinn threw her a blanket draped over a nearby chair. "Cover yourself, Yolanda."

Yolanda? Dulcy's heart skipped a beat. This was Yolanda?

Dulcy openly stared at the only other woman Quinn had brought out to his ranch, trusted with his heart. Thick black hair hung to the middle of her back. Dark eyes glittered dangerously. A full, red mouth was pursed in anger. She looked at Brad, cooing something to him, then pointed at Quinn. "I told you he was a very angry, very jealous man."

Quinn made a sound.

Dulcy felt her ire rise. "Quinn didn't hit Brad because he's jealous, you moron. He hit him because we've all been worried sick about him for the past two days."

A shadow of amusement lit Quinn's eyes as he looked at her.

"Moron? Why you—"

The other woman flung herself in Dulcy's direction. Dulcy squared her feet, but impact never occurred. Brad had caught her by the waist and pulled her back. "There will be none of that, Yolanda."

Quinn crossed his arms over his chest. "Dulcy and I are returning to the ranch. That's where I want to see you," he pointed to Brad, "in no more than a half hour."

Brad sank back to the mattress and ran his hands through his tousled blond hair. Dulcy found it hard to believe that the man before her was the same one she'd known. Where was the guy who had wanted to wait for their wedding night because he respected her? Her gaze shifted to Yolanda, then back to him again. More than likely he hadn't slept with her because he was too tired to do anything but sleep, period, when the Mexican bombshell was done with him.

She swallowed hard, barely aware when Quinn grasped her arm and tugged her toward the door.

IT HAD TAKEN BRAD an hour and a half to make his way to the ranch and he'd had Yolanda, thankfully fully dressed, in tow. But Quinn refused to have a discussion that was long overdue right then. No. He had told Brad he'd contacted his mother, Beatrix, and that they would wait until she got there before proceeding with any explanations. Dulcy had been grateful for the temporary reprieve. She hoped the time would give her a chance to work through the shock of it all. But here it was three hours later and she was still shaking.

She sat in the bathroom, where she'd been for at least the past hour, door tightly closed and locked, gripping the closed commode for all she was worth. She hadn't been able to sit in the living room a moment longer, watching Quinn stand in the corner like a dark sentinel and Brad and Yolanda share the couch across from her.

My God, had everything really come down to this? Her and Quinn? Brad and Yolanda? Three days and how many man-hours spent looking for Brad while he was off schtuping Quinn's ex-girlfriend mere days before their wedding? Dulcy smoothed her hair back, trying to find a way to return to some sense of normalcy, to get a grip on all that was going on and figure out a way to work herself into the picture. Or, more preferably, out of it.

This was just all so…bizarre.

Surprisingly, even after all she and Quinn had done together over the past few days, she felt betrayed by Brad's behavior. But above and beyond everything else, she knew a relief so complete her legs barely supported her. A relief that Brad was all right, yes. But also a relief that she wouldn't have to marry him now. And she wouldn't have to be the bad guy in the breakup, either.

She knew it was selfish, but she felt better knowing that both of them had been equally bad, even if it appeared Brad had been bad for much longer than she had. Possibly even for the entire duration of their dating and engagement. She shook her head in confusion. But why then would he propose to her, when he was so obviously in lust, and possibly in love, with another woman? It didn't make any sense.

A slight turn of the knob. Dulcy stared at it, wondering if Quinn had finally come in search of her. When she'd excused herself an hour ago, she had secretly hoped he would follow. She'd needed assurance that this didn't change anything. That he still felt what she'd glimpsed in his eyes earlier. Still felt what she'd sensed from the beginning.

But he hadn't followed. And there she'd sat in the bathroom, alone and confused, wondering if she'd ever find the courage to leave the room again.

The knob turned again and the door opened inward.

Dulcy saw the familiar hands and the key they brandished, and was instantly on her feet. Why wasn't she surprised that Esmerelda had a key?

The old woman entered the room and stood there for a moment. She glanced behind her and closed the door. She shook her head slightly, eyeing Dulcy.

"Everyone has arrived," Ezzie told her quietly.

Dulcy leaned against the wall.

If Esmerelda expected some sort of response, she didn't indicate so. Instead, she stepped to the sink and picked up the brush lying on the tiled countertop. Without saying a word, she stood in front of Dulcy and began brushing her hair.

Dulcy's throat closed so tightly she couldn't draw a breath.

"There, there." Esmerelda's hands stilled, and she gently pressed Dulcy's cheek against her slender stomach.

Dulcy gave herself over to the windstorm of emotions ripping through her, not having known that's what she was going to do and distantly scolding herself for doing it. Why was she crying? Because of Brad? Because it appeared that everything over the past five months had been a lie? Because she had ultimately found him in the arms of another woman when she'd been afraid for his life?

No. She knew that wasn't what was at the root of her grief. It was the uncertainty of what existed between her and Quinn.

As unreasonable as it was, she realized she had been hoping that their time together would stretch indefinitely—although logic dictated that eventually, even soon, it would come to an end. Aside from Brad's reappearance, there was the fact that the nature of their relationship would have come into question with the coming and going of her wedding date this Saturday.

Still, so long as Brad was missing, and she had the excuse of staying with Quinn to look for him, well, all had been right with the world. In a strange sort of way.

Finally, her crying jag slowed. Her breathing began to even out. And the dampness on her cheeks began to dry.

The fabric of Esmerelda's gold lamé jogging suit was at odds with the woman's softness and compassion. She began to gently smooth her hands over Dulcy's head. Dulcy was so grateful for the human touch that she nearly started crying anew.

The old woman didn't appear in a hurry. She merely stood there patiently, saying nothing, holding Dulcy, not demanding an explanation, but merely showing quiet acceptance.

Dulcy finally found the strength to pull back.

Esmerelda put her fingers under Dulcy's chin and lifted her face to get a better look. Without a word, she reached for a washcloth, wet it, then began running the cool, cleansing cotton over Dulcy's hot cheeks.

Five minutes later, under the careful, gentle attentions of Esmerelda, Dulcy's face looked somewhat normal, her hair was back in her usual French twist, and her blouse and skirt appeared as though they were fresh from the cleaners.

Dulcy began to step from the room, then hesitated. She reached out, took the old Native woman's hand in hers and squeezed, saying nothing for a moment. She offered up a feeble smile. "Thank you."

She tried to tug her hand free, but Ezzie held tight. "All this...the reemergence of your fiancé, this changes nothing," she said so quietly Dulcy almost didn't hear her.

Dulcy looked down to where their hands were joined, not trusting herself to hold her gaze. "You're wrong, Ezzie. It changes everything."

QUINN FELT AS THOUGH his body were bound with rope from neck to foot, preventing him from moving in the way that he'd like, stopping him from doing what he wanted.

When Dulcy finally reentered the room, his stomach tightened to the point of pain. It was obvious that she'd been crying. And the way she refused to meet his eyes worried him more than Brad's disappearance ever had.

A short time before, Beatrix had shown up at the ranch, her trusty bodyguard Bruno in tow. But more surprising was the presence of Dulcy's senior partner Barry Lomax. Quinn couldn't be sure, but he'd bet dollars to doughnuts that Barry's interest in Beatrix wasn't solely professional.

Beatrix was crooning to Brad as if he'd just survived an awful car crash. If she ignored the woman standing next to her son, Brad appeared not to notice. Or care.

Quinn's gaze slid to his ex-girlfriend. Yolanda had always been an incredible-looking woman. Born in Mexico, she had the sleek, Latin features of an Aztec goddess. The biggest problem he'd had with her was that she'd wanted to be *treated* like a goddess. She was great in the sack, but awful when it came to intimacy. Near the end of their relationship he'd also realized that she was bitter to the core. Bitter about her poor upbringing. Bitter about the life she had to live. Bitter about those who had, when she had not. He hadn't blinked at Ezzie's dislike of her when she moved in. Hadn't even put two and two together when random items began disappearing from the ranch house while new pieces of jewelry began appearing on her person. What had opened his eyes was seeing Yolanda slap Ezzie across the face while in one of her infamous fiery rages. But that rage was nothing compared to what he saw when he confronted her.

He'd immediately packed up her stuff, stuck her into the truck and driven her into town, but not fast enough to avoid hearing her flaunt all the wrongs she'd inflicted on him without his even knowing it.

Then, apparently, she had set her sights on her next victim. Brad.

Suddenly, Beatrix appeared to reach her capacity for concern and stepped back, her expression instantly changing. "How could you do this to me? And who in the hell is this?"

Quinn crossed his arms. Here it comes.

Brad grasped Yolanda and hauled her to stand in front of him. Quinn squinted, finding his behavior interesting.

"Mother, I'd like you to meet Yolanda Sanchez. Yolanda, this is my mother, Beatrix."

Yolanda held out her hand. "It's a pleasure to finally meet you, Mizz Wheeler," she said in her thickly accented voice.

Beatrix kept her eyes focused strictly on her son ignoring Yolanda's proferred hand. The smile she gave him was decidedly deadly. "Your fiancée and I have been very worried, Bradley." With an ease provided her from years of training, Beatrix put her arm around Brad and skillfully maneuvered him away from Yolanda and toward Dulcy.

Quinn instantly snapped straighter. He glanced at Dulcy to find the blood draining from her face, her eyes as large as saucers.

"But all's well that ends well. Isn't that how the saying goes?" Beatrix said.

"Mrs. Wheeler," Dulcy said, shaking her head and taking a step back.

"Mother," Brad said simultaneously, trying to work himself free from Beatrix's death grip.

Quinn cleared his throat, gaining everyone's attention. "Beatrix, I think there are some other matters you might want to hear about surrounding the reason behind Brad's disappearance."

Beatrix raised her chin. "I need to know nothing except that my son is all right."

She *knew*. Quinn wasn't sure how she knew, but he was one-hundred-percent certain that Beatrix was aware of the financial trouble Wheeler Industries was in.

Beatrix half hugged her son. "And that this wedding we've all been looking forward to will take place."

"Wedding?" Yolanda circled Brad until she was standing between him and his mother.

Quinn rubbed his chin with his forefinger, waiting for the inevitable explosion.

"What wedding?" She pointed toward Beatrix. "Tell her

there izn't going to be no wedding, Brad.'' She ran her hand down the front of Brad's shirt and smiled. ''The only person you're going to marry is me. Isn't that right, *miho?*''

The moment of truth. Quinn crossed his arms and waited.

Brad looked from his lover to his mother. Then opened his mouth and said, ''That's completely right, baby.''

Quinn stared at his friend as if he'd gone insane. Yolanda grinned. Beatrix looked ready to throttle someone, and she didn't appear to care who.

But Beatrix wasn't done. Taking Brad by the ear, she led him away from Yolanda. Despite Dulcy looking decidedly uncomfortable, Quinn couldn't help but be amused.

''Brad, we have an agreement,'' Beatrix whispered. ''Your part is to marry Dulcy.''

Dulcy dropped her hand. ''What? What did you mean by that? What agreement?''

Quinn hated that an entire room and five people separated him from Dulcy. He wanted to place a reassuring arm around her shoulders and pull her to his chest. He wanted to erase the tension from her brow.

Quinn cleared his throat. ''Tell her.''

Dulcy finally looked at him, and in the depths of her hazel eyes he saw a pain so deep it made him wince. He began to shake his head, to tell her he hadn't known—had only *suspected* what was going on. But she looked quickly away from him and back to Brad and Beatrix. The pain disappeared from her eyes and she stepped more confidently forward.

''Someone had better tell me what's going on. I don't care who.''

Barry was the one who looked uncomfortable now. ''Dulcy, Wheeler Industries is in trouble. Deep financial trouble.''

Dulcy looked confused. "I still don't understand what any of this has to do with my marrying Brad."

Brad looked at her, an apologetic expression on his face. Quinn wanted to sucker punch his best friend again.

"I'm sorry, Dulcy. Really, I am. If not for Yolanda, I would have loved to spent the rest of my life with you. You're a great girl. Witty. Beautiful. Funny."

Incredibly sexy, amazingly responsive, with an infinite capacity for love, Quinn silently supplied.

Dulcy's cheeks reddened. "Well, thanks, Brad. I'll sleep easier knowing that," she said quietly, sarcasm lacing the words. "Now tell me about this agreement between you and your mother."

Yolanda was the one to step forward. Quinn clenched his fists, wanting it to be anyone but her to tell Dulcy the truth.

"Tell her, Brad," Quinn ordered.

His friend glanced at him and frowned. "Dulcy, it was your family's money that was going to make Wheeler Industries solvent. As soon as we were married, I was going to tell you of our problems. Then, of course, you and your family would step in and take care of things."

Dulcy stared at him as if he were speaking a foreign language. Then something happened that not even Quinn expected. She laughed. Out of the corner of his eye, Quinn also noticed Barry cover his own smile with his hand.

"Let me get this straight. You were going to marry me, Dulcy Ferris, of the Albuquerque Ferrises, for my family's money?"

Beatrix hiked up her chin. "Why else do you think my son would be interested in a woman of your questionable morals?"

Rather than seeming insulted, Dulcy finally gave in to the laughter shining in her eyes. "That's funny. Because I was marrying Brad for *his* money."

Quinn narrowed his eyes. Her comment went against everything he knew about Dulcy. Never could he see her being as shallow as his best friend apparently was.

Barry folded his hands behind his back. "Perhaps Wheeler's changing of hands is for the best," he said carefully. "Because if either of you had bothered to check, you would have discovered that the Ferrises lost their family fortune over two decades ago."

"What?" Beatrix said, staring at him malevolently.

Barry shrugged, smiling at Dulcy. "Sorry, Trixie. If you had been up front with me, I could have told you that. The only asset of worth Dulcy's parents own is the house they live in. And even that is mortgaged to the hilt. Their net worth is well in the red."

"Trixie?" Brad repeated, eyeing his mother and the older attorney. "Did he just call you Trixie?"

"Oh, shut up, Brad," Beatrix said. She turned to Dulcy. "Is this true?"

Dulcy nodded. Then let loose an unintentional, inelegant snort so loud that even Quinn grinned. She put her hand to her mouth, murmured a quick "pardon me" then said, "Oh, yes. Very true. Exceedingly true. It puts the *T* in true."

Barry grinned. "I think you've made your point, Dulcy."

"Why you lying little no-good excuse for a bride," Beatrix said from between tightly clenched teeth.

"I take offense," Dulcy said. "While you might be right about the second part, when have I ever lied to either you or Brad? Did you sit me down and ask for a net worth accounting? Did you ask me whether or not my family had money?"

While Quinn found what was happening intriguing, he couldn't help but wonder why he hadn't guessed that Dulcy's family wasn't wealthy. From what Brad said, to the vibes Dulcy herself gave off, you would have thought she was raised in the same type of environment as Bradley Wheeler III.

Beatrix stared at her for a long moment, then turned on Yolanda. "I don't suppose your family has money?"

"I have enough money to pay someone to bust your knee-caps, if that's what you're asking," Yolanda said, her expression warning that she was a breath away from taking on the job herself.

"Whoa," Brad said, grabbing Yolanda.

"Speaking of kneecap breaking," Quinn said, "you might want to check into Bruno's background." Coincidentally, the Neanderthal had disappeared the instant he confirmed that Brad had, indeed, been found. An associate of Tucci, the flower deliveryman? Quinn suspected so. "I think he's connected with the nonaffiliated people to whom you owe money, Brad."

Beatrix looked around, sighing in exasperation. "Brad, what is he talking about?"

The man had the decency to look abashed. "We can talk about that later, Mother."

Quinn's guess was that the conversation would come sooner rather than later. One thing Brad had working in his favor was the remoteness of the ranch. If Bruno was contacting Tucci, it would take the other guy a while to get out there, which gave Brad plenty of time to disappear again—until he was ready to face the rest of his problems.

Actually, Quinn wondered how the knowledge of Brad's penniless status would affect Yolanda's interest in him. More than likely she didn't believe that a man of Brad's caliber could ever actually be broke. And perhaps she was right. People like the Wheelers always managed to find their way out of tight spots, emerging all the wealthier, and smelling like roses.

He glanced beyond the threesome to where Dulcy had

gone suddenly quiet again. She stepped toward Barry, who lowered his head to hear something she had to say. Then she walked toward the door.

Quinn's stomach tightened and he moved to go after her.

"Quinn, ole chum, ole buddy, ole pal of mine," Brad said, patting him on the arm and stopping his progress. "I owe you one."

Quinn squinted at him. "You owe me nothing."

Barry said something to Beatrix, who in turn slapped him across the face. Strangely, the action merely served to broaden Barry's grin as he followed Dulcy out the door.

"Oh, but I do," Brad insisted. "Not only are you the one who brought Yolanda into my life, though in a roundabout way, but, because of you, I no longer have to hide out in that shack behind your house."

Shack? Quinn's muscles suddenly ached to do some more hitting of his own. He eyed his ex-lover and his ex-best friend. "I hope you two are very happy together. You deserve each other."

With each step he took toward the door, his heartbeat thumped more heavily, until he finally stood in the open threshold watching Barry drive away, Dulcy in the passenger's seat staring stalwartly forward.

"Damn."

14

HOURS LATER Dulcy sat curled up on her overstuffed sofa in her apartment, a pillow crushed to her chest, late-night talk show host Craig Kilborn springing his five questions on an actor she vaguely recognized. Not that she was paying close attention. Mostly—between well-planned attacks on her refrigerator—she sat staring at the television screen without seeing anything.

She blinked and brought the contents of her coffee table into focus. An empty carton of ice cream with a wooden spoon sticking out of it. A ravaged box of a dozen chocolate-covered doughnuts. A bag of Doritos she'd abandoned for something sweet. A tub of soft butter she'd slathered over a half loaf of zucchini bread her mother had sent home with her after her last dinner there.

Dulcy groaned and sank lower into the sofa's soft cushions. She'd hoped to distract herself from the chaos churning through her, or at least eat her way into a sugar coma. Instead her stomach now felt as bad as the rest of her.

Nothing Barry had said or done on the long three-hour drive back from Quinn's ranch had helped. Not even her fear that he thought she was devastated by Brad's actions could jar her from her silence. And while his comment that Viagra was the greatest thing since sliced bread hadn't earned him any more than a blank stare, the information had sunk in enough for her to decide it fell firmly into the "more information than she wanted to know" category. She hadn't had the stomach to ask him about "Trixie" after that, but got the distinct impression that whatever had happened between the two was well over.

A tear rolled down her cheek and plopped onto the pillow beneath her chin. She absently rubbed the dampness away. Damn seeping eyes.

Okay, so she'd fallen for Quinn. Hard. Which, she rationalized, should make her feel better about the whole situation. Had she come away feeling nothing, had their relationship been about nothing but the sex, then she would have had something to worry about. What she was going through now was proof that she wasn't the bad-girl she had feared she was. She was nothing but a simple woman looking for a simple relationship. Love. Commitment. Great sex.

She rubbed her nose and sniffed. Two out of three wasn't bad.

What had she expected? That Quinn would get down on one knee and propose to her the moment they found Brad? She clamped her eyes shut. One thing did bother her about what had happened. Her entire lack of control over everything.

A soft knock sounded at her door.

Dulcy reached for the remote and pressed the mute button.

Another knock.

She sank lower into the cushions. Given the late hour, there were only a handful of people it could be. More than likely Barry had called Jena and Marie, told them what had happened and asked them to look in on her. Maybe if she pretended to be asleep, they would just go away.

Another knock, this time more insistent. A few minutes later, the doorbell rang.

Dulcy put her hands over her ears. But even as she did so, she knew it wouldn't work. Finally she pushed the pillow aside, straightened the old University of New Mexico T-shirt she wore, stalked to the door and swung it open.

"I'm fine. Why don't you just go home? We'll talk about this—"

Her words trailed off as her gaze caught on a long, muscular pair of jeans-clad legs, slid down to a pair of familiar cowboy boots, then moved up past a soft chambray shirt and into Quinn's somber face.

Dulcy raised a shaking hand to her tangled hair, her entire body instantly humming to life, her heart expanding to beat painfully against her rib cage. "I...I thought you were Jena and Marie."

"Are you really fine?" he asked quietly, his dark eyes shifting as he looked her over.

"Depends on your definition of *fine*."

"The normal one would do."

No, then, she wasn't fine. She was a mess. A big, fat, sloppy, emotional mess.

"Can I come in?" he asked, shifting from boot to boot.

Dulcy glanced behind her. But it was more than the empty cartons and crumbs littering the coffee table that concerned her, or the muted images flickering across the television screen. Her apartment was her last bastion. The only place Quinn hadn't stamped with memories of his presence, his kisses or his lovemaking.

She gripped the door frame. "I don't think that's a good idea."

He nodded as if he understood. She wondered if he did.

"You left the ranch before I had a chance to talk to you," he said simply.

"Oh? And what would you have said?" Dulcy scanned his striking face, fisting her hands to keep them from reaching up to smooth the lines of worry from his forehead, tug his dark hair free. "I'm sorry?" Her voice quavered. "Goodbye?"

"Dulcy…" He reached out for her.

It took everything she had to step away from his touch. "No, please, don't." She took a deep breath, ordering herself not to cry. "I just need some time to think, okay? Everything…everything happened so damn fast. I have to find a way to process it all."

He stood silently watching her, no expression giving away his thoughts.

"I just feel like I've had so little control over my life lately, you know?" she whispered, suddenly desperate to make him understand. "Brad's disappearance and reappearance. Us…" She looked everywhere but at him.

"Sometimes control is overrated," he said.

She stared at him. "Control is the only thing that makes my life bearable, Quinn, don't you see that? If anyone can see that, understand that, it has to be you. The way you were raised…the difficulties you've faced. You know both sides of the fence. I do, too." She steeled herself. "When you touch me, something happens. Something wild. Something so completely uncontrollable it scares me to death."

He appeared ready to reach for her again, but instead shoved his hands into his jeans pockets. "So that's it, then? Is this where we end?"

Dulcy's heart plummeted. "What?"

"We. You and me, Dulcy. Us. And there is 'an us.' No matter what you tell yourself, something happened between us over the past few days. Something more than that uncontrollable something you mentioned."

"Sex," she whispered. "It was just sex."

His eyes narrowed. "Is that all you think it was?"

She closed her eyes and nodded, even though she knew she was wrong, wrong, wrong.

She felt his fingers on her face and looked at him in surprise. His brown eyes were full of warmth, of softness, of every second of the time they'd spent together.

"You're wrong. But that's not for me to tell you." He dropped his hand and looked down the hall toward the stairs. "You know where to find me if you change your mind."

Dulcy's chest threatened to cave in on itself as she watched him walk away, his proud back disappearing down the stairs. The outside door slammed, and she winced. Then she closed her own apartment door and slid down it to sit on the floor.

FRIDAY MORNING Dulcy sat back in her office chair and stared at the multicolored pile of cards in the middle of her desk, compliments of Mona, who'd said they arrived in the morning mail. She randomly fingered one, a muted purple envelope, and separated it from the rest. *The Johnsons,* the return address read. The Johnsons were dear friends of her parents, which meant the card inside would be sappy and apologetic. "Sorry to hear about the breakup of your engagement," the words would say. Or "There are a lot of fish in the sea. Don't give up because you got a rotten one."

She grimaced. Over the past three days, since she and Quinn had discovered Brad's little love nest, the news had already made the rounds of Albuquerque's social circle. Had done so even before Barry dropped her off at her apartment. She'd dragged herself inside to find a frantic message from her mother waiting on her answering machine, who had been looking for reassurance that the gossip was just that, gossip.

She opened the card and wondered what it was about broken engagements that everyone associated them with death. Sorry about your loss…. Condolences… This, too, shall pass… Card companies didn't even have to be especially original in the variances. She hadn't even known you could buy cards that fit this specific occasion.

She blindly reached for her ever-present coffee cup, just as the phone rang. The contents of the cup went spewing all over the cards. She snatched up the receiver at the same moment she reached in her drawer for a pile of napkins to sop up the mess.

"Hello?"

When no one immediately responded, she could feel a jitterbug dance in her chest. The same dance it had been doing ever since Quinn had left her apartment the other night.

"Hello?" she said again.

"Miss Ferris?"

Dulcy's hands slowed and the jitterbug died. Much as it had every other time over the past three days that she'd answered the phone or her apartment door or looked up at a knock on her office door, hoping it would be Quinn. And it wasn't.

Not that she expected it would be. By telling her that she knew where to find him, he'd knocked the ball fully into her court. There would be no calls from him. No more surprise visits. If there was to be anything between them, she would have to be the one to initiate contact.

The caller was following up on a claim Dulcy had filed the day before but for which she neglected to include the supporting documentation. Promising to fax the information right over, she hung up the phone, made a valiant attempt at saving the soggy mass of colored envelopes before her, then sagged in her chair.

Okay, so she supposed it might not be a bad idea to call Quinn. Just to let him know that she didn't blame him for what had happened. But for the life of her she couldn't figure out what she might say. *Hey, thanks for the memories.*

Do you want to be friends? Or *Oh, look, your ex is with my ex. How about a date?* Or the even more vague *So…where do we go from here?*

Dulcy leaned back and picked up the garbage pail next to her feet. Positioning it even with the desk, she swept the destroyed cards into the bin, ignoring that she felt better as she did it. Were you supposed to respond to these cards? Acknowledge the well-wishers? Thank them for their thoughtfulness the same way you thanked them for wedding presents?

She topped the mess off with her empty coffee cup and dripping napkins, then tucked the wastebasket back under her desk.

What upset her more was that all along she had been terrified about what would happen when everyone found out she'd been "doing" the best man. Ironically, no one even knew about her and Quinn. Well, except for Esmerelda. And Jena. Instead, Brad ended up the bad guy. And as luck would have it, the public was turning him into an unlikely hero of sorts. New Mexico's most eligible bachelor chose love over an arranged marriage.

Dulcy slapped her hand against her forehead and groaned. She had little doubt that if the opposite had happened, if she and Quinn had been found out, she would have been painted as the harlot of the century. The friendship-ruining hussy who, while her fiancé was missing, was seducing the best man. Pictures of Yolanda and Brad were splashed all over the society pages, beaming at photographers, always touching as if they couldn't keep their hands off each other. This news far eclipsed the other two-sentence piece noting that Wheeler Industries was as good as bankrupt and that another competing company was making a move to take it over.

But not even that was really bothering her. No. She didn't care what happened with Brad from here on out. She and

Brad had never been a love match. She knew that now because she had something with which to compare the cold union. Rather, what caused the ache in her heart was that it was as though the magic between her and Quinn had never existed. With no one around to acknowledge it, to ask about it, to add "Congratulations on bouncing back," "Way to go on boinking the best man" comments to their cards of condolence, it was as if it had all been a figment of her imagination. A rip in reality that closed back up the instant Brad was found and she sent Quinn packing.

Is that what happened when your secret fantasies became real? And where *did* she go from here? Did she spend the rest of her life mooning over a guy who couldn't keep his hands to himself when they were together but was now making sure they weren't even within touching proximity?

"Hey."

Dulcy peeled her hands from her eyes. "Hey, yourself," she said to Jena, who stood leaning against the doorjamb.

"You look like shit."

"Gee, thanks."

"Don't mention it." Jena pushed from the door, then poured herself into one of the two visitor chairs in front of the desk. "You probably shouldn't be here, you know. I think after all that's happened, a few days of major R and R wouldn't be out of the question. In fact, that's exactly what you should do this weekend. Take off. Have some fun."

Dulcy winced. She had a lot of fun the past week. And just look at where that had gotten her.

She glanced at the yellow legal pad on the corner of her desk. It was filled with all the steps she'd taken to cancel the wedding arrangements. She thought she'd covered everything. After tomorrow it all would be moot, anyway. One o'clock would come and go, and she and Brad wouldn't be anywhere near an altar. She grimaced. Well, at least she wouldn't be.

Jena opened the jelly bean jar on her desk and fished out a couple of red ones. "What about the honeymoon to Fiji? Did you get the money back?"

"Nope." She eyed the two envelopes lined up beside her mousepad. One held the plane tickets; the other held the engagement ring she would mail to Brad. "Special fare. Nonrefundable."

Jena slowed her chewing. "Are you going to go?"

"Where?"

"To Fiji, of course."

"Nope." She fingered the envelope and the itinerary inside. Then she tossed it to her friend. The envelope seemed to stop in midair, then drift down into Jena's lap. "Be my guest."

Her friend looked like a ten-year-old on Christmas morning. "No way."

Dulcy smiled for the first time in what felt like forever. "Way." She shrugged, then turned around and took a bottle of sunblock from a drawer in the cabinet behind her. It landed on top of the tickets. "They come with a price, though."

"Uh-oh."

"Sit shotgun with me at the meeting with Mandy Mallone later this morning. I'm afraid if I go in there after…well, you know, all that's happened with me, I just might make her fiancé eat the prenup agreement, if everything's not in order."

Jena shrugged. "I'll go just to watch you do that."

"You're supposed to *stop* me from doing that."

"Then, forget it."

Dulcy laughed. "Be there at eleven."

Jena picked up the tickets and the sunblock. Halfway to

the door she hesitated and gave a deep sigh. She swiveled on her heels, then placed the bottle and the envelope on the desk in front of Dulcy. "As much as it kills me, I can't do this. You should be the one to take that trip, babe. Not me." She crossed her arms as if to keep her hands from snatching the tickets back. "A piña colada on a sandy beach is just the ticket to get your mind off everything." She grinned. "Grab that hot guy of yours and go."

Dulcy swallowed. "I don't have a hot guy."

"Yes, you do."

"Whatever."

Jena told her she'd see her at eleven, then left her office.

QUINN LEANED against the mahogany monstrosity of a desk that befitted the president of Wheeler Industries. That which wasn't packed into boxes was stacked next to an overflowing garbage can near the door.

He'd agreed to meet Brad there at nine. He didn't know what his friend had to say, but curiosity had gotten the better of him. That, and he was going stir-crazy out at the ranch.

He absently rubbed the back of his neck. It was harder than hell being in the city and knowing Dulcy was only a few blocks away. But he could understand her need for time, which was how he chose to interpret her saying it was over between them. Actually, she hadn't suggested it was over. He had. Right after his pride had taken a major dent when she stepped away from his touch.

It wasn't every day a woman found out her fiancé, or rather her fiancé's mother, had been interested in her only for her money—albeit money she didn't have. But to discover that that same fiancé was in love with another woman, too, well, that was enough to send anyone off on a search for a stretch of uninterrupted reflection time.

The problem was, he was having a hard time giving it to her.

He'd been through enough in his lifetime to know that even if you played by the rules, there was no guarantee it all would turn out right in the end. And he and Dulcy hadn't exactly played by the rules, which gave him double the worry about any future with her.

The sound of whistling heralded Brad's arrival. Quinn crossed his arms watching his friend enter the office carrying another box.

"Good, you're here," he said, then grinned.

Quinn grimaced. "Getting fired suits you."

"I didn't get fired, I resigned."

"Yes, as soon as the company was taken over by the highest bidder."

Brad slid a pile of files into the box and waved a hand. "Details. I never was very good with those."

"And the shylock?"

"The shylock? Oh, you mean Tucci." The smile finally left his face. "To tell you the truth, I haven't thought about what I'm going to do with him yet."

Quinn cocked a brow. "Don't you think that's something you should worry about?"

Brad moved around, putting more items into the boxes. "That's not why I asked you here."

"Why *did* you ask me here?"

Brad put a mantel clock down, then stood. His grin was too wide, too knowing. "I saw you."

"Saw me what?"

"With Dulcy. On the back of that horse." He shook his head. "I didn't even know that was possible."

"The horse or Dulcy?"

Brad chuckled. "Both."

Quinn leaned back on his hands. "Why didn't you say

anything the other day? It might have saved you some trouble if you had just focused the blame on the two of us.''

"Not my style.''

Quinn already knew that. Recent behavior aside, Brad was a stand-up guy. The kind you called in an emergency. The type you could trust with anything. It had been an heroic action so many years before that had started their friendship, but it was those solid qualities that maintained it.

Quinn cleared his throat. "You know I could help you out with Tucci.''

"Help me out? How?''

"Even the account.''

"You mean pay him?'' Brad looked at him long and hard. "If you told me ten years ago that this is where we would be standing right here, right now, I would have laughed my ass off.'' He shook his head. "No. Thanks for the offer, bud. It means more than you know, but I'll take care of Tucci.''

"You know where I am if you change your mind.''

"Yeah, I know where you are. Exactly where you shouldn't be.''

"How so?''

Brad crossed his arms and rested them on the back of one of the two leather wing chairs in front of his desk. "I've known you for a long time, Quinn. I know the last thing you would do is boink my fiancée, unless you were serious about her.'' He glanced at his watch. "You should be with her. I can only imagine what she's going through right now, after all that's gone down.'' He reached out for the paper folded back to the Society section and tossed it at him. "Can you believe how everyone's reacting to me? I got three cushy job offers yesterday and another one this morning.''

Quinn skimmed the grainy black-and-white photo of Brad and Yolanda, then put the paper back on the desk.

"The thing is, Dulcy is a great girl. I would never have caved to mother's demands, otherwise. I mean, who wouldn't want a piece like that hanging on your arm, waiting for you at home, warming up your bed every night." He shook his head. "Only, I'd already met Yolanda."

"Or Yolanda met you."

Rather than be insulted, Brad grinned. "Trust me, I'm not going into any of this with blinders on, Quinn. I know her past. With you. With others." He shrugged. "But what can I say? I love the girl. And if she ends up taking everything I own—" he motioned toward the boxes "—or rather, all that I don't own, so be it. I made that decision the instant I decided to tell mother I wasn't marrying Dulcy. What I couldn't live with was wondering what would have happened if I never gave us a chance, you know? Maybe she does love me. Maybe we'll rent a two bedroom apartment on the wrong side of town, have two-point-two kids and live happily ever after." He grinned. "Or maybe we'll just have a few months of great sex and she'll leave me for the next target. I don't know. But I'm sure going to have a lot of fun finding out."

Quinn shook his head. He couldn't live with that kind of risk. He wanted to know that the woman he chose to spend his life with was as committed to him as he was to her. Was as true and truthful as he would be to her. Living his life without knowing what tomorrow would bring wasn't his style.

If that was the case, what was he doing here with Brad, instead of going after Dulcy? By letting the dust settle, giving her time, wasn't he contradicting his usual mode of operation?

He pushed away from the desk. "That road might be okay for you, but I operate a little differently."

Brad made a clucking sound. "Who would have thought. Quinn Landis is a coward."

Quinn laughed. Not chuckled. He'd been called a lot of things in his life, but a coward wasn't one of them.

Brad crossed to stand in front of him, his expression as somber as Quinn had ever seen it. "I just want you to know that I meant neither you nor Dulcy harm. And that I don't hold whatever it is between the two of you against you, either."

"Big of you."

Brad grinned. "Yeah, isn't it?"

He slapped Quinn on the back. "Come on, let's get out of here and go get something to eat. I'm starved."

Quinn was hungry, too. But not for food.

Nonetheless, he followed his friend out of the office for what would probably be the last time.

A HEADACHE. A monstrous, temple-throbbing, skull-crushing migraine. That's what Dulcy felt coming on, as Mandy Mallone and her fiancé launched into another argument, the third in ten minutes, across the conference table from each other.

Jena leaned closer to Dulcy and whispered, "You can feed him the papers anytime now."

Dulcy stared at her and her friend shrugged.

"At least it would shut one of them up." She leaned back in her chair. "If ever I needed a reminder of why I don't believe in marriage…"

Jena had made her comment to Dulcy, but the arguing couple heard and instantly stopped arguing.

"You don't want to get married?" Mandy asked Jason

after a long pause, during which the ice in the water pitcher could be heard melting.

"The wedding's tomorrow, Mandy," Jason said, clearly exasperated.

"What kind of answer is that?"

"Yes, Mandy. I still want to marry you. There, is that answer enough for you?"

Dulcy winced and glanced at her client, whose eyes widened in shock. Either that or she'd gone a little heavy on the mascara that morning.

Jason Polansky's attorney, Steve Saragin, leaned forward. "So long as you sign the prenuptial agreement." He slid the papers toward Mandy for the third time. Mandy appeared to blink back tears as she stared at them. At least she wasn't pushing them away, as she'd done on the other two occasions.

Dulcy moved to smooth her hair, and was startled to find it wasn't pulled back. For some odd reason she couldn't seem to bring herself to do anything the way she usually did it.

"She's going to cave," Jena whispered to her.

Dulcy blinked and noticed Mandy reaching out for the papers with a shaking hand.

Dulcy slapped her hand on top of the papers. Jason and his attorney groaned, Mandy looked at her with that doe-eyed optimism that made Dulcy wonder how someone so street-smart could be so fiscally gullible.

The way she saw it, if she allowed her client to sign the papers she was essentially signing the death warrant for their relationship. Who could go into a marriage with this poor excuse for a document hanging over their heads? Six months, or maybe a year, down the road she would probably be sitting in the same room with Mandy and Jason, tearing apart the same agreement over a petition for divorce.

Dulcy looked up. "May I have a word alone with you, Jason?"

She knew it wasn't normal protocol for the opposing attorney to ask to speak to the opposing claimant alone. But Jason was an attorney. And he was also a guy in love, from what she could make out. Although a screwy guy in love.

"No way," Saragin said. "Whatever has to be said can be said in present company." He glanced Jena's way and grinned. "Unless, of course, Ms. McCade would like to leave."

Dulcy's gaze never wavered from Jason's. "Do you want this wedding to happen or not? If you're sincere in your response that you still want to marry my client, I'd suggest you do as I ask."

Jason quickly looked to Saragin, who shook his head, but she could tell she had him. One word from her either way, and Mandy either did or did not sign the papers.

Dulcy got up. "Let's go to my office." She took the agreement from the table in case Mandy got antsy and signed the sucker anyway, then led the way from the room.

Once in her office, she closed the door.

"So, what do I have to do to get you to allow Mandy to sign those papers?" Jason asked.

Dulcy crossed the room and leaned against her desk. "First I have something I'd like to ask you."

He grimaced.

"You really didn't think this was going to be easy, did you? What do you think I am, a wet-behind-the-ears law school grad?"

Jason shrugged. "It was worth a try."

Dulcy lifted a finger. "That's exactly what I'm going after here."

"I don't get you."

"Do you love Mandy, Jason?"

Dulcy already knew that he did. Ever since she'd returned from Quinn's ranch, she'd been bombarded with phone calls. From Mandy, from Jason's attorney, and from Jason himself, begging her to stop giving Mandy advice that would keep them apart.

"I don't see how that's any business of yours."

Dulcy crossed her arms. "Since it's my job to look after my client's best interest, I think it is."

"Fine. Fine." Jason ran his hand through his thick dark hair and murmured, "Yes, I love Mandy. More than you can know."

Dulcy guessed that she did know. And it was that emotion she was planning to use to her, and their, advantage.

"Then, forget the contract," she said point-blank.

He blinked at her. "Are you nuts? Do you have any idea how much I'm worth?"

"Unfortunately, yes. Down to the last penny."

"So you know how much I stand to lose in a divorce."

"If you make Mandy sign that, you'll lose her."

"You don't think she'll marry me?"

She shook her head. "Oh, she's going to marry you, all right. Tomorrow. In front of God and everyone. But the reason she'll be doing it isn't for your money or for what she stands to gain financially. She'll be marrying you for you. Because she loves you. And because you love her."

"So what's the problem, then?"

Dulcy stared at the ceiling and sighed. "That contract undermines everything honest about your love. Don't you see that, Jason? Make her sign it and it will turn into an acid that will corrode your entire marriage."

"I'll take it under advisement."

Which essentially meant no deal.

Dulcy genuinely felt sorry for him. Not because he couldn't see past the dollar signs swimming in front of his nose, but because he wouldn't see where she was coming from until it was too late for him to turn back.

"Let me tell you about my situation," she said, then swallowed hard.

She was banking on the fact that everyone and their brother knew what had happened over the past few days. Brad's disappearance, and reappearance. And her unequivocal silence on the matter.

Jason narrowed his eyes, apparently wondering where she was going with this.

"Don't worry. I'm not asking for a shoulder to cry on." She gave a humorless laugh. "And if I did cry, it wouldn't be for the reason you might think." Her gaze trailed to the window and the city beyond. "My situation…well, it was a simple matter of the loss of control you're trying to impose with that prenuptial agreement."

"You mean Brad with that hot salsa chick."

Dulcy found his description distantly amusing. "There's that. But that's not what I'm referring to. No, I mean me with the best man."

Jason stood up straighter. "What? It didn't say anything about that in the papers."

"Nope. It won't either, because I don't plan on talking to them or any other members of the media." She sharpened her gaze on him. "Do you want to know why I'm telling you this?"

"Does it matter?"

"I think it does."

He grimaced. She smiled. "You should have thought more about the price before you came in here with me."

She rounded her desk but didn't sit down. "A week ago I had complete control over my life. I was going to marry a great catch and, let's face it, I've got a damn good job." She looked down at her hands. "Then I lost that control. I met a man who made me want to do things that I...well, that I thought I would never have done in a million years. And I couldn't help myself. I...I was forced to give up a bit of that control. Who am I kidding? I had to forfeit all of it in order to get what I wanted. And that was him.''

''So when's the wedding?''

She shook her head. ''There's not going to be one.''

''I don't understand.''

''Neither do I. Well, not fully, anyway.'' She stepped to the window and looked out. ''You see, losing that control scares me to death.'' She realized that she'd given up control in other areas of her life but couldn't bring herself to give in to it when it came to the whoppers. ''I know if I see him again, I'd give anything to be with him. Anything. Everything.'' She shivered, imagining Quinn's hot hands branding her skin.

''Which brings me back to you.'' She turned to face Jason again.

''What were you thinking about just now?''

''Wouldn't you like to know.''

He grinned.

''Admit it, Jason. The only reason you want that damn prenup is to try to maintain some of the same control I just talked about. Emotional control. Being with Mandy makes you feel helpless, weak. And that scares you.''

He glanced away.

''I'm right, aren't I. Don't make the same mistake I'm making, Jason. While you're marrying your girl, and I've left my guy, eventually we're both going to end up in the same place.''

''Alone.''

''Yes,'' she said quietly.

For a moment he stared at her without really seeing her.

She wasn't sure what she'd said that had driven her message home, but she was pretty sure she'd succeeded.

"Shall we rejoin the others?" she asked, picking up the prenup from her desk.

He got up and led the way to the door. Dulcy touched his shoulder and handed him the papers. He stared at her. Her answer was a smile.

They entered the conference room to complete silence. Then Jason tore up the prenuptial agreement and told Mandy he loved her.

15

THE PINK LADY LOUNGE. One o'clock on a Saturday afternoon. Quinn grimaced, just then realizing it was the time that Brad and Dulcy would have been getting married at Our Lady of Perpetual Hope Cathedral. Was it significant that Dulcy had summoned him here now? Or coincidence?

The heavy bass of the music pulsated as he spotted the black woman from his previous visit bumping and grinding for the dozen or so men who'd chosen to have lunch there, though he suspected the limited food menu wasn't what they'd come for. He tucked his hand into his jeans pocket and pulled out the fax he'd received the day before. Actually a re-fax of a fax. It had gone through to the ranch, and Ezzie had immediately contacted him to fax it through to his hotel. It read simply, "Pink Lady at one. Saturday." It was signed, *D.*

The same bartender from the other day slid a beer bottle in front of him and moved the peanuts within reach. "Still searching for that guy?"

"Nope."

She smiled. "Good."

The door opened. Quinn squinted against the sudden bright sunlight. The new addition wasn't Dulcy. He took a long pull from the condensation-dotted bottle, then rolled the glass between his palms. At least now he'd have an explanation for the dampness of his palms.

The truth was, he wasn't sure what to expect. For three

long days Dulcy hadn't been in contact with him. Then she sent this bizarre request. A meeting in a familiar place to give him the final shove off? He was afraid the chances of that happening were better than her declaring her love for him in this joint. He grimaced at one of the men who hooted near the stage, then bummed a cigarette off the guy sitting two stools up from him.

It had been years since he'd smoked. And this was his second cigarette since Dulcy had entered his life. No, he didn't plan to take up the habit again, but so long as he was sitting here breathing in others' smoke, he might as well get some enjoyment out of it. He inhaled a deep drag, then let the smoke out in a long, thick cloud.

"That's Ebony, everybody. Show her how much you love her by giving her a big hand."

Quinn clapped without enthusiasm. The door opened again, and he stared in that direction. Not Dulcy.

He glanced at his watch. Where was she? He never considered that she'd get him there and then not show up. He motioned to the barmaid then slid a newspaper clipping from his back pocket. He'd only kept the one page and it was folded back to a copy of Brad and Dulcy's engagement announcement photo. Alongside it was another photo of Brad and Yolanda on the courthouse steps after a quickie wedding ceremony the previous evening. Beatrix Wheeler was a scowling presence behind them.

He flashed the picture of Dulcy at the bartender, his thumb over Brad's face. "Have you seen this woman come in here?"

"Encouraging. You're looking for a woman. That's good."

Depended on what Dulcy had to tell him.

The bartender squinted at the grainy picture, a deep-set frown on her face. Then she put on the reading glasses hanging around her neck by a gold chain. They made her look closer to what he guessed was her age.

The announcer's voice boomed through the joint. "Okay, guys, we have a special treat for you this afternoon. A first timer! They all have to start somewhere, right? Let's give a warm hello, how do you do to delicious, decadent, delectable...Dulcy!"

The barmaid grinned at him, slid the paper from his hands and pointed behind him.

Quinn slowly turned toward the stage. Nothing. The platform was empty. Music began pumping through the sound system. Still no stripper. He rubbed his tired face. There was no way that the Dulcy due to take the stage was the same Dulcy. Hadn't she, herself, told him the last time they were there that she would never, ever strip for him? And having come to know her, seeing firsthand all that she had gone through, he could never see her giving in to that naughty side he'd viewed so much of.

The door opened. He glanced that way. No Dulcy.

An enthusiastic shout went out near the stage. He glanced to find a head of teased blond hair peeking through the metallic beads at the back of the stage. The air in his lungs froze along with the last puff he'd taken from the cigarette. If he had any doubts that it was Dulcy, they were extinguished when she appeared to be pushed from behind. She stumbled center stage in a tight blue pinstriped pantsuit and towering stiletto heels, looking like a virgin on prom night. Then she snagged his gaze and a slow, sexy smile tugged at her red, red lips.

Dear Lord.

Quinn nearly choked on the smoke trapped in his lungs.

Then Dulcy moved.

Slowly. Uncertainly. She stepped nearer the oval circle at the front of the stage, her steps unsure. A female voice sounded behind her. She glanced that way, made an *O* with her mouth, then looked forward again. Sliding her hands down her body, she caught the button holding the jacket closed and appeared to have a problem undoing it. Then the jacket finally sprang open, revealing the shiny gold bikini top she wore underneath. With more finesse than Quinn would have thought possible, she let the jacket fall back off her shoulders, then smoothly down her arms. She caught the material in her right hand, gave it a couple of swings and launched it in his direction. It fell short, landing squarely on top of the balding head of another onlooker.

Next came the pants—specially designed pants that, with one yank, cleanly broke away, revealing that her bikini bottoms matched the top. His gaze devoured the length of her long, long legs in the fishnet stockings and black heels. Another shout from behind the curtain and she put one leg forward, keeping it bent at the knee, then did a simple roll of her hips that sent the fire in Quinn's lungs speeding straight for his groin.

Dulcy's blond curls had been worked so that they fell over her brows, cloaking her expression in seductive mystery. She stepped forward, reaching her arms up high to grip the metal bar. Her breasts pressed dangerously against the shiny material, her nipples engorged and protruding. Quinn's gaze skimmed her toned abdomen, then fell lower still to where the tiny triangle of fabric barely covered her plump womanhood. She ran one hand down around her left breast, over her stomach, and then her fingertips dipped into the elastic of the bikini bottoms. Quinn found it impossible to breathe. And his heart doubled in size, thundering against his rib cage.

While her awkward movements were provocative, the sexy shadows in her eyes were revealing. In that one moment Quinn knew that her brave display had nothing to do with sex. It had everything to do with her finding control in lack of control. Of giving herself over to love. Love for him. Love for them.

He slowly rose from the stool and started to make his way to the stage.

SWEAT, HOT AND LIQUID, trickled down the middle of Dulcy's bare back, sending a shiver right after it. She felt exposed and vulnerable and—she swallowed hard—powerful as hell. But beyond the stage fright that had nearly kept her from going through with her plan, the only thing that mattered, once one of the strippers had pushed her through that curtain, was Quinn. She'd met his gaze and her anxiety had vanished. All that mattered was him. Her need for him. Her love for him. Her longing to have him back in her life.

Dulcy could pinpoint the exact time the clouds in her head and heart had blown away, making her decision crystal clear. When she'd watched Jason Polansky rip up that prenuptial contract and his bride rush across the room and into his arms, blubbering like a fool. She realized that when it came to love, real love, the victims were all fools. Sweet, wonderful, irresistible fools who had no more control over their hearts than they did over the weather. And she'd known what she had to do.

Now she watched Quinn push from his stool, and her heart pitched. She forced her feet to move to the other side of the pole in a swinging motion she'd only practiced once with the help of the girls in the back. She'd found it amazing that they'd been so welcoming, transforming a plan that was nothing but a wispy fantasy into sexy reality.

Quinn moved closer to the stage. Every cell in Dulcy's body reacted.

Never had she felt so connected to another human being.

He was the shadow to her light. The action to her reaction. He made her want to say, do and be all the things she had only dreamed of. He made her yearn to be her.

Tearing her gaze from where he was making his way to the stage, she slowly turned around and bent at the waist, propping her hands against her knees and thrusting her bottom into the air, grinding her hips in a decadently provocative way she'd watched the other strippers do. Displaying herself in a way she would never have imagined herself capable of. And growing incredibly hot knowing he was the one man on earth who wouldn't tease, taunt or ridicule her. She trusted him implicitly. And while she still questioned her ability to trust herself, trusting him was a good start.

She rose and turned back to face him. She was surprised to find him standing before the stage. The man her jacket had landed on hurried up next to him, waving a bill. Quinn thrust a hand against the guy's chest. "Uh-uh, buddy. This one's all mine."

Dulcy's breath caught in her throat and her limbs froze. She could do little more than gape at the thoroughly dark and aroused and proprietary expression on Quinn's face. He lifted a hand and slowly crooked his finger, indicating for her to come to him. And she did. Oh so willingly.

He caught her around the waist and pulled her flush against him. She slid the length of his aroused body until she was standing in front of him, off the stage. His eyes were nearly black in the darkness, his pulse pounding at the base of his neck. "Does this mean what I think it does?" he asked, his fingers splayed across the small of her back, setting her skin on fire.

She smiled. "I don't know. What do you think it means?"

"You want me. Bad."

She laughed, pressing her hips more firmly against his. "That, too."

A couple of *boos* sounded from the small crowd. A fumble sounded over the speakers, then the announcer said, "Looks like we lost Dulcy. But don't look now, Candy's stepped in to take over."

Quinn grinned, standing cemented to the spot. "You mean there's more?"

"Oh, yeah. Much, much more," Dulcy whispered. Her gaze slid to his mouth, his provocative, delicious mouth, and she gently pressed her lips against it.

"Tell me," Quinn said, his voice gravelly.

"I want you. In my bed. In my life," she said. "I love you, Quinn Landis. And I think you love me." She slid her hand between them, then around to the back of her bikini bottoms, tugging out the envelope she'd hidden there. She held it aloft. "I want you to go on my honeymoon with me. Tomorrow. Fiji. So we can talk about where we go from here."

Quinn was silent, his face intense as he seemed to gauge her intent. Then he cleared his throat and bent to kiss her thoroughly. "For how long?"

"Ten days."

His grin made her knees go weak. "Not enough time."

"Oh?"

"No." His lips sought and found the sensitive area at the base of her neck. He pressed a kiss there, on her jaw, then ran his tongue the length of her bottom lip. "I have a suggestion of my own."

Dulcy moved to ask what, but couldn't seem to force the word out of her mouth. She stood spellbound, waiting for him to go on, her senses swirling.

"We make it a true honeymoon."

Dulcy's knees did give out.

Quinn caught her and held her tightly against his chest. "Are you asking what I think you are?"

He nodded. "I'm telling you I love you, more than the air that I breathe. And I want you, Dulcy Ferris, to marry me, Quinn Landis. Now."

She glanced around. "Here?"

He chuckled quietly. "I think we'd have a hard time finding a preacher on the premises. No. Not here. But somewhere. Soon. Very soon." He moved until his mouth rested against her ear. "I want you in my life. Not just for the next ten days, but forever. I want to make love to you until you can't get out of bed. I want you to have my, our, children."

"Children?" She wavered. "As in plural?"

He nodded, amusement and love shining from his eyes.

In that one instant, Dulcy saw the rest of her life unfurl in front of her like the best fantasy of all. She saw herself keeping her apartment in the city, where she would work three days a week, then spending the rest of her time at Quinn's ranch with him, Esmerelda and what would eventually be the additional members of their family.

"Is that a yes?"

She nodded emphatically, not trusting herself with words. Tears flooded her eyes and desire pooled in her stomach.

"I didn't hear you."

She tried to swallow the emotion choking her throat. "Yes. I said yes."

He swept her up into his arms and strode purposefully for the door. "That's what I thought you said. Now, let's get out of here."

HARLEQUIN®
Temptation.

It's hot...and it's out of control!

This spring, the forecast is hot *and* steamy!
Don't miss these bold, provocative, ultra-sexy books!

PRIVATE INVESTIGATIONS by Tori Carrington
April 2002
Secretary-turned-P.I. Ripley Logan never thought her first job
would have her running for her life—or crawling into
a stranger's bed....

ONE HOT NUMBER by Sandy Steen
May 2002
Accountant Samantha Collins may be good with numbers, but
she needs some work with men...until she meets sexy but
broke rancher Ryder Wells. Then she decides to make him a
deal—her brains for his bed. Sam's getting the better of the
deal, but hey, who's counting?

WHAT'S YOUR PLEASURE? by Julie Elizabeth Leto
June 2002
Mystery writer Devon Michaels is in a bind. Her publisher has
promised her a lucrative contract, *if* she makes the jump to
erotic thrillers. The problem: Devon can't write a love scene to
save her life. Luckily for her, Detective Jake Tanner is an
expert at "hands-on" training....

Don't miss this thrilling threesome!

HARLEQUIN®
Makes any time special ®

Visit us at www.eHarlequin.com

HTH